KINSHIP COVE: CUDDLES & COFFEE

VOLUME ONE

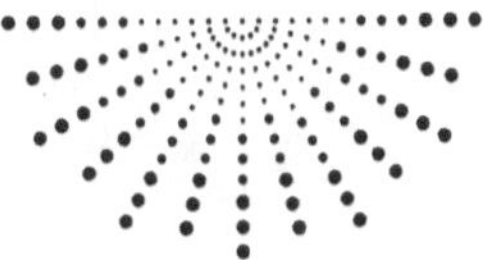

ELLIS LEIGH

FRAPPÉ FOX

KINSHIP COVE: CUDDLES & COFFEE

A town cannot live on baked goods alone, and a teacher won't find their mate in a book. Welcome to the Kinship Cove Diner, where a good cup of coffee comes with every fated mating.

It sucks to be invisible. In the diner my family owns, I'm just the sister who gets stuff done. My entire skulk seems to forget about me on a weekly basis. So color me tickled when the fates drop my fated mate—a hunky, nerdy-hot wolf shifting professor—directly in my path. But not all matings go as planned, mine included.

He's smart, he's hot, and he's decided to use our bond for research instead of actually getting to know me. And did I mention he used to buy my best friend's worn undergarments? Thanks for that, fates.

· · ·

Undies aside, my wolf shifter professor is about to learn his toughest lesson ever—never go up against a fox shifter in a battle of wit or will. We're sneaky, smart, and not afraid to take an opponent to the mattresses to win a battle.

1

MISTY

I swear to the fates, if my skulk adds even one more fox kit, I'm out.

"Tawny!" I stormed across the kitchen at the Kinship Cove Diner, my family's restaurant for four generations, and busted through the doors that led to the private party area. "Someone take this child before he finds himself inside a hot oven."

The child in question—Phillip, age six—giggled. "You wouldn't cook me, Aunt Misty."

I wouldn't. I would threaten to, though. "I might mistake you for one of the roasts, Philly Bo-Billy. You should hang out in here where it's safe."

"But all the old people are in here. I want to be with you. You're more fun."

Damn right, I am. "You can come back and help me get the desserts ready later, okay? Right now, there's too much going on."

Tawny, my oldest sister and mother to Phillip, smiled as she took her son from my arms. "C'mon, little man. Let's go see your aunts and uncles."

His pouty bottom lip hurt me a lot more than the way my sister didn't bother to say hi or thanks or who are you. I swear, my entire family wouldn't notice if I went missing unless they needed something.

"Misty!"

Like dinner to be served.

"On it, Mom." I hurried past my mother, trying really hard not to cower under her glare. The woman was a workhorse and had raised her children—all eighteen of us—to follow her commands no matter what. As each litter of kits grew into adulthood, they worked a little less and a little less, moving on to jobs outside of the diner and growing their own families with mates and kits. Being part of her youngest litter put me firmly in the worker group, whether I wanted to be there or not.

I pushed through the swinging doors and raced into the kitchen, ready to get the dinner finished, plated, and served. Thankfully, my closest sister—in age and in general compatibility—was right there with me.

"I pulled the roasts out of the ovens to rest," Tilly said as she wiped her hands on a cloth and looked over the disaster area that was the Kinship Cove Diner kitchen on our weekly family dinner night. "Potatoes are warmed and ready to go, green beans are in serving bowls already under the heat lamps, and the bread is in the baskets. You want to start slicing the meat while I start bringing out the first course?"

"Perfect." I headed for my station—the only one even remotely clean. Tilly had kindly placed one of the roasts beside it, knowing I'd carve the side of beef for the family. There was something very methodical and almost soothing in the activity—I liked the focus it took to cut neat, even pieces. The order of it.

Unfortunately, when you had a family as large as mine all in one place, chaos tended to follow them.

"Oof." Tilly's exclamation came a second after our oldest brother—Robbie, though he told everyone in town to call him Robert because he liked to pretend he was more important than any of us thought he should be—shoved through the doors. My sister fell to the floor along with eight baskets of fresh bread.

Chaos. Always.

"That's why the doors have windows in them," I said, shaking my head as Robbie—no way would I call him Robert—helped Tilly to her feet.

"Everyone is waiting." Robbie scowled at the bread on the floor, looking more like the victim than the perpetrator of the crime. "What's taking so long?"

Two parents, eighteen children, sixteen mates, fifty-seven grandchildren at my last count, and ten or so random aunts, uncles, or cousins who sometimes joined us in our weekly dinner tradition. What took so long? Feeding one of the largest skulks in the country, that's what.

"We're trying to feed a hundred people in one seating in a kitchen not designed to do so, without enough help to get all the work done on time. You want us to go faster? Get some of our siblings back here." I pointed my knife in his direction. Not really at him—though he'd probably tell my mother I'd tried to stab him or something. He always had been the tattletale of the group. "If you can't get anyone to lend a hand, just stay out of our way."

Robbie huffed and puffed as I knew he would, but he turned without a word and stormed back into the dining room. As usual.

"Okay," I said, wiping off my hands and joining Tilly to assess the damage. "Change of plans. You get the beef sliced and into the serving dishes, I'll bake some of the frozen rolls from Cake-ily Ever After."

"Mom will be mad they're not our recipe."

Mom got mad about a lot of things, specifically whenever those things reminded her that I worked at the bakery down the street more than in the family restaurant.

"She'll just have to suck it up. Otherwise, they get no bread."

Tilly's eyes grew wide, a shocked expression crossing over her pretty face. An exaggerated one for sure. "Oh, the horror. No bread." She placed the back of her hand against her forehead, hamming it up as I did my best not to laugh. "Whatever shall we do?"

"We shall cut the meat and bake the other rolls, that's what. Are you starring in the next play for the community theater? Is it a gothic romance or something?"

"I am, but not a gothic. Just a romance. I get to kiss a llama shifter."

By the fates. "Yeah. That sounds...fuzzy." And not at all like something she'd be able to do if she ever found her mate. A male would never let another male touch his mate, let alone kiss her. Or him. Or them. Thankfully, Tilly had yet to find her Mr. or Miss Right, though I had a feeling it wouldn't be too long. I trusted my gut in these matters—it never lied to me.

"Girls," our mother yelled, not even bothering to open the doors and come inside the kitchen. "Where is that bread?"

"Go," I hissed.

Tilly swung into action while I raced through the kitchen to the walk-in freezer. Trays of the yeast rolls I helped make at the bakery sat in the far corner. We stocked them to serve with our minestrone soup on Wednesdays—the texture was perfect for sopping up some of the broth. I loved them. Mom tolerated them. Beggars couldn't be choosers, though. I didn't have time to remake the rolls from scratch, so these would have to do. Thankfully, they only took a few minutes to warm through.

By the time the rolls were ready and I had the mess of the original bread cleaned up, Tilly was done serving all the food and everyone was in the dining room. I loaded the baskets of rolls onto a tray and headed out, not really surprised to see everyone eating already. No one said a word to me as I moved from table to table, setting the baskets in the middle. Not one *Thank you* or *How are you* or *What's been happening*. Not one use of my name.

Typical.

What wasn't typical was the fact that the room was full. Not a single chair sat empty. Not a space saved for me. Even Tilly had found a spot next to our great aunt who always talked about the feral cats on her farm and smelled as if she'd been bathing in menthol. No one had saved me a seat.

One of my sisters' mates—which one I couldn't have said because they all ran together in my mind—yelled from the far end of the room. "We need more bread over here."

No name. No please or thank you. No manners. And still no spot for me to sit with my family and eat the meal I'd prepared for them. Family dinner night was always my least favorite night of the week simply because of how much work it took to make the meal, but this was beyond anything I'd expected. My family was tight—close and protective of each other—but lately, I'd felt left behind by them. Invisible, even. Not unwanted, mind you, just…overlooked. And tonight proved that by far.

Why am I even here?

My mother didn't look up as I walked past her. No one did. They all kept up their conversations, their laughing and bragging and complaining, as I headed for the back door and pushed through it into the cold night air. They needed more bread? They knew where the kitchen was. I was done being their servant for the night.

I didn't need to decide where I was going. I didn't put any thought into my path at all. I simply started walking and ended up at the back door of my favorite place in the entire world—the Cake-ily Ever After Bakery. Owned by the human Chance sisters, the place had become a respite for me. A center of friendship and comfort that had been growing more and more scarce within my family's diner. It was another home to me, and I was happy to be there.

"Misty. I'm so glad you were able to come by." The excitement in Coco's voice welcomed and warmed me before I'd even closed the door. The oldest of the three Chance sisters, Coco had been the one who'd hired me to run the customer service segment of the business, not that I'd given her a choice in the matter. I'd pretty much just showed up to work and stayed put. Eventually, she'd grown to love me as I'd known she would.

She'd also taken the time to teach me how to bake whatever I wanted. She was a classically trained pastry chef and could make just about anything. Whenever I binged my favorite British baking show, I would pick a particular dessert to try, and she'd spend far too much time showing me exactly how to make it and giving me the why behind every step. She was a good human to know.

"No family dinner tonight?" Ginger, the middle sister and the one who threw traditional baking a curve ball with her wild flavor combinations and amazing cupcakes, gave me a huge smile. "I figured you'd be surrounded by all those foxes tonight and unable to escape the boredom of family functions—no offense, sisters. Hey, where's your coat?"

"I didn't think it was that cold out," I said, washing my hands and looking around at the mess that was the current state of the kitchen. It was cleanup night—an event the girls held monthly where they spent an evening in the bakery deep-cleaning and organizing all the bits and bobs they used on a daily basis. One of the only nights you'd find the girls at the shop past closing, especially since they'd all recently found their mates. Something I'd been happy to have a hand in. "I left dinner a little early to come help."

"Hey, Misty." Madeleine, the youngest Chance sister, came strolling in from the front carrying an armful of sheet trays. "Want a cookie or some coffee? I can grab you something since I'm on *clean out all the cases* duty."

And just like that, all was right in my world. Something so basic as being seen, as being asked how I was doing, as being offered something that might make me happy—those simple niceties were at the heart of family. While I loved my fox family more than I could state, I adored these three as well. Sometimes I needed a break from my skulk, and the Chance sisters gave that to me without question. There was nothing like being home in the bakery with my favorite human sisters.

"I'm good. If I have any more caffeine, I might just go running down Main Street naked, singing some old classic rock ballad at the top of my lungs."

Ginger shrugged. "Wouldn't be the first time."

Yyyyyeeeeeaaaaahhhhh. She wasn't wrong. And I wasn't doing *that* again. "No more naked Misty talks. Where are we, and what can I do to help?"

Three hours, an untold number of cookies, and four cups of coffee—decaf, of course—later, I stood in a spotless kitchen with the three sisters. "We really outdid ourselves this time."

Coco nodded. "This kitchen looks amazing. Too bad it'll seem more like a war zone in about three days."

"Two," Ginger said with a grin. "I give it two days."

Madeleine, ever the positive one, disagreed. "I say five. The high of having such a nice work space will make us more apt to put stuff where it belongs."

"Sure thing, Pollyanna." Ginger bumped her younger sister's shoulder with her own. "I'm so ready to go home."

Coco's smile turned a little teasing. "That's a first. Guess having a dragon shifter to curl up with makes home more appealing."

"Damn right, it does. And don't pretend like you're not itching to see your wolf man. We all know you and Magnus are practically inseparable."

They were. They really, really were. All three girls had found shifter mates—a wolf for Coco, a dragon for Ginger, and a bear who also happened to be the mayor and pack alpha of our funky little shifter town for Madeleine. Me? I was the lone mateless female in the group. Though, I had a feeling that wouldn't be for long. Not a feeling, really... more like a premonition.

A sixth sense of impending doom.

Dramatic but likely accurate with my luck. I'd been experiencing a desire over the past few months, a need within me that screamed mating pull. I'd also been avoiding it like the plague as I worked to make sure the Chance sisters found their happily-ever-afters. They deserved good mates in their lives to love and be loved by. Me? I wasn't up for being forced to care for another being right then.

Until the fates threw a mate right in my face and made him dance, I wasn't dealing.

"Guys are here," Ginger said, looking at her phone. "Everyone ready to head out?"

Coco nodded. "Need a lift, Misty? We can drop you off on our way."

"I can walk."

"It's freezing outside." Ginger slipped into her own thick winter jacket and threw me a raised eyebrow. "And you, my friend, didn't bring a coat."

Because I'd been too busy trying to escape the mess of family dinner night to bother. "Yeah, okay. If you don't think Magnus will mind."

"I have no idea what you're assigning to me, but I certainly will not mind." The man himself—an older, silver fox of a wolf shifter in a long, black wool coat—swept into the kitchen and beelined it to Coco. "It looks amazing in here. Did you get everything done, beautiful?"

Coco hummed as she rose onto the balls of her feet to place a soft, gentle kiss on her mate's lips. "Definitely. Are the guys outside?"

"Yes. They didn't want to leave the door unprotected. Jericho's been on edge all night."

Madeleine's bear shifter mate. The youngest Chance sister suddenly looked worried. "Is everything okay?"

"I believe so, but perhaps we should hurry along home. Something has his senses in protective mode."

Wonderful. Just what we all needed—an overprotective bear making everyone jumpy. The girls rushed to get their coats, while I quickly made sure the front door was locked, the coffee machine turned off, and all the lights dimmed to our night settings.

"Thank you so much for your help tonight, Misty," Coco said as we stepped out of the back door. "We never could have done—"

But her words were cut off by the throaty, booming growl of a bear shifter defending his mate. Jericho created a wall of flesh before Madeleine, his head up and his fur sprouting through his human skin as he likely fought not to change forms. Kingston—Ginger's dragon shifter —didn't fight the urge, shifting fast and flying just slightly off the ground directly in front of his mate. Magnus grabbed Coco and even tugged me behind him as we all stood and stared at—

Were we being attacked by Mr. Rogers?

The man looked like some sort of professor. Or librarian. Or... retired fisherman with his thick sweater and graying hair. What he definitely didn't look like was a threat.

"Is that a cardigan?" Ginger asked, looking downright horrified. "Calm down, boys. No one wearing a cardigan is a danger to us."

"You," Jericho said, a growl evident in his voice. "I want you gone."

"Ryder?" Madeleine peeked around the arm of her mate. "What are you doing here?"

"What's going on?" Kingston asked as soon as he shifted back to his human form. Fully clothed. Only dragons could do that—the rest of us ended up butt naked. I was seriously jealous of his ability.

Once Kingston was firmly back on terra firma with two legs and no scales, Magnus relaxed a little and I was able to get a good look at the man before me. Brown dress shoes, dark jeans, a plaid collared shirt—thick cardigan over it, of course—with a suede bomber-type jacket topping off the look. If he were human, I'd put him in his mid-to-late-forties, but as he seemed to be a shifter, he could be anywhere from forty to two hundred. You just never knew, but the gray-tinged scruff on his cheeks definitely set him apart from most men I knew. And the glasses—thick, dark-rimmed, and oddly sexual. Seriously—professor material. Maybe an engineer or physicist. Some sort of super smarty. Way too nerdy to be—

The man in question looked my way, and our eyes locked for a brief moment. First impression—wolf shifter. Definitely wolf, what with the way his eyes pinned me in place like some sort of prey animal. Second impression? I was so very screwed.

Fate could be a cruel mistress—there were moments when she whispered and others when she screamed. This time? She smashed me over the head with what felt like a cast iron skillet.

Mate.

Without thinking, I jumped in front of Jericho, spreading my arms wide. "Don't hurt him."

The man—Ryder, though there was no way that was his real name—frowned, not meeting my gaze anymore. Starting more at my shoulder as he asked, "Who are you?"

Before I could answer, Jericho growled again, pushing Madeline back another step as he said, "But he used to buy your panties."

What the… I spun, staring hard at the bear shifter. "Did you just say he bought Madeleine's *panties?*"

By the way her face turned bright red, I guessed that was true. Huh. I never would have thought she had it in her to do something so… naughty. Had she not sold them to *my* mate, I might have congratulated her.

I still likely would. Tomorrow.

Jericho snarled, darting glances over my shoulder. "He did, and they're no longer for sale."

"Jericho, please." Madeleine patted her mate on the chest. "I'm sure there's a logical—and non-panty-related—reason he's here."

Yeah. That made sense. Sort of. I turned back around, looking Ryder-not-Ryder up and down. Finding it hard not to notice that he didn't look at me in the same way. *One step at a time, fox.* "Why are you here? Because her panties are off the market."

Professor no-name shook his head, still staring at my shoulder as if it was a puzzle he wanted to figure out. "I did use to buy her—" he glanced up when Jericho growled "—merchandise. But I don't think it was because of her." He stepped closer, obviously sniffing. "I think it was because of you."

That made so much sense. Not.

"So you—my mate—bought her panties. Because of me." I huffed, pacing in front of the Chance sisters and mates brigade. "Am I the only one seeing something wrong with this picture?"

"I'm still stuck on the fact that little Maddy sold her goodies to men." Ginger tutted, shaking her head and grinning at her younger sister. "Well done, ya whore."

"Shut it," Madeleine said as Jericho snarled deeper. "It was to make extra money to fix up the house. Nothing more, nothing less."

Oh, right. Matilda—the dilapidated home on the edge of town she'd bought in some misguided effort to stay connected to Jericho when he was refusing their mating bond. Who needed to watch soap operas when I had so much local fodder?

Coco's frown deepened. "What did you do with the panties?"

"Don't ask." I crossed my arms over my chest—my high beams had to be blazing considering it felt like a whole ten degrees outside—and cocked my head. "So, you bought another woman's panties to help get your rocks off, and now…what? You needed another hit?"

Jericho might as well have been a broken record with how loudly he snarled. Again.

"No, not anymore," Cardigan Guy said, shooting a worried look in Madeline's general direction. "I thought my obsession with the panties was because of her, but now that I see you…"

"Now that you see me…what? You realize the error of your ways?"

"No, I just think perhaps I was buying from the wrong girl."

"I don't sell my worn underwear—" I patted Madeleine's arm "—not that there's anything wrong with that."

"This whole situation is wrong," Ginger said. "I'm still not understanding why you're here."

The guy shrugged, his cardigan nearly bouncing up and down with the movement. "I'm really not sure. Something called to me, and I had to come here. I kept trying to avoid it, but sometimes it would get too strong. Tonight, it was too difficult to resist."

"The fates called to you," Coco said with a nod. "They knew your mate was here."

"There's no such thing as the fates."

Everything went still, all six of the people beside me staring at the man as if he'd just vomited up a selkie coat. With equal parts horror and intrigued. Didn't believe in the fates? That meant he didn't believe in the sacred connection between two people destined to be together—between us. Which fit—the man could barely look at me. In fact, I might as well have been invisible for all the good the mating bond seemed to be doing me.

First my family forgot about me, then my fated mate had no interest in me. Talk about punching a girl when she was down.

"So...you feel the pull but don't believe in the mating bond?" Kingston sounded just as dubious as I felt. Minus the heartbreak, naturally.

Ryder shrugged. "I prefer logic to instinct, and my logic tells me you can't form a deep connection with another person based solely on some fated mates hocus pocus."

It's just a bunch of hocus pocus. The words reverberated in my head, and just like that, my world went completely sideways. Again. Thanks, fate. "Well, isn't that just peachy. I guess we're done here, then."

"Misty, wait." Madeleine reached for me, but I was gone. Cooked. Fried. Tired and angry and over being everyone's shadow.

Not that I would tell them all that in mixed company—maybe in the morning over coffee and cry-my-eyes-out cupcakes, though. I had a feeling the sisters would be waiting for me at work.

Tomorrow. I could talk about things tomorrow. Tonight, I needed to retreat. "I'm going home."

"But, Misty," Coco called as I hurried down the alley toward the sidewalk. "He's your mate."

I didn't have a lot to say to that. Just one word, really. "Unfortunately."

2

MISTY

The problem with renting a small house in the woods on the west side of Kinship Cove seemed to be that the setup of said house was not conducive to pacing. Sure, I had walked about ten miles through my living room and kitchen since I'd gotten home, but the path wasn't exactly easy to navigate.

"Son of a biscuit muncher." I grabbed my foot, rubbing my toes. The same ones I'd rubbed four times already for kicking the same table leg. Let no one ever be able to say I wasn't persistent.

Sidelined by the pain in the toes I'd likely broken, I plopped onto the couch and stared at the ceiling. My mate—the man fated to be mine forever—didn't want me. He hadn't even tried to stop me when I'd stormed off. Not that I would have stopped, but a little *hey, wait* might have been nice. No one had tried to stop me from leaving the restaurant earlier either. From the fireplace into the fire—from a family too large to pay attention to me to a man who would rather pay attention to someone else. Quite possibly, my friend Madeleine.

He used to buy her panties.

Ugh. Triple ugh. Ugh to the 415th power. Who would want to deal with *that* sort of nonsense? If I accepted this mating, he'd be around my work. Would I need to be worried about him thinking of Madeleine's panties instead of mine? True, mine left a lot to be desired. Utilitarian white cotton was made for comfort, not visual effect. I could buy nice panties, though—sexy ones. Scraps of lace and satin that would likely ride up and make me uncomfortable. What would be the point if I wasn't the person he wanted to see in them?

"In summation," I said, talking to no one but beginning to hate the silence, "my mate did not try to stop me from leaving him behind the night we met." I raised my arm and extended one finger. "Strike one. It has been determined that said mate was not there for me but for Madeleine. Or her panties. Whatever." I extended another finger. "Strike two."

"So, if he gets to three, is he out?"

I bolted upright, nearly jumping off the couch until I saw Madeleine standing in my hallway. "Hey."

"Hey." She took off her coat and laid it across the chair in the corner. "I knocked, but you might have been..."

"Talking to myself?"

"Yeah. That." Her lips turned down, and she had trouble holding my gaze. This had to be hard on her, though it wasn't exactly a picnic for me. Panty-incident aside, she was my best friend. The closest Chance sister to me. And this whole mate thing...it hurt. A lot.

But so did the thought of anything coming between us. "Why are you here?"

"I wanted to talk to you about what just happened. About Ryder."

Yeah. That. "No way is that his name."

"Right?" She leaned forward. "I've always called him Ryder-not-Ryder in my head."

"Same."

She smiled for a second, but it didn't last. Not surprisingly. "I'm so sorry for this. If I'd have known..."

"You'd never have sold your panties to my mate?"

"Yeah. That."

"Understood. Panties, though? Like...worn ones?"

Her cheeks turned bright red. "Yeah, well...there was some decent profity in it, and I was usually able to ship them, so nothing got personal. I used a fake name and info, kept everything super quiet, and earned a little extra money. It had seemed like a good idea at the time."

"But Ryder-not-Ryder showed up at the bakery." Which meant… Oh. Ooohhhh. "You met him in person."

If her expression turned any more uncomfortable, she might cause a portal to hell to open just to escape this conversation. "He was local and one of my first customers. I thought it'd be okay. Plus, he never gave me the creepy vibes of some of the guys I sold to. I mean, not as strong of a creepy vibe."

"You're selling worn underwear, but *they're* creepy."

"They're buying worn underwear over the internet so…yeah. They are."

"Touché." I rolled back, staring up at the ceiling once more. "I don't know what to do."

"Talk to him. I realize I might not be the best example of being forward and confrontational—"

"You've got that right."

"—but I think this situation warrants it. He was really upset that you'd left so quickly."

Hold up. "He was?"

"Yeah. I think he was trying to run after you, but Jericho and Kingston went all big-brother mode on him."

I turned my head, almost smiling. "Did they beat him up for me?"

"No, but I'm pretty sure they scared him half to death with their threats."

"Good."

"Go to him." She stood, grabbing her coat and giving me one more frown. "He's staying at the hotel in town. Said he'd be in Room 315. Waiting for you."

My mate was waiting for me. That thought made my heart jump a little. "Thanks. And, Madeleine?"

"Yeah?"

"Let's never talk about my mate and your panties again."

"Deal."

She closed the door behind her, leaving me alone in my house once more. Alone and quiet—too quiet. No one needed that much silence to get their thoughts in order, especially not after hearing their mate was likely waiting for them. He'd tried to follow me after I'd left the bakery. It wasn't his fault a bear shifter and a dragon shifter had decided to give him a good scare. They'd scare me too, if I didn't know they were both big softies for their mates.

Okay, that was a lie.

No one scared me.

Kingston and Jericho were totally teddy bears for their mates, though. That was the truth.

And maybe mine would be, too.

Fifteen minutes later, I walked out of the elevator on the third floor of the hotel. The hall felt endless as I worked my way to the right door, my heart pounding and my hands sweating the entire way. Granny panties and sweaty palms...I was quite the catch. Of course, he had lied about his name and bought worn underwear off the internet. Not exactly a position to judge from.

When I reached the end of the endless hall—seriously, why so long? —I took a deep breath, gave the girls a little fluff, and issued myself a mental pep talk that involved not killing him or getting naked. The only two options in my mind. Once convinced neither would happen—yet— I knocked on the door to room 315 and waited. And waited some more. And began to wonder if I'd heard Madeleine wrong. I had just raised my hand to knock again when the door swung wide...

And I died a little.

Ryder-not-Ryder stood in a pair of baggy gray sweats and...nothing else. His hair was wet—on his head and the graying bits on his chest— and his glasses slightly fogged. I'd obviously caught him post-shower. Post-naked time—his, not mine. I couldn't help but stare, to look him up and down and take it all in. Every single inch. My fox stood up and took notice too. She chattered in my head, sassy as ever and looking like a vixen on a mission. I swatted her back, though. He might be our mate, and he might have that whole sexy daddy-slash-professor thing going on, but there would be no humping. I darted a glance at his bulge. Unable not to.

No humping…yet.

"Hi," I said, holding out my hand. "I'm Misty. Fox shifter, bakery worker, and apparently, the best friend of the woman you used to buy worn panties from."

He blinked, barely focusing on my face between looking away once more. "I'm Clark. Please come in, Misty."

I followed Clark—totally called the whole not-Ryder thing—inside and took a seat on the only chair in the room. No-humping rule firmly in place even if my inner fox was exceptionally unhappy about that. Hussy.

Clark tugged on a T-shirt and ran a hand through his hair before settling on the end of the bed to stare at the floor. And then we sat. In silence. For some very long minutes. Awkward minutes. I didn't do well with those.

"So," I finally said when I simply couldn't take another second. "You like to buy worn panties."

He coughed, his eyes growing large. "Uh…not really."

"But you bought" —*if he used a fake name, then so did Madeleine*— "hers."

"I did, yes. But more for research than physical stimulation."

"Does that mean jacking off? Because I'm assuming your research involved spanking the monkey, which definitely falls under physical stimulation."

A growl slipped past his lips and he looked up to catch my gaze for just a moment, sending a chill up my spine and my inner fox to chattering. He choked it off and looked away again quickly, though. "Sorry about that."

"About what? Your wolf responding to me talking about your masturbatory habits?"

"I'm not sure it has anything to do with my wolf."

I sat back, my brow pulling tight. "No? Because my fox is responding to your animal side right now."

Understatement. She was about ready to crawl out of my skin. But Clark didn't seem as affected.

Or perhaps he didn't find me as attractive as I found him.

Which would suck.

Clark frowned and pushed up his glasses, his eyes darting in my direction and then away. "I don't allow the animal side of myself to overtake the more civilized side."

I'd met a lot of shifters in my life—ones who embraced their animal sides a little too much and ones who tended to swing to the other side of the pendulum, ignoring their animal for their human side. It was quite obvious where Clark fell on that spectrum.

"Civilized." The word tasted sour on my tongue, the meaning behind it making my stomach turn. "You feel your animal soul is uncivilized."

"Of course."

Asshole. "Okay. So…you do realize that I have an animal side as well, right? Because my fox is not uncivilized. She's amazing. And she would never accept a mate who thinks less of her."

He blanched, looking at least somewhat regretful. "I'm sorry, Misty. I obviously hit on a sensitive subject, but it wasn't my intention to upset you. That's not why I came to Kinship Cove or why I wanted to talk to you."

The whole not looking at me thing was really getting under my skin. "So then, why are you here?"

"I've felt a pull to be here for months. Especially after I started buying…"

"Panties." Yeah. I still wasn't over that one.

"Yes. After I started buying the products. I thought perhaps it was some sort of instinctual response to the seller, but I've since changed my hypothesis."

Hypotho…what? "So, what are these changes?"

"I think I craved the products because there were hints of your essence on them."

The hell? "I never touched her panties."

"No, no. Not… I just meant because she spent time near you, I was able to discern your essence under hers."

I'd heard of powerful noses, even knew a Bassett hound shifter once who could have put most other animals to shame with his sniffer, but that was a bit of a stretch. "So, your wolf recognized its mate's scent underneath hers."

"I think I should tell you up front—I don't believe in mates."

No fate and no mates. Lovely. "Of course you don't."

H didn't seem to appreciate my deadpan tone. "There's no scientific evidence to back up the claim of some supernatural force pulling two people together. Shifters simply believe that legend and then happen to fall into it. Perhaps there is an attractant—I've certainly been drawn to this area for a few months—but that doesn't mean we have a fated bond to last a lifetime. It could be something as simple as pheromones."

My mate didn't believe in fated mates. He didn't seem to desire an *uncivilized* shifter partner, let alone me. He didn't seem to want a mate at all because he refused to believe in the bond between them. I didn't know what to do with that information other than cry, which I certainly wasn't about to do in front of him. But when I got home?

Hallmark movies, ice cream, and fuzzy pajama time. For real.

But until then, I had to hold myself together. "So then, what are we doing here? If you don't want a relationship with your mate, what do you want?"

"Intercourse."

He did not… "You don't want a mate, but you want to have sex?"

"Yes." Another push of his glasses—seriously the things obviously needed to be adjusted—and a quick glance in my direction before staring at what seemed to be my foot. "I tend to develop erections around your scent, which seems to be a sign that my inner wolf is interested in you. I'd love to research this further if you'd be open to it."

I was almost afraid to ask. "Research how?"

He leaned forward, catching my gaze for just a second before dropping his eyes to my shoulder. "I'm proposing a biweekly schedule for approved sexual activity that would likely keep those urges at bay and still give both of us plenty of time to live our lives. I could research the connection and figure out the root cause of this pull I feel, and you could work with me to prove the fated mate idea as false."

Clark's statement pretty much became Charlie Brown's teacher's voice in my head after the fourth word. Three syllables that wouldn't stop playing in my head. "I'm sorry—did you say *biweekly?*"

"Yes. I'm sorry—do you not understand? I know it can technically mean two things. For this case, I was considering the every-other scenario. A fortnight, if you know—"

"I know what it means, you jackass. What I don't know is why I'm still sitting here." I rose to my feet and stormed toward the door, looking to escape. To run home. I had ice cream there. And weapons. Because right then, I wasn't sure which I needed first. *Bi-fucking-weekly, my ass.*

Clark followed me, though. All the way out into the hallway. "What about our arrangement?"

The sex. Without the mating. Because he didn't believe in that.

And I hated him a little bit for it.

"Look at me," I said, the growl evident in my voice. My fox growing a little uncivilized just for him.

Clark did as I asked, his eyes locking on mine even though he certainly didn't seem to like it. Didn't seem comfortable looking directly at me. Which was fine—he never had to look at me again. I only needed this one moment to be seen and then I could bee invisible once more.

But I'd take advantage while I had his attention.

"Why don't you take the erections my scent evokes and go fuck yourself?" I began walking backward as I gave him my best smile. "Biweekly."

And with that, I turned, shoved open the door to the staircase, and ran downstairs. And if a few tears fell before I made it to my car...well, no one could blame me. Right?

My mate—my fated other half—didn't want me, which meant pain and hopelessness in regard to my own future. Shifters didn't refuse matings—it simply wasn't done. They'd get sick. They'd die alone eventually.

Clark had just destroyed my life and his, and he wasn't smart enough to know it yet.

3

CLARK

Women had always been a mystery to me. No, not a mystery—I liked mysteries. Liked solving them, really. Women were an unsolvable conundrum that simply refused to fit into place in my mind. My draw to a particular woman—the little fox shifter named Misty—made no sense to me. She was gorgeous, yes. Of course. Way too pretty to want to spend time with a man like me. She was also snarky and sarcastic, brassy and bold. She was the exact opposite of me, yet there was nothing I wanted more than to figure out why I couldn't stop thinking about her. Stop dreaming of her scent. Why she was slowly driving me mad.

Out of habit, I opened my computer and began listing what I knew about her. I'd first noticed that something was off inside of me, that the mental cage I'd kept my wolf in since I was a child seemed to be weakening, about four months prior. I'd taken a trip to Kinship Cove for the day and had ended up not wanting to leave. When I did return to the college where I lived and taught, I couldn't get the town out of my head.

I'd assumed at first that it was some sort of seasonal hormone shift, being that I had a beast living within me. My mother had raised me to control the wolf, to cage him up and not let him overtake my logical thoughts. Shifting hadn't happened until I was in my twenties—and rarely happened since that first time. I didn't like losing control to him. I lived in a world of science and logic and reason—he lived in a world of base desires like food and sex.

Sex…didn't sound so bad right then.

"Hydrogen, helium, lithium, beryllium, boron, carbon, nitrogen…" I chanted the periodic table out loud first by atomic mass then by year of discovery, letting my mind wander back to the problem at hand. The one named Misty.

I'd been drawn to a bakery in Kinship Cove, the one where my wolf had woken up for the first time in a long time and demanded something of me. Had pushed my human side to the back and nearly taken over. He hadn't succeeded. The control of my human mind was undoubtedly stronger—likely from starving the beast of any sort of control for so many years—but the mutt had still figured out a way to overpower me at times. He'd force my thoughts back to that place, that town, that bakery. Back to the scent that wouldn't let us go.

So, I'd studied and researched the town and later the bakery, had figured out who owned the place and then hacked my way in to their computers to know more about them. The three sisters had seemed quite uninteresting until I'd dug a little deeper into the youngest one's browser history, specifically the links and records from her phone. I'd discovered that Franny—such a horrible name for a woman named Madeleine—was looking into selling her intimates online to strangers. I'd monitored her activity until that first pair hit the auction site. I'd purchased that pair for research, of course. Thinking maybe, just maybe, I could build some sort of professional relationship with the girl so I could explore my call to her store. That hadn't happened, though. I'd barely made it back to my door from the mailbox with the garment in hand before an erection—so large and so uncomfortable, I'd thought for just a moment that I'd been drugged—had demanded all my attention. And by attention, I meant my hand. A lot of time with that damned erection in my hand. Too much time.

Once I'd finally spent myself a dozen times, I'd written up a research log on what had happened. My experiment results list, while short, had led me to assume that Madeleine was the one whose scent tugged me toward the bakery. Of course, I had to test that hypothesis, so I bought another pair. And another. And then...well, let's just say I became a regular customer. And a person who suddenly hated how fast he ran out of hot water.

And yet, those panties had never quite scratched my itch. Never quite soothed my beast. No matter how many times I'd bought them.

I'd bought them a lot, too. Paid top dollar for them. Even convincing the young Franny to meet in person multiple times so I could determine if proximity mattered. All for nothing—I'd gone down the wrong path. It was Misty I should have been studying.

"Misty, fox shifter, beautiful..." My chant shifted gears, my mind filling with thoughts of the woman who was supposedly my mate. I'd overlooked her at the bakery—a stupid mistake on my part and one that would plague me for weeks as I rewound every interaction with Madeleine and tried to put the pieces together in a new pattern. I should research the little fox shifter, should hack my way in to her computer and phone to see what I could find out. I was about to, actually, when suddenly my fingertips were no longer fingertips. They were claws.

"Beast, no—"

But my words turned to a growl, fur sprouting and my body changing until I stood on all fours. My wolf howled in my head, his own thoughts accessible to me in a way they'd never been before. And they were totally focused on one thing.

Misty. Mate. Claim.

I was forced into a passenger role as the wolf padded through the hotel room, opened the door with an impressively large paw, and raced down the stairs and through the hotel lobby. Once outside, the beast ran fast and hard, scenting Misty and following her trail. Hunting her down. My human side was unable to stop him. This action—this moment— seemed to be based solely on an instinct I had no say in.

It didn't take long to catch up with the fox shifter. She'd pulled over at a scenic overlook and was sitting on the hood of her car, staring up at the sky. And crying. That made my wolf see red at the idea that someone had hurt her. But, me? I was far more curious. Why would she be crying when she was the one who'd refused to participate in my experiment?

My wolf huffed, forcing his thoughts in a direction that showed me things like mates and affection, like pack dynamics and puppy piles, like companionship and sex. Lots of sex. He wanted his mate, to take care of her, to love her. I huffed, doubting that was real. Forcing my thoughts to hotels and beds and computers where I could research.

My wolf won. Again.

We slipped along the edge of the overlook until we stood directly in front of Misty's car, watching her. She stared right back, our eyes locked in a way that made human me uncomfortable. My wolf loved it, though. Needed that connection. Craved it.

Even upset and tear-streaked, Misty's inherent beauty spoke to me. So soft, this woman. So lovely. Perhaps I should try a little harder to convince her to let me research our connection. Perhaps I should look at my wolf's ideas as more than antiquated hormonal pulses.

Perhaps I should lose the fur for a bit.

It took much more energy than I would have liked, but I shifted back to my human form.

My very naked human form.

I'd forgotten about that part.

And Misty wasn't polite enough to ignore it. "Welp, you certainly weren't lying about the whole erection thing, were you?"

I crossed my hands over my groin, every inch of my body in tune with hers. Too many inches. "I'm sorry that I was curt before. I'm...new to all this."

"To the whole being a shifter thing. I can tell."

"I've known about my wolf since I was a child."

She shrugged, moving over and patting the empty area of hood next to her. Indicating I should join her, which of course, I did.

"You may have known about him, but you never learned about him."

"I studied—"

"You can't study being a shifter. You have to live it." She stared up at the stars for a long moment, quiet and calm. No longer crying. "Why do you want to treat this—me—like a science experiment?"

I gave her question the time and thought it deserved, even though the answer was easy to me. "Science makes sense, and logic is necessary. I love research, always have. I like solving puzzles."

"And you see me as a puzzle."

"More my draw to you than you yourself. You're…a woman."

She rolled her eyes. "Gee, thanks for noticing."

Hurt. She was hurt. By my words. "I'm sorry. I'm horrible at this. I don't mean to diminish your femininity as if I were only just noticing it. You're stunningly beautiful. Breathtaking, really."

She turned to stare at me with an inscrutable expression on her face, one that made my wolf sit up and take notice. One that had my heart pounding in my chest. I held her gaze for as long as I could, which wasn't that long. The pull to her was just too strong when I looked into those dark eyes. The need to do more too hard to resist. What was it with this woman?

"I'll make you a deal," she said finally, watching me long after I'd been forced to move my gaze to her sexy-as-fuck shoulder. "I'll let you research this whole mating pull with me if you allow me to teach you about being a shifter, including what the fates and being a mate means to us."

"I don't believe in—"

"Then you have nothing to worry about." She went back to looking at the stars, her chin up this time and her expression hardening. "You'll never feel anything for me anyway."

My wolf whined for some reason, the hard edge in her voice scratching at something in my human senses, too. I pushed past the discomfort, though. She was willing to give me what I wanted, and all I had to do was learn about being a shifter. That could only add to my overall research of shifter dynamics. I liked research.

I liked the idea of spending time with her in any way I could, too.

"You've got yourself a deal."

4

MISTY

I am an idiot. A raging idiot. A raging idiot without a lot of choices.

You know what sucked? My life. That's what. For two days, I'd paced and fretted and berated myself. I'd questioned what I was thinking every single second I was awake. I'd fought the almost overwhelming urge to haul ass over that mountain and track down the man the fates had thrown into my path like some sort of boulder. And while doing all that, I thought about my decision. Accepting it. Coming to terms with it. And in the end, I held strong. I would become a willing research subject instead of a mate.

By the fates, suck was too weak of a word choice.

My reality had taken a turn for the worse with my mating, and that hadn't been something I could have seen coming. I mean, I'd heard of imperfect pairings—I had a brother mated to a human social media influencer who also happened to be a vegan. Talk about a mismatch. I figured mine took the proverbial cake, though. Clark didn't see me, didn't believe in mates. There was no future with him, and yet there was no life for either of us without our bond. I could torture myself physically or emotionally—deal with the pain of trying to deny a mating bond, or deal with the hurt of knowing my own mate had no real interest in building a life with me. Decisions, decisions.

Ah, bullshit. The decision was easy enough. I was no sadist in the physical sense, and I could cut off any sort of emotional connection that might develop on my end. I would spend my time teaching Clark about shifters and stuff. *Stuff* being sex. Unemotional, casual sex. With a hottie professor my fox had a distinct and specific attraction to. One that focused around the whole…sex thing. Not that I could blame her. That erection he'd come walking up to me with when I'd stopped to give my tears a chance to dry? Impressive.

If you can't mate them, ride them.

"You okay?"

I looked up, meeting Coco's concerned eyes. "Yeah, of course. Why?"

"Because you've been staring at the eclairs for a solid five minutes."

Seriously…impressive.

"I'm fine, just preoccupied." I glanced at the clock, and my heart jumped a bit. Research time. "And late. I have to go."

"Hot date tonight?"

I wish. "Something like that."

Coco cocked her head, her brow furrowing. Her concern apparent on her pretty face. "You okay, Misty?"

How to answer that? No one else had asked—not my father when I'd run into him, not my brothers when I'd dropped off food at their houses because they were too darn lazy to pick it up. No one.

I loved these Chance sisters. I could also be honest with them. "Not in the least, but there's nothing anyone can do to help, so just ignore me."

Coco's frown deepened. "You know that'll never happen."

"I do, and I love you for caring. Just…I don't have the mental capacity to deal with a Chance sisters inquisition right now."

She gave me a long, concerned look—holding completely still much like an animal would—before nodding. "Understood. I'll leave you alone. You know you've got us, though, right?"

My heart was full—I had the best friends ever. "I do."

"Then go forth and suffer alone. Call me if you need a shoulder to cry on." She winged an eyebrow up in a seriously impressive arch. "Call Magnus if you need someone to bury the body."

But words were less important than that expression. "You learned that eyebrow trick from me."

"I did."

"It looks good on you."

"Thanks. I meant what I said."

"I know. Shoulders and bodies. I've got it." I paused for just a second before diving for her and giving her a big hug. "Thanks."

She hugged me back, sniffling suspiciously before shoving me away. "Get out of here, fox. Go be your sneaky self. And don't forget your coat."

"Yes, *Mom*." Grabbing my coat—because the temperature really had been dropping lately—I hurried out the door and down Main Street before turning toward the water. *Don't throw up. Don't throw up.*

I was totally going to throw up.

But I had no time for regurgitating. I was meeting Clark for our first educational session. He'd seemed excited about the plan when I'd offered up the option of meeting right away instead of waiting for two weeks. Biweekly was for losers—thankfully, he'd agreed. For this event, at least. Okay, so maybe a response of *That sounds fine* was more placating than accepting. Maybe. Who texted that response to a *Want to meet up to talk about shifters* text? Clark did, apparently.

The man himself appeared at the end of the block wearing a dark, wool pea coat and gray beanie. I almost had to chain up my fox inside myself to keep her from exploding—the man was hot. Like, movie star, silver fox, still got it hot. He had a little scruff growing below those dark glasses he wore and a very serious expression on his face that made him seem almost dangerous. Not that he was. To anyone but me.

"Hi," I said, doing my best to control the need within me to touch, to feel, to hug. He didn't seem like a hugger, and my fox would snuggle the stuffing out of him if I let her loose. "You find it okay?"

He nodded, those eyes I wanted on me so much looking past me instead. Rendering me invisible once more. Talk about taking a girl down a notch or two.

"Yes, thank you. Though—" his nose wrinkled, and that dangerous expression grew harsher "—it's quite pungent down here."

I nearly grinned. "I know. Come on, I'll show you why."

We headed all the way to the water, to a pier that sat at the edge of the wharf. The ships didn't come to this particular pier anymore for numerous reasons, one being the source of the stink.

"Clark, meet the seal shifters of Kinship Cove." I swept out my arm, indicating the water in front of us. It took Clark a second or two to realize he needed to look down, not out, but he eventually saw them.

"What are they doing here?"

"Enjoying the last days they can of decent weather before they come out of the water for winter."

He looked disgusted. "Why do they smell so bad?"

"Because seals are stinky. Cute, though."

He whipped around, frowning. Eyes meeting mine for exactly two-point-five seconds—and making me feel as if I'd been punched in the gut—before he looked away.

"You think they're cute?"

"Of course. Look how tubby they are. They embrace their chub, and I think that's adorable and awesome." I waved at the seals, trying hard not to think about the fact that I'd said chub to a man who might be showing me his own chub—again—shortly. Maybe. *Get your mind off of sex.* "Hi, guys! My mom got her hands on some beautiful lox this afternoon, so tomorrow there will be freshly made bagels from Cake-ily Ever After on the menu. Make sure to stop by the diner."

The seals below hissed and grunted a little in response, which was really all I could expect from them. The water was too cold for them to shift just to talk to me. They'd freeze their bits off.

"Did you choose to show me the seals so you could sell more bagels tomorrow?"

I waved at the seals again, then grabbed Clark by the arm and walked him toward town. "No, though that really should have been my plan. The salmon lox thing was a coincidence."

"I don't believe in coincidence."

"You don't believe in a lot of things," I said, wrinkling my nose at the leftover eau de seal shifter. "Doesn't mean they're not true."

"So, if you weren't there to sell things, why on earth would you subject yourself and me to such a stench?"

"Because it's a reminder that you're not human." I turned the corner, keeping pace with him as he slowed his steps. "Humans wouldn't smell that so strongly. They wouldn't abandon entire areas because of the odor either. That reaction to the scent of them? That was your wolf senses in play."

His brow pulled down, his eyes unfocused as they stared at the sidewalk before us. "But I'm in my human form."

"Doesn't matter. Our animals don't just disappear when we're human, no matter how much you might want them to."

"So, you're trying to show me my animal side is always there."

"Sure. That seems like a good lesson."

"Those seal shifters had a purpose, then."

"Oh no," I said, grinning. "They just hang out there being lazy and making a nuisance of themselves. They're excellent examples of stinky things being stinky, though."

He laughed and caught my eyes once more. Loud and somewhat brash, the sound rolled across my senses and made me grin. He hadn't laughed with me before, and I liked it. Liked the sound and the look of him grinning and the knowledge that I'd done that—had made him happy, even if for just a moment. Liked the way my insides went molten when those eyes stayed on mine. I liked *him*.

Quit falling for your mate.

"C'mon, professor," I said, dragging him along the road as I shoved my fox—and my own emotional needs—into the very back of my head. "There's a great coffee shop up the way. I'll buy you a cup."

"Shouldn't I buy you one? You're the one doing me the favor."

"Nope. My town, my treat. That's the way this works." I didn't mention that him buying me coffee would feel too much like a date. I didn't mention that spending time with him made me ache for more, for a true mate. I didn't mention that seeing him laugh was a bright spot in my day. I didn't mention how much it hurt when he refused to grace me with his full attention.

I didn't mention any of that stuff because I was a raging idiot and an emotional sadist. For real.

We ambled along the road, taking our time on our way to grab a coffee. Being that I'd been raised in Kinship Cove and had worked in the diner almost since I could walk, I knew most of the town. People stopped to say hello, to smile, and to look over Clark in curiosity. I introduced him as a professor in town for a research project and kept moving, not wanting any of them to get the wrong idea. Well, the right idea—he was my mate—with the wrong sort of ending. There would be no Clark and Misty after our research was done. No happily ever after with kits and a house and all that domestic crap. Not really.

I might need to put some Baileys in my coffee.

"So," Clark said once we'd reached the shop and ordered our coffees —latte for me, espresso panna for him. "While seeing the seals was quite an interesting experience, I can't see how that teaches me about being a shifter."

"How many people did you meet on your way to the wharf?"

"None."

"And how many on our walk once we left?"

His eyes met mine. Holding there for far longer than usual. Drawing my fox to the forefront in an instant. "Eighteen."

How was I supposed to speak when he was looking at me? Really looking? Oh…right. "Hang on—you counted?"

He broke our gaze, making my fox deflate and my heart stop pounding. "It's a habit. I still don't see what this has to do with shifters."

Of course he wouldn't. I took a sip of my latte, organizing my thoughts. Yup, definitely should have asked for Baileys.

"Shifters are not always like their animal selves. You're a wolf— wolves are pack animals, so perhaps a large group of wolf shifters doesn't seem abnormal to you. I'm a fox—we don't pack, but in Kinship Cove, we stay close and connected much like humans do. Even solitary animals come together to form groups for safety, for comfort, and for community. We have all types of shifters here—from mice all the way up to a dragon."

Clark huffed. "I quite remember him."

"Good, because you likely won't ever see one again. He's the only one *I've* ever met, and I grew up around here. My point is, shifters need other shifters. Kinship Cove is a place where we can all be who we really are—and who we are is a family."

"Technically not." His smile softened his words, made him seem almost to be joking. Did the good professor joke?

I definitely did. "You can take your technically and—"

He looked up, gutting me once more as he steeled me in place with a look. "Go fuck myself?"

Bingo. "Biweekly."

His grin grew larger, his eyes—a deep blue with flecks of what looked like gray—staying locked on mine. Suddenly, the tension between us grew. The pressure of our animal sides trying to push us to complete our mating making it harder to breathe. Harder to not simply attack him and tear his clothes off. To not kiss that grin right off his handsome face and pay for that mistake later.

That big, awful, ugly mistake.

"So," Clark finally said, still not tearing his gaze from mine. "About biweekly."

He wanted to talk about intercourse. *Let's talk about intercourse, baby.* Man, that just didn't flow like using the word sex would. "I was wondering when we'd get on that subject."

He seemed almost taken aback. He also looked down, focusing on the table instead of me. Releasing me from his magical gaze. "I apologize. I don't mean to—"

"How about tonight?"

Okay, so *now* he seemed taken aback. "Excuse me?"

"The first biweekly appointment—does tonight work?"

"Yes. Of course. Sure." He coughed, almost as if he'd just choked on his own spit. Which could have happened—I was basically setting up a date to have sex with him. That couldn't be a normal occurrence.

Oh my fates, what if this was normal to him?

Stop thinking.

"Great." I grabbed my coat, thankful we'd gotten our coffees in to-go cups seeing as how staying around Clark at this point would be an impossibility. "So tonight, we research why my scent has such an effect on you."

"Why?"

"That's what we're out to learn."

"No, I mean—" he held the door for me but blocked the way, essentially trapping me in the vestibule with him as he once again stared at my shoulder "—why are you agreeing to this so easily?"

Because I'd take what I could get for as long as my heart let me. Because I might as well get something out of this crazy mating before the denial of our bond drove me over the edge. Because just a glance from him set my skin on fire and made me feel seen for the first time in a long time.

Because sometimes a girl just wanted to get laid. "I'm teaching you about mates, and mating is a part of that."

"So...sex?"

One side of my mouth quirked up. "That's sort of the idea."

"Tonight."

"Yes. I can be at your hotel by say...seven. Does that work?"

He released the door so we could walk outside, looking almost flustered. "Shouldn't I buy you dinner or something first?"

If only. "Why bother with formalities? This is just about research, right?"

Clark frowned. "Right."

"I'll see you at seven then."

I walked away, not looking back. Unable to get the frown I'd just seen out of my head. This was a mistake—a big, bad, horrible, worst idea ever mistake.

Which meant I needed to buy something sexy to wear. Sexy lingerie and bad mistakes went hand in hand.

5

MISTY

My razor had never gotten such a workout.

I twisted, I turned, I pulled, and I removed every bit of hair I could discover from my neck down. Why? It wasn't like this was my first time—I wasn't some blushing human virgin with puritanical ideas about waiting until marriage. Ha. I was a shifter—a fox shifter. We fornicated like rabbits at times.

Okay, not that bad, but seriously, female fox shifters weren't called vixens for nothing.

In essence, I'd had sex plenty of times, but something about this night with Clark felt different. New. I was going to have sex with my mate. Who didn't believe in mates. And therefore, didn't want me as his.

But I was still going to ride him like I stole him.

No matter how much it hurt in the end.

"It's fine," I mumbled, looking in the mirror as I rubbed a pint of lotion into my skin. Softer...I needed to be softer. "It's totally fine. I can handle this."

Man, I was a good liar.

I was just starting to hyperventilate a little bit at the thought of what was to come—the good, the bad, and the likely-to-get ugly—when my phone rang, Ginger's face appearing on my screen from my contact log.

Perhaps she'd finally read the text I'd sent her earlier. The one that contained only three words—*thong or commando?*

I tapped the screen to answer the call. "What's up, dollface?"

"So...there's going to be sexing tonight."

"I don't know what you're talking about." *Best liar ever.*

"Really? Because that's not what I heard."

"Who the heck is talking? I didn't tell anyone—" My teeth rattled with the force I used to snap my jaw closed. "You tricked me."

"I don't know what you're talking about."

Basically, I wasn't the only good liar in the bunch. Not surprised, to be honest. "Ginger, I swear to the fates, if you're messing with me—"

"Fine," she said before I could threaten her with something super crafty and evil. Like...replacing all her moisturizer with edible lube guaranteed to bring all the single shifter men to her door. Not that I'd investigated the right scent to do such a thing. Or whatever. "I didn't hear a thing. Though you texted me about underwear choices that don't involve an entire yard of fabric—I figured sex was a pretty clear indication."

"Really? I didn't think my question was all that brazen."

"Asking if your pussy lips should be flapping in the breeze or not is awfully brazen, my friend. Totally a dead giveaway. Plus, I'm pretty much psychic when it comes to fucking. I can sense the rise in hormones."

She couldn't...I didn't think. "Impressive."

"As is how good you are at lying to yourself."

"What do you mean?"

"He's your mate. You won't be able to hit it and quit it."

My stomach dropped, my inner fox chattering unhappily in my head. I had to take a breath before I could answer her. "Friends with benefits is doable at this point."

"No."

"We're going to meet up biweekly."

"What the fuck is biweekly?"

"It means—"

"I know what it means—though really there are two meanings, so a little clarification on whether that's twice a week or once every other week might be nice."

I huffed a laugh. "Once every other week."

"A fortnight between fucking? You poor thing. And why is any sort of time frame even being discussed along with sex? Are you scheduling hookups?"

Hookups. Not matings, not dates, not anything normal. Just...sex. "Yeah. For research."

"Misty." If Ginger had sounded any angrier, I'd have been afraid. As it was, I was sort of thinking I'd call in sick tomorrow. And maybe the next day. I definitely needed at least three days away from the sisters.

"It's fine," I said, already working on my absenteeism excuses in my head. Sore throat. Cramps. A giant eagle chased me down and sliced my arm open. Hey, it could happen.

Ginger, meanwhile, was stuck on the Clark and me thing. "It's so not *fine*. You deserve more than biweekly fuck fests."

I wanted more than that too, but Clark didn't. He wanted research.

Which meant I was going to research his dick like no other. "I'm good. I can handle this."

"Bitch, you're more than just good. You're fabulous. But are you sure you're okay with this? Are you ready for the fallout?"

Ready for Clark to disappear? For him to decide our research was done? Or for him to keep coming back, ready to settle for twice-a-month physical interludes with no personal connection, no snuggling and curling up together? No true mating, just an occasional visit to ward off the worst of the mating denial pain.

Was I ready?

I was going to have to be. "I'm ready. I know what I'm getting into."

Ginger blew out a breath, causing a little static on the line. "Then I'll leave you alone about it. Call me if you need saving, though. I've got a dragon shifter, and I'm not afraid to use him."

"You use that dragon enough already."

"True. But Kingston won't mind if I call off our nightly freak fest for a little search and rescue mission."

From the background, I heard a deep, rumbly, "The fuck I won't."

"Sounds like he disagrees with your assumption."

"Well, there goes my foot rub," Ginger said, sounding more than a little pouty. "I should go. He gets cranky when I ignore him for too long."

In Ginger/Kingston speak, that meant he got anxious if he didn't have her naked and underneath him every few hours. Or in front of him. Or on top of him. This one time, I walked into the kitchen at the bakery, and…

Well, that's a story for another time.

I gave her the same advice I'd been giving myself all day. "Get yours, girl."

"Back atcha."

I ended the call with a tap, clinging to the phone as if somehow it would tell me what to do. I was pretty sure Siri's answer to "Should I or should I not fuck my noncommitting mate?" would be something along the lines of "I don't understand the question."

To be honest, neither did I. A mate who didn't want to be mates. Who didn't believe in the concept or understand what could happen if one tried to ignore the bond. I'd seen shifters suffer through horrible seizure-like episodes while trying to break a mating. Had watched our town alpha—Jericho, of Madeleine and Jericho—deal with a depression lesser men would have fallen victim to when he was stupidly trying to ignore his mating bond. Shifters couldn't stop a mating bond. But Clark —well, he didn't fully embrace his shifter side, so he thought the entire phenomena could be boiled down to pheromones.

If that were the case, there would have been some aged shifters brewing that shit up on the daily.

Only I would be cursed with a mate who would even consider such a thing as *mating doesn't exist*.

By the fates, what was wrong with that man?

Still, there was no denying the pull to be with my mate, no use trying to stop it. I might not ever get everything I wanted—a true mate, partner, and father to a litter or two of adorable, crossbred kits—but I was going to take what I could get for as long as I could. Impending heartbreak be damned. So I got dressed into some seriously sexy clothes, I put on some seriously sinful red lipstick, and I gave myself a seriously intense look-over in the full-length mirror. Hair done, makeup ready, lips looking like they were meant for sucking things, dress showing every curve, legs bare and ready to be spread.

Heart...tucked deep inside the fortress I'd built around it.

"It's research time."

6

CLARK

It's just research. It's just research.

I chanted those words to myself as I paced my hotel room. They didn't help. My stomach stayed knotted, and my skin still felt clammy. Tonight was more than research. I didn't know how much more, definitely *more*…but in what way? I'd had sex before. Twice, in fact. Two totally different people. Both times had been pretty good. I mean, not like *the greatest event in my life* good…but good. Fine. Lovely, if not slightly messy. How much better could sex be with a shifter woman than a human?

Mate. My inner beast huffed, growling the word in my mind. *Mate.*

"No such thing." I started to pace again, but a knock at the door sent me scampering in that direction. I waited a few seconds to answer, taking a deep breath and preparing myself to see Misty again. Beautiful, sexy, funny, sarcastic Misty. My not-mate. And yet the only woman I'd ever met whom I simply couldn't stop thinking about. Who inflamed my soul and made me want to throw logic out the window. And whom I was about to have sex with.

Lord help me.

One last deep breath and a quick adjustment to my already hard and aching self, then I was ready. I swung open the door and tried to smile, but I was pretty sure every muscle in my body turned to stone in exactly zero point five seconds. Every. Single. Muscle.

She is so fucking hot.

The thought startled me in its baseness, but there was no other way to describe her. No better word. Beautiful was too trite, pretty too simple. Cute was all wrong for sure, and exquisite trivial. No… Misty was all of those things but more. She was hot and totally fuckable.

And I was standing there staring at her instead of inviting her inside.

"Hi." I coughed, the word coming out on a breathy sort of sigh. "You look lovely."

Hot, my wolf growled. *Mate. Hot. Sex.* A sensation unlike any I'd ever experienced tickled my mind, the feeling of my inner beast…moving around. As if he was a real being living inside my head instead of some whisper of spirit. I sensed movement and emotion, need and desire. Misty had awakened him from a long, deep slumber. She was what he'd been waiting for. What he wanted.

Mine.

"Did you get your work done this afternoon?" She slipped out of her coat, making my knees go weak. Skin and red and…curves. Have mercy, the woman was a siren. A dangerous creature hell-bent on destroying me. Or at least my control.

"Some of it," I replied, the lie rolling off my tongue easily. As if I could work when I'd been so worked up. When I'd known I would be having sex with her later. I couldn't have worked if my life had depended on it. She didn't need to know that. "Did you have a nice time after we went for coffee?"

"I did. Dealt with a few issues at the diner, went shopping for a few thongs, and then took a nice, hot bath."

Do not think about her ass in a thong. Do not think— "Thong shopping?"

Yeah, those two words proved I wasn't thinking, all right.

"Yeah," she said, pouting those bright red lips of hers. "But I didn't find anything I liked, so I figured I'd just go without."

Without…as in…was she not wearing panties? I liked panties—*I think we all know I like panties*—but her in that dress with nothing underneath? If I hadn't bit my tongue, I would have moaned. And then come. And then moaned again.

Death by vixen. That would be the title of my memoir.

"Uh…" *Think, think, think. You have a PhD—there is a brain somewhere inside of you. THINK.* "Can I get you something from the minibar?"

"No thank you. I'd prefer a clear head for our research."

"Research." Hypothesis: If I have sexual intercourse with my supposed mate, then my level of pleasure should increase tenfold. "Right. So…you've been thinking about the research?"

I met her gaze for the first time, nearly stumbling at the immediate sensations that overcame me when our eyes locked. At all my inner wolf threw at me in that moment. Need, desire, arousal, lust—her eyes on mine were pure sex, and I had a hard time keeping mine from looking elsewhere to escape her.

I had a hard time looking anywhere but at those bright red lips, to be honest.

She smiled, lips turning up in such a sexy way, the look that of a predator, then stood and sauntered over to me. Sauntered—because there was no other way to describe the way she moved. Hips rolling, breasts jiggling, eyes locked on mine even though I could only dart looked her way. She teased with every step, exuded confidence with every foot covered. Yeah, that was a saunter for sure.

"Oh, I've been thinking about our *research*, all right. Have you?"

She pushed me back until I was seated on the end of the bed. And then she…well, she…there was no easy way to describe this. She straddled me. Hoisted a leg and settled directly over my very hard, very neglected…groin area.

Sweet mercy. "Yeah. I've been…thinking."

Her lips kicked up a little higher, that smile turning a bit more devilish. "Thinking is good. Doing is better."

Oh hell. My inner wolf bounded back and forth in my head, making me dizzy. Throwing off my equilibrium. I did my best to leash the beast, but it was hard work. I was having trouble concentrating, what with the sexy female on my lap with her legs spread and her dress hiked up to show off…

Yup. Pantiless. Nothing but warm skin.

Pretty sure I came a little bit when I saw that.

"Tell me something, Clark," Misty said, leaning closer and biting her lip. "What do you like?"

You. This. How out of control I feel. "Everything. I think."

"You think? Okay, that's a broad question. Tell me this instead—what do you want to do?"

As if I could choose just one thing. "I…I'm not sure."

"Anything. You can tell me anything."

Those lips. My god, did they entice me. "Well, there's one thing I've never done."

"Hmmm, I don't mind butt stuff, but maybe not for our first time."

"Yeah. Sure. I just—" My wolf froze, his tenseness overriding my own feelings. "Wait…is that an option?"

She shrugged, the strap of her dress falling down and revealing all sorts of soft, hot skin. "Maybe later. I did promise you a full research opportunity."

And that, my friends, was the moment I died. Or it felt as if I'd died. Whatever. My heart leaped in my chest, and my lungs stopped functioning. Death by vixen, part deux.

Before I could pull my thoughts together enough to form words and sentences, Misty took over again. Rolling her hips into mine and leaning close to whisper, "Tell me what you want."

My vocabulary failed me, for I could only think of two tiny little words.

"Your mouth."

Misty grinned, those lips all I could see. "You want me to suck you, Clark?"

I…where…what…huh?

When I didn't answer, Misty scooted back, dropping until her knees rested on the carpet. "Have you ever had a blow job?"

Her fingers brushed across my…self, and I whimpered. That made her smile even wider.

"I'll take that as a no." She spread my legs, inching between them.

Opening me up to her invasion. "Where's your wolf, Clark? Why isn't he growling at me yet?"

"I have him on a leash." True, but odd at the same time. He'd never demanded my attention before, so thinking of him as trying to now, as being a separate entity inside of me, felt off. Wrong.

But Misty felt so very right.

She ran her hands up my thighs, teasing me with fingertips that just barely brushed the sides of where I was so hard for her. Staring up at me the entire time. "You could let him out to play, you know. You might like it."

I shook my head, my hands going to her hair. Unable not to touch as a growl filled my ears from within. "I don't think that's a good idea."

Misty unfastened my pants and pulled my...cock, there was no better word than cock in that moment...from inside, blowing over the tip as I took a breath and held it. As I struggled to hang on to the leash around my wolf. As I did my best not to fist my hands in her hair and force myself inside her mouth.

Between those thick, red lips.

Into the heaven I knew had to be waiting for me within them.

Misty looked up at me when I whimpered, all wide eyes and open mouth and sin and salvation right there at my feet. And I finally fell—I looked right into the eyes of the temptress, and I didn't look away.

Such gorgeous, heart-stealing eyes.

Her grin turned wicked, her tongue peeking out to lick the tip of me before she whispered her own version of magic words. "Let your wolf out, Clark. I want to see you lose control."

That leash—the one I'd imagined tying my inner wolf to me and helping me keep control? Well, it snapped.

Gone.

Destroyed.

And my wolf took control.

7

MISTY

Asking to see his wolf might have been a bit sneaky—heck, showing up dressed to seduce and playing the vampy little vixen wasn't exactly playing by his rules—but the ends justified the means. I needed him to let go, needed the smarty-pants human side of Clark to crack just a little. He'd neglected his animal side so long, I wasn't sure if his wolf would even respond.

He responded, all right.

Clark grabbed me under the arms and lifted, twisting his body and swinging me onto the bed. Practically throwing me up the mattress. When his eyes met mine once more, I could finally see the beast within. See how that wolf was running more of the show now. Pushing Clark to act. That was just what I wanted.

"Come to me." I inched up the bed, tugging my dress higher as I moved. Making sure my legs were spread just enough for him to know. To *see.* "I want my mate. Come to me."

Clark growled but did as I said, crawling over me on all fours. Covering my body with his as he refused to break our gaze. His voice barely more than a growl as he said, "You're playing a dangerous game, Misty."

I wrapped my arms around his neck and yanked him closer. "I know."

Kissing Clark was like… Have you ever seen videos of buildings being imploded? There's a huge boom, and the entire structure is sucked inward just a bit. There's this moment then, when the world goes still for a split second, before a waterfall of *everything* comes crashing down. That was our kiss. Clark's lips met mine, and the world stopped. Our first kiss, and all I could do was inhale and wait for the crash. The first time our lips touched, and suddenly everything felt right in my world. Mostly because all that world included was Clark and me, his wolf and my fox. No families, no jobs, no research. Just us.

With my exhale, a wave of lust so strong I couldn't breathe swept over me. The crash. Finally.

"Misty," Clark grumbled before kissing me deeper, diving in for more and hotter and wetter. I responded in kind, sliding my hands under his sweater and dragging my nails down his back. Relishing the way his entire body responded to my touch. The way his skin felt against mine. When I reached the waistband of his pants, I kept going. Working my way underneath the fabric. Grabbing handfuls of flesh as I moaned and he rocked his hips into mine. As he shoved my dress over my breasts so more skin could touch, more heat could build. More friction could happen. So we had simply *more*.

Dry-humping. We were dry-humping on a hotel bed, half naked and slightly out of control. Like some sort of human teenagers after the prom story. Quaint, but not what I wanted. I wasn't a teenager—neither was Clark—and we certainly weren't human.

"Naked," I gasped once Clark moved his lips to my neck. "I need you naked."

He groaned and bit my neck hard enough to make me tremble. To make me gasp. For three seconds, I thought maybe—just maybe—he was giving me a claiming bite, but that wasn't to be. His wolf might have been driving the car, but Clark was still navigating. The man who didn't believe in mates.

Stop thinking, keep feeling.

I tugged Clark's sweater up, pushing it over his shoulders with his assistance. He shoved his pants down and off with a little help from me. Such warm skin, such joy in connection when he was bare with me. Finally, with eyes still locked on mine and making me feel truly seen for the first time, he dove forward, and then he was on top of me, naked. And he felt so damn good, but it wasn't enough.

"I want to see you," I whispered, tracing patterns onto his skin. My fox practically screaming into my mind as I made him stop. "Please. For research."

I was sure I only imagined the flinch at that word.

"Of course." Clark rose up, kneeling over me. Legs spread around mine and cock jutting up against his belly. Toned and strong but not bulky, the man exuded the air of someone who took good care of themselves. Who ate grilled chicken and broccoli or a salad every day for lunch. I sat up, my dress falling to cover more of my skin, and ran my hands over his chest, tracing the muscles there. Taking my sweet time to learn him. Doing my own research in a slightly different field than his.

"You're strong."

"Does that surprise you?"

"Not really, no."

"Do you like it?" Clark wrapped his hand around mine and tugged it down, over his rippled abs. "Do I please you?"

So much beast in that voice, so much of his wolf influencing him. He sounded like a shifter with a mate, not a professor performing research. He sounded like he could be mine.

With a smile, I circled his cock and stroked him once, twice, three times. "I think you'll please me just fine."

Clark groaned and his head fell forward, rocking with my movement. His thighs trembling a bit. My word, the man was sexy. Half out of control but still holding back. Obviously wanting so much more but not taking. It was a total tease to see him like that—to know there was more. That he hadn't let go just yet.

Time to change that. "Where do you want this to happen?"

He looked up, eyes locking on mine again and breaths coming fast. "What?"

"The first time I make you come. Where would you like it? My mouth, my hand, or my pussy?"

A fire lit inside of his eyes, something burning bright and hot as he stared at me. As his features moved just enough for me to see the changes. His structure sharpening a bit. His wolf pushing a little closer to the surface.

"You first," he said as his hands slipped under my dress and tugged upward. As he undressed me with a yank of fabric over my head. "I want to make you come first, but I get to choose the how."

"Oh, you do?" I ran a nail over his jaw as he took me in, as he stared down at me and growled softly. So hot, this man. So mine. "That doesn't seem fair."

With a wicked grin, Clark grabbed my wrists, pulling my hands over my head, and shoved me back. I lay before him, naked. Shivering a little under that heated stare. Trembling more when he let go of my arms and placed his hands instead on the inside of my knees. When he pushed them apart.

"I've wanted to taste you since that first scenting." He crawled forward, keeping his hands in contact with my thighs. Kneading my flesh as he leaned in to kiss and lick his way north. "You have driven me crazy for months, little fox. It may be selfish of me, but there's nothing I want more than to have you come on my tongue right now."

I arched as he ran a finger all the way up, as he teased and tickled me where I was so wet for him. As he moved close enough for me to feel his breath *right there*.

"So very selfish," I said, gripping his hair as he gave me a soft kiss directly over my clit, making me gasp and clench and need. "I guess I can forgive you that, though."

"Good. Because you smell like sin, and I'm not leaving this spot until I've gotten my fill of it."

And then he was on me. No gentle lead-in or more teasing. Nope. Clark dove in and went to work, licking, sucking, biting, and all around assaulting my pussy. The man was good at loving me with his mouth, too. Learned in the art of pussy-eating. And like any good student who had put in the work to master a subject, he wanted to show off. And he did. He *so* did.

I arched and tugged and cried and tried to control the man, but he wasn't having it. This was his show, his dissertation. I was merely the very appreciative audience. The moaning, writhing audience.

"Clark, oh." So good, so very good. I was going to lose it. To fall into an abyss of pleasure and lust and heat and need and —

With a growl, he slipped two fingers inside of me. Filling me up as he flattened his tongue and licked me from opening to clit, as he owned every inch of me.

Dead. I was dead. Gone. Building falling.

"So wet," he mumbled, adjusting his position to lift my hips off the bed and hold me before him like some sort of feast. Like an offering. "I want to lick up every drop."

Me? I was past words. The man had me lifted up. Off the bed. Had me splayed before him and was eating me as if I were his last meal. As if this were his only chance. I tugged and wiggled and moaned his name over and over again, chasing that high. That feeling of intense pressure then release.

Waiting for another implosion.

It came when Clark surprised me. The man seemed so inexperienced, yet he knew how to work my body well. Knew exactly what to do to drive me that much higher. Even twisting his hand so his thumb could press against my asshole. Not enter it, just...push. A bit of pressure. A tease.

A make-her-come-immediately sort of action.

I exploded around his fingers, yanking his face against me and riding his tongue as my body shook and fell apart. As the world shrank to nothing but him and me and that feeling of intense pleasure. That moment in the implosion when the world stopped. When silence reigned for one long, glorious moment.

Clark pulled me through every pulse, treated me past every point of no return, and dragged me through the longest orgasm of my life. He was a growling, writhing mess when I finally pushed him off me.

"Too sensitive," I said, grabbing his shoulders. Tugging him up me once more. "Come here now. I want you inside me."

"I thought I got to choose where I wanted to come for this first time." Clark softened his words with a smile as he capitulated, laying his body over mine and lining us up. Staring into my eyes as if I was more than a research project for him.

Oh, there was no way to save my heart now. None. And I was okay with that…for the moment.

"You do," I said, reaching up to run a finger along his jaw. Basking in that blue-gray stare as I arched my back and took him inside. "You choose inside my pussy. Don't even pretend like that's not what you wanted."

"You can read my mind now?" He sighed and pushed deeper, nudging his way in. Killing me slowly in the best possible way.

"No. Your body." I arched and moaned, wanting so much more. Needing him deep. Knowing there were ways to make him lose that blasted control. Words I could say. "Besides, I can suck you off later. I want to come around that big, thick cock of yours."

"Dammit, Misty." He plunged forward, that control snapping a little more. That wall between him and his true self crumbling brick by brick as he thrust all the way in. "You're so hot inside. Oh shit, so tight."

He lost all sense of rhythm and control, bucking his hips against me and moaning with every thrust. I let him, knowing he needed this. Needed to get one good fuck out of his system before he could begin to refine his style. Before he could figure out how to finesse the pleasure instead of forcing it.

Still, I wanted more. I had a feeling I would always want more. So I grabbed his hand and slipped it between us, leading his fingers to my clit.

"Rub," I said when he opened his eyes and looked at me, surprised. "I want you to feel me come on you. Rub, and I will."

"Oh god, again?"

Poor, misguided man thinking women only came once. He'd learn. "Yes. Again. Make me come, Clark. I want you to feel me."

He growled long and deep, rubbing my clit as his lips came back to mine. As he kissed me, letting me taste myself on him. Letting my fox smell the scent of the two of us together. This was right and good and so very hot, especially when my body clamped down on his cock. When my orgasm slammed over me and I yelped a filthy curse that made him moan. When he came right after me, groaning and growling and pressing deep inside as he filled me up.

As he collapsed on top of me, holding me close and whispering my name.

As he ran his fingers through my hair and snuggled so sweetly.

As the reality of biweekly sank in and my heart began to ache.

That wouldn't be enough. Sex every other week without my mate to come home to every day? It would never be enough.

At least, not for me.

Ever.

What had I just done?

8

CLARK

Waking up with Misty in my arms was unlike any experience I'd had before. Sex with her had also been different. Not mechanically, though the girl *was* exceptionally flexible and coordinated. She'd crawled and rocked and bent and twisted herself into pretzels all for our enjoyment. And I'd enjoyed it all. Greatly.

No, mechanically, sex hadn't changed. Emotionally? This was an entirely new realm of knowledge. Never before had I felt as much as I did with her, never had I cared so much either. This girl had burrowed her way into my heart, and I was pretty sure I felt for her in a deeper, more meaningful way than I'd ever thought possible.

My wolf stretched in my mind, his fur brushing along my nerve endings. An odd sensation for sure. No more cage—no more leash. Just him completely free in my mind. Definitely new, but not something I minded. He seemed to fit there.

He also really loved the little fox shifter in my arms. *Mate. Mine.*

Still such odd terms, but the words didn't bother me as much as they had the day before. They didn't seem as foreign. They felt…somehow within the realm of possibility under a new perspective. Like string theory, proven false but brought back to life as superstring theory.

Misty rolled closer to me, nuzzling against my chest. Those dark eyes I suddenly wanted to stare into forever meeting mine. Something that had been making me feel uncomfortable because of how locking our gazes brought my wolf forward. Something I never wanted to avoid again, wolf or no.

She smiled. "Hi."

One word, and I was dead. "Hi. It's still early, my little fox. Go back to sleep."

"I can't. I never sleep this late." She stretched, pressing her body against mine. Teasing me with her warm flesh and soft curves. *Vixen, indeed.* "What are you doing up?"

I ran my hands down her back to her thighs and all the way up again. Pulling her tighter against me. Wanting to rut into her but holding back. Mostly. "Thinking about you."

"Good thoughts, I hope."

I rolled her under me. Kissing my way down her neck to her breasts, teasing the hard, pink tips with my tongue. "Always good thoughts."

She arched and tugged on my hair, something I never would have thought I'd enjoy but that made me want to ravage her. I liked her demanding—loved that she knew what she wanted and wasn't afraid to show me. I didn't have a lot of experience, but I was one hell of a student. I'd read all the books on sexual satiation and technique—I'd studied *She Comes First* as if prepping for a final exam. Study and books couldn't teach me everything, though. Couldn't give me the knowledge to know what every sigh meant, why she arched at times and shook at others. Couldn't tell me how her heartbeat would be a pulse I craved to feel against my skin. Only being with her would, and I was ready to put in the time to learn more. Study harder. To become a PhD in all things Misty.

I sucked her nipple into my mouth and bit down on the tip. Not too hard, just enough to make her moan. To make her start to shake. To warm her up for more. Still focusing on her breasts, I slipped a hand down farther. Teasing the flesh between her thighs. Finding her wet and hot and ready for me. Perfect. Two fingers inside, and those thighs I wanted to live between rose, creating a little den for me right there on top of her body. Giving my wolf an immediate sense of security and safety and trust.

She wrapped herself around me, and I was home.

"Clark," Misty gasped as her body responded to my touch, as she began to writhe on my fingers and rock into my hold. "Please. I need you."

"Want to feel you come first. Give me one, then you can ride my cock."

She groaned long and loud, rocking harder. Fucking herself on my fingers. I'd never been one for any sort of sexy talk. The words had never come easily to me. At least, not before Misty. With her, I suddenly knew what to say, knew what to do. Everything was about her pleasure, and that focusing gave me a deep dive into *Dirty Talk 301: Sexing up a fox named Misty*. Course completion achieved. Level up.

"I'm so close." Misty moaned and grabbed my hand, pressing it harder against her clit. Forcing my fingers deeper inside her body.

"I feel you. Come for me, baby. I need it. Then you can have my cock. Then I can fill you up and make you come over and over again."

And she did. Come, that is. I was more than grateful, because as she clenched and shook and chanted my name, I slipped my fingers out of her and replaced them with my cock, driving him home in one thrust. Pushing deep inside of her to feel that pulsation. Enough for me but not for her. She'd taught that lesson, and I'd memorized the theorem. I pressed on her clit with my thumb, giving her the added pressure she needed, and started moving. Loving the way her legs wrapped around my hips, the way she grabbed my shoulders as if she needed something to hang on to. That something was me, and I'd make sure she got what she wanted. Make sure I got something for me too.

"Turn over." I rose off Misty, smacking her ass as she flipped onto her stomach. Pulling her up to her knees so I could get a good view of those curves. Of the dip of her waist and the swell of her hips. Of her perfectly bitable ass. "So beautiful."

"You're not looking at my face."

"I know. Every part of you is beautiful." To punctuate my point, I leaned over to bite her ass cheek, then reared back and slid home once more. We'd done this last night. Just once, but the position had made an impression on me for sure, had become a favorite within seconds. I didn't like that I couldn't see her face—I'd need to buy a mirrored headboard for that, something I'd already added to my mental to-do list —but I loved how deep I could go, how much Misty thrust back against me. How I could make her moan with my cock inside of her and my body wrapped around hers. This was a position meant for us. Obviously.

"That's it, little fox. You love it when I fuck you deep, don't you? Love feeling my big cock all the way inside you. I want you to come again for me, show me how much you like this. How much you want me to keep fucking you."

"By the fates, Clark." Misty groaned, coming around me with a sudden clench of her pussy that nearly made me crawl out of my skin. There was no holding back. I thrust deep and came, my entire body going white-hot, every nerve ending alight just for her. For us. Our union.

Mate, my wolf howled. *Mine.*

Fate and mates and forever. Hypothesis, not theory. Unable to be proven true, but not able to be proven false either.

"That was…" Misty sighed and stretched, laughing quietly. "Well done, professor."

Gripping her ass, I chuckled and tugged her against me. Relishing the feel of her hot skin on mine. Living for that touch. "Excellent research, fox."

She stiffened in my arms, but I stroked her back and she relaxed again. Curling into me and hanging on. I closed my eyes, thinking about another round, happily lying on the bed next to my mate and enjoying a few minutes of peace and quiet, when my world suddenly went sideways.

Misty got up.

Left the bed.

She grabbed her clothes off the floor.

And started putting them on.

"Where are you going?"

"I have to work at the diner today. Besides, you got what you came for." Harsh words in an even harsher tone. Flat and emotionless and just plain wrong. She leaned over me, her eyes suddenly not meeting mine. Her lips dry as she kissed my cheek. "Hope you enjoyed your research. See you in two weeks."

She was gone before I could find the words I needed to make her stay, practically running from the room as if this space had become dangerous. As if the only place she wanted to be was *not here*.

I was left alone—naked in the bed we'd shared, with no knowledge of how to make her come back.

She'd walked away.

It was only research, I thought. Just an experiment to determine why I felt so drawn to her. To investigate that connection and find the root cause of it.

Only research.

So why did her leaving hurt so badly?

And why was my wolf howling horribly in my head?

MISTY

Biweekly was bullshit.

Research was a crock.

And I was a raging, sadistic idiot who should have known better.

I'd spent two weeks suffering without my mate, on edge and completely distraught. My chest hurting more and more each day. But just as I could admit I was an idiot of epic proportions, I was also stubborn as hell. No way would I break down and go to Clark when he obviously wasn't coming for me. Not happening. So I waited, and I suffered.

And I made everyone around me almost as miserable as I was.

Even the customers had noticed my grumpy side come out. The Chance sisters had allowed me half a shift at the counter before they'd moved me into the back to deal with the baking instead of the people.

Good call—I may have threatened a man who asked for an iced cappuccino with my claws.

Iced cappuccinos are not a thing. Ever.

I'd been upset and cranky and altogether in a foul mood enough that even my own mother had noticed. Don't get me wrong, my mom was amazing and kind in her own way, but when you had so many kits, little things like my bad mood tended to slip past her. Not this time, though.

"Are you okay, Misty Rain?"

She full-named me. Yeah, she'd noticed my mood. This wasn't good. "I'm fine."

Her look sharpened, the mom side of her on high alert, it seemed. "You've been sulking."

Understatement. "I haven't sulked."

"Sulkers always claim they don't sulk. But they do. Why has a sulky sulker taken over my baby?"

My sigh was big enough to earn a raised eyebrow, one I was helpless against. "I met my mate."

Her face lit up, her smile growing wide and high as my stomach sank into the floor. "Oh, that's wonderful—"

"He doesn't believe in the fates and thinks mating is something other than a forever connection between two people."

My mom was an expressive soul. Her face, her body language—she transmitted her mood in muscle twitches and eyebrow raises. The look she gave me was one I'd never seen before. Worse than the time one of my older brothers had gotten into trouble and she'd had to bail him out of a human jail. Worse than the look I'd gotten when I'd *borrowed* my father's car to go cruising with friends. Without asking. And drove it into a ditch. The look on her face could only be described as a thundercloud, and one heck of a storm was coming.

"How is that possible? Is he stupid?"

I wish. "No. He's really smart, actually. He's a college professor."

"Well, he seems stupid to me. What man wouldn't want such a mate as you? Who could possibly turn down someone as kind and caring, as sweet and—"

"You're thinking of Tilly. She's the sweet one."

"I'm thinking of my Misty, who went to work a second job at a bakery owned by humans because she knew they'd need help when their mates found them. Who made a deathbed promise to those girls' parents to take care of them and worked hard to see that through." She grabbed my hands like she had when I was a child and too upset to speak, leaning closer. Locking me in place with a look so filled with love, there was nothing else in the room. "I'm talking about my most generous child. The one who has always put others' needs before her own. Who cooks for all of us at our weekly dinner and never complains about helping out her old mother who just wants a single night off. I'm speaking of my devilishly quick-witted daughter who deserves so much more than she's been given."

Oh. Tears. They were a-comin'. "Stop it, Mom."

"I will not. I'm livid on your behalf. I have a right mind to track this professor down and give him an education on mating he won't soon forget." She huffed, letting me go so she could pace the kitchen. Her lips twisting into a scowl that would have scared her grandkids. Heck, it scared me. "Why would the fates give you a man who didn't deserve your kindness? I want to have a word with him."

"Mom, you can't—"

"I can. You introduce me to this man. I'll set him straight."

She would, too. Because that was what she did—sure, she worked and ran a business that took up way to much of her time, but she took care of her children, too. All eighteen of us. She had a sharp tongue and the attitude of someone who'd fought hard all their life, but there was a sweetness to her when it came to her kits. No one messed with her skulk.

But I didn't want my mom fighting my battles for me, didn't need her to talk to Clark about mating and the fates. He didn't believe in the concept—end of story.

End of our story, at least.

I kissed my mom's cheek because she looked about ready to explode. "I know you're upset, but it's fine. I'm dealing with this and am ready to turn my back on the mating. No matter how much hurt that brings."

Anger faded into utter sadness, a look no one wanted to see. "Oh, Misty—

Don't cry in front of your mom. "I have to go."

"You don't."

"I do. I have a date."

"To see him?"

Him. Clark. "Yes."

She pursed her lips and pointed her finger at me. "Bring him back with you, Misty. Let me meet this man. I may not be the smartest fox in the forest, but I can still put the fear of mom in anyone."

Yeah, no shit. I'd been afraid of my mother almost since birth. "Maybe someday."

Because the idea of my family meeting my mate only to never see him again was too much even for me to deal with. My mom had said I'd been sulking—I had a feeling my mood was only going to get worse.

Because this whole biweekly thing?

It was bullshit.

Times a million.

9

CLARK

Two weeks was far too long. I'd tried to honor the agreement, but the idea of Misty being hurt or lonely or missing me for even a moment ate at my inner beast until I couldn't take it anymore. When that happened, the two of us made a trek over the mountain to the little city on the cove where she lived.

Four times, my wolf had stolen control, shifted us to his animal form, and ran us right to Misty's front door. He'd whined and paced until he'd finally seen her, even if it was just a glimpse through a window, then he could settle again. Usually under her bedroom window where we'd sleep the night through before running back over the mountain as the sun came up. If any of her neighbors noticed a large, gray wolf skulking around outside her house, they certainly didn't do anything to scare us off. Misty clearly didn't notice, something that bothered both me and my wolf to no end. Him especially as all he had to do during the day was obsess over where Misty was, what she was doing, and if she smelled as good as she had the last time he'd scented her.

No doubt about it, my wolf had an addictive personality, and his drug of choice was the little fox shifter. Our fated mate.

I know, I know. I don't believe in mates. But after the third time we'd crossed the mountain and lay sleeping peacefully under Misty's window, I began to see that maybe—*just maybe*—my hypothesis that mating was more of a pheromone-based attraction thing was way off. I went back to the college the next day and began diving into my research. History, sociology, biology…anything and everything that might lead me to a new conclusion. I asked questions of people I respected and then cornered students in my classes to ask them about shifter mating as well.

Sidebar—never ask a college kid about mating and mating habits unless you want graphic, *graphic* details.

In the end, after much discussion with the shifters at the college where I taught—both the educators and the students—and after feeling the pull the past two weeks so strong and unbearable, I was a convert. I'd been convinced. Hypothesis proven true—theory of animal shifter mating connection as dictated by some mythical force known only as the fates achieved.

I may have joined a cult, and I was *not* about to call my dad.

Bad side to this discovery? All of my peers and most of my students now knew I was an idiot when it came to shifter customs and needs. Thankfully, I agreed with them. There was no turning my back on this mating connection, no walking away from it or treating it like a casual sort of thing. Misty needed to be mine. Permanently. On a daily basis. And she would be—I'd tell her I was an idiot and that I wanted her all the time.

As soon as I finished this class.

"Okay, students. You've all asked for a special lecture on string theory, and I'm here to give you a slower-paced, deeper, and more personalized lesson than I normally teach. Let's get to it." I stood behind the podium, giving the five students in the room—all good ones who simply couldn't process things the same way or at the same speed as some of their peers could—a chance to settle in and open their computers. Once they were ready, I was too. "In the year 1919, a virtually unknown German mathematician named Theodor Kaluza suggested a very bold and, in some ways, very bizarre idea."

I fell into the rhythm of the words, the cadence of teaching something I'd taught for years, but today…something felt off. A need, a yearning. A distraction. One I couldn't lay at the feet of the students or the lecture. "He proposed that our universe might actually have more than the three dimensions that we are all aware of. That is in addition…"

The feeling within me grew, setting every nerve ending on fire. Making me want to race out of the building and take to my wolf form. Which I simply could not do, so I focused hard. Dug deep to pull out the words I'd recited numerous times over the years.

"Now, when someone presents a bold and bizarre idea, sometimes that's all it is—bold and bizarre, but it has nothing to do with the world around us. But this particular…"

The words flowed from my mouth, but my mind had focused elsewhere. On the one person in the world I wanted to see more than any other. The one tied to me in some cosmic way that I'd been too stupid to accept at first. Misty. She was here. On campus. Close. Early.

Maybe—just maybe—she'd been feeling as anxious as I'd been since we'd been apart. Maybe—just maybe—I had a shot to fix my own failure and claim that woman as mine.

I spoke faster.

MISTY

My hands were clammy as I pulled onto the college campus. Nervous. I was totally nervous. Not because of the college itself—it looked nice. I'd never been to college, having already been assigned a job in the restaurant and needing to help the family after I graduated from my shifter high school. I didn't regret that decision at all, but college seemed fun enough. The Ivy League-looking brick buildings and cutesy little signs directing people around the campus weren't intimidating. Not at all of my world, but I'd never been afraid of celebrating differences.

No, the school itself was fine. Knowing my mate taught here, though —that was different. He belonged in a place like this. With his theories and hypotheses, his relying on research and proof instead of instinct and gut, he fit right in. I did not.

"Maybe that's why you're just research material, you dumbass."

Sometimes, I hated when I talked to myself. Inner me could be a real bitch.

Once I found a parking spot close to the building where Clark had said he'd be teaching, I turned off my brain and tracked him by feel. By the connection between us. I put all my energy into that bond, blowing it up, wondering if he felt the intensity. Curious if he'd think it was pheromones or something so basic instead of a deep connection to one another.

The energy to keep us linked sapped my strength, a lack of sleep over the past two weeks wearing me down faster than anything else. Four nights—only four nights had I gotten any sort of real rest, and even then, I'd flipped and flopped in my bed. Restless. Needy. The rest of the two weeks? Nada. No sleep. Just a deep, pounding need rattling my inner self until rest became an impossibility. I needed to sleep. I needed my mate.

On the third floor of the science building, I heard Clark's voice. Strong and smooth, the sound soothed something inside of me. Pushed away all the tiredness and anxiety at meeting him today. That was my mate. Mine. And even if he pushed me away, even if he only wanted me to research the hypothesis of mating, I needed him. I needed that connection.

For now.

I slipped inside the classroom and watched from the back, settling into the shadows so he wouldn't see me. I knew he had to sense me, to feel me close, but he didn't falter. He simply kept teaching, kept talking. Something about...strings. The subject didn't matter, though, because all I could focus on was how sexy he looked. Graying hair rumpled, glasses on, sleeves rolled up those strong forearms, and wearing a freaking sweater vest. I wanted to lick him.

As soon as these kids left the room, I would.

"Well, it turns out that Einstein and Kaluza and many others worked refining this framework and applied it to the physics of the universe as was understood at the time, but it didn't work." He walked along the front of the room, looking good enough to eat. As much as I loved hiding from him, I was ready to end this game. I couldn't wait to get my hands on him, to rumple my naughty professor even more. To feel the muscles under that sweater vest, to see the beast in his eyes behind those dark frames. These children had no idea how much of an animal he could be. Especially not the girl who made the mistake of putting her hand on his arm as she asked a question.

Oh, hell no.

My growl was automatic and unstoppable, soft but there. Clark's head whipped up, his eyes finding mine immediately. Every student in the room went still. This was a shifter college, after all—a place where I was surrounded by my own kind. They all knew what the sound I'd just made meant. A predator was in the room—and she wasn't happy with them.

"Sorry," the girl said, jerking her hand back from Clark's arm and packing up her computer. "I wasn't thinking."

"It's fine." Clark kept his eyes on mine, kept that look burning into my skin. "We're done here, folks. We'll reschedule another time to finish this up. If you still need more help, I suggest you look up the TED Talk on superstring theory. We can discuss it at the next session."

Within seconds, all the students were gone, leaving out a side door instead of walking past me. Smart kids. I waited until the door closed behind them, then rose to my feet.

"She touched you."

Clark leaned against a desk, casual but striking. Waiting for me. "She did."

"I didn't like it."

"The touch wasn't meant to be sexual."

My growl rumbled through the room, louder this time. "She doesn't get to touch what's mine."

I almost flinched, almost wished I could pull that word back. He didn't want a mate—he wanted a fuck buddy. That was what I'd agreed to. I couldn't help it that my inner fox was territorial as heck and that he was my territory. I couldn't help that at all.

Thankfully, he didn't seem bothered by my claiming of him. In fact, he almost seemed…interested. "In my class, we don't growl, young lady. It's rude and unprofessional. Behavior like that could affect your grade."

Oh. Teacher-student role play. I was down for that. "I'm sorry, professor. I couldn't stand the thought of someone else's hands being where they shouldn't."

"She's just a student."

"Then what am I?"

"You're my little fox." He tugged me close, his hands coming to grip my ass. "Look at me."

I did—I looked right at him. Gazed square into his pretty gray eyes and melted a little. He held my look, never faltering, never looking away. He'd always looked away, though. Or…had he? The night we'd met for research…the morning after…he'd stared right at me as we'd been fucking, but I'd written that off as an in the moment thing.

Apparently, it was *not* an in the moment thing.

When had that happened?

Clark leaned closer, scenting me. Growling softly under his breath as he said, "I've missed you so much, Misty. More than you know."

I clutched at his arms, hanging onto my ghost of a mate. If only his words were true. They couldn't be, though—he wouldn't miss a research partner like he would a fated mate. And that's what I was—a research partner. Still, the thought was nice.

I pushed aside all the feelings of what I was missing out on, shoved them into the farthest, darkest closet in my mind to deal with later. Research time, sexy time. I needed to sink into the moment, so I sank to my knees.

"Come on, teach. Let me show you how much I want to earn that A grade on my research project. I'm a diligent student and quite detailed with my experiments." I looked up at him, grinning, holding on to his cock as he stared down at me with fire burning behind those eyes that never budged from mine.

Too much emotion in that look. It was time to dive headfirst into research mode.

"You can spank me if I didn't take thorough enough notes from our last lecture, professor."

MISTY

Waking up with Clark after a night of naughtiness should have been sweet. It should have brought me comfort. Instead, all I got was pain. Not physical pain, but emotional. My heart ached, and even my fox's hopeful chattering wasn't enough to stop it. I had thought I could stay casual, teach him about mates and mating, keep the relationship physical. I had thought I had it in me to deny the mating pull.

Then I'd fallen asleep in his arms.

And I'd woken up realizing I had been wrong.

So very wrong.

Snuggling was not just research. The comfort of laying my head on his chest was not just research. This entire thing *was not just research.*

The need to complete the bond, to let him bite me and to link us together forever, was too strong to resist in that moment. I struggled with the urges, the refusal of my base instincts making me ache in ways I never had before. Making me want things I couldn't have. Resisting him when his scent surrounded me and the heat of his body warmed my own was simply not something I could do.

It didn't help that the man was so sweet at times. Sure, our first meeting had been a train wreck, but since then? He'd been caring and concerned. He'd been attentive. He'd even bought a few bottles of a wine I'd mentioned I liked to have on hand for me to drink for our research weekend. The man didn't drink, so that was all for my benefit. That's not something you do for a research subject, not that I'd ever been one before. Still, it seemed too far over the line of casual. His sweet words, his gentle hands, the wine, the laughs, the snuggling—too much. It was all too much—exactly what I'd always wanted and nothing that I could actually have. The bastard had teased me with perfection but wouldn't give it to me. I was supposed to be his research subject.

Just his research subject.

But it hurt too much to accept that.

While Clark slept, I slipped out of bed, quickly picking up my clothes and tugging them on. I had no intention of stopping once I got on the road to Kinship Cove, so no one would see my walk of shame. They wouldn't notice my leftover eye makeup or the mussed hair that told the story of Clark's hands tugging, pulling, and fisting the long strands. No one would see any of that—just my car speeding away from the college and back to the safety of the cove. A fox alone once more.

A quick glance around the room to make sure I hadn't left anything behind, and I was ready to escape. Just a few more steps and—

"Where are you going?"

Busted.

I turned, taking in the sight before me. Clark, completely rumpled and groggy, slowly sitting up on the bed with the sheet around his waist. So hot, this man. Why couldn't he be the least bit unattractive? That might make things easier.

Okay, fine. Nothing would make this easier. "I need to go home."

He frowned. "Why?"

Might as well be honest. "I can't do this anymore."

His brow tightened, and he reached to put on his glasses as if he needed to *see* what I was saying. "I don't understand."

"It's too hard, Clark. My feelings are too hard to control."

"Misty, I—"

I shushed him, needing him to stop talking. Needing him to go back to sleep so I could leave without feeling as if my heart were being ripped from my chest. "I get it. You don't want a mate in the true sense of the word. I do, though—so all of this snuggling and waking up together won't work for me. I thought it would, but I was so very wrong about that. I can't bond with you physically and hold back the emotional tie. I'm just not strong enough to do that." I took a breath, backing toward the door as I straightened my shoulders. Time to rip that bandage off. "It's not going to be easy, but we'll figure out some sort of arrangement that keeps our beasts sane and our lives separate. I'm sure somewhere there are others who have been in this same situation. Not all matings end up with two people in love forever, you know? We'll research that— how they handled it. How often they had to meet and the minimum contact needed. We'll make this arrangement more...contractual. No extras, no emotions."

I couldn't look at him, so just as he'd once done to me, I stared at his shoulder. That was better because I couldn't bear to see whatever expression was on his face. Disappointment? Irritation? Anger? Nothing? The options were endlessly awful. I grabbed my bag, rushing for the door, every second spent with him as he sat and said nothing digging a bigger hole in my heart.

He's not stopping you.

And he wouldn't. I knew that because I was just a research subject. I might disappoint the student within him, but I wouldn't be doing much to the man. A fact that half killed me. Humiliation burned in my veins as I headed through the bedroom and into the living area. Clark had taken me back to his apartment just off campus—a cute place with lots of comfy furniture and books and cozy nooks. A place I never wanted to be in again.

Not long now. Just one more door. I can do this. I can—

"Hey," Clark said from behind me. "Wait a minute."

I yanked the front door open, unable to follow his command. Knowing if I stopped, I'd stay. And I'd hurt more when I finally left Clark's *research facility*. "Can't. It's family dinner night, and I'm late already. I'll see you around, teach."

"Misty, wait—"

But I didn't. I couldn't. I may have been an idiot about how I'd handled this whole thing, but I refused to stand there and give him time to tell me how he'd only meant our weekend together to be about research. And it should have been—it was my fault I'd stayed for more. My fault that I'd fallen asleep in his arms and woken up with the dream of truly being his playing in my head.

All of this was my fault for wanting more than he was willing to give me.

I wouldn't be making that mistake again.

CLARK

Stunned stupid.

For the first time in my life, I finally understood such a statement. I'd been stunned stupid by Misty's sudden need to escape. Unable to find the words to get her to pause or to calm the situation. I'd woken up in the middle of a fire and had thrown gasoline on it instead of water with my inability to speak. See? Stupid.

I might not have been able to think of what words to say to Misty to calm her down, I still might not know them when I saw her again, but I could at least try. And that was what I was going to do—try. As soon as I caught up with her. Because biweekly wasn't going to be enough. Waiting two more weeks to see her wouldn't be enough. Nothing would ever be enough when it came to that woman.

I drove over the mountain road linking the college town to Kinship Cove, speeding through curves and over rises at a pace far too fast for the conditions. It would be worth it, though. She'd gotten a bit of a head start on me, but I'd track her down. Catch up with her. I had to. I needed to find her. Needed to tell her that the research project was off. I was an ignorant asshole for even suggesting such a thing and had no qualms about admitting my mistake. I wanted my mate. Not to research, but to love. To take care of. To bond with. I wanted Misty, and I'd do anything to make her want me too. She was perfect for me. I could try to be perfect for her—starting with telling her how much I didn't deserve her.

As soon as I rolled into Kinship Cove, I headed for the bakery. I wasn't sure, but it seemed as if she might be there. I felt a tug in that direction as well, my wolf guiding me that way. I'd trust his guidance at this point—he definitely knew more than I did.

Sadly, when I walked inside, it wasn't Misty at the counter. It was the one sister—Ginger—and her dragon shifter mate.

And they were obviously not happy with me.

I couldn't blame them, but I also couldn't take the time to explain. "I need to find Misty."

Ginger huffed a snort that was a clear *fuck off*, wiping down the counter as if the world weren't ending right there in front of her. My world—not hers.

"If it's so important to you, use your mating bond. You'll feel her."

The dragon eyed me like prey, staring hard. Distracting me. My inner wolf growled and snarled at the man, but I held him back. Needing the dragon's help. "I get slight tugs, but otherwise I don't feel her. It's more…static."

It was the dragon who replied. "You're not so good at this whole shifter thing, are you?"

"No," I admitted. "Not at all. But I'm willing to learn. For her."

He shot a quick glance at Ginger, who still looked ready to murder me where I stood, then directed those hard eyes back to mine. "Go wolf."

"I'm sorry?"

"You might suck at this shifter thing, but your wolf knows what to do. He'll also know where to find Misty. Go wolf."

"But…it's the middle of the day, and there are people."

He shrugged. "It's a shifter town—they're all used to seeing animals walking the streets. Bring out your wolf. He'll take you to Misty. You just have to trust him."

Trust the beast inside of me. Trust the animal instincts that seemed to be overtaking my life. Trust…fate.

Misty was worth it.

"Thanks," I said, hoping like hell I was strong enough to let go. My wolf practically snickered. He was definitely ready.

"Oh, and Clark?" The dragon called just before I opened the door.

"Yeah?"

"You fuck with Misty again, and I'll spit roast you." He glared my way, his expression deadly. "That girl is family to us, and we defend our family at all costs. Understand?"

I looked him dead in the eye. "Completely. I have no intention of messing this up."

I raced outside, taking a deep breath before handing over the reins of my mind to my inner wolf. He surged forward, not at all timid, and landed on his paws in a full run. Yeah, he knew where to go. He also knew how much we had to hurry. The ache in our chest was not my own. He knew it, and so did I.

We sped up as we hit the alley running behind the businesses on the main street through town. Running faster without fear of things like cars and people and being out in the world on four paws instead of two feet. We needed more speed, though. I couldn't allow my mate to hurt like this for long. I could feel her pain inside of me, rebounding through me. Our bond pulling us together even as I berated myself for being such an idiot. I'd put all my energy into building that bond, caring for it, if it meant I got Misty in my life. I'd do anything.

My wolf veered back toward town and headed straight into a small restaurant at the end of the street, bypassing the humans waiting in line for a table. An older woman eyed me as I passed, tutting.

"Human forms only, sir."

I stayed wolf, though. Ignoring her request. The place smelled like Misty. She was here. Somewhere. I just had to find her. Thankfully, the wolf knew exactly where to go. We beelined it for the doors to the kitchen and shoved our way through them. It took me about two seconds to find Misty in the melee of the space. In the chaos of a busy kitchen in full serving mode. So many people. Only one mattered.

We stopped right next to her, sitting down. Waiting.

"Clark?" She looked confused. She also looked as if she'd been crying. I couldn't have that. I wanted to shift—to hold her and talk to her—but there were a lot of people there. If I shifted, I'd be naked—an obvious flaw in the dragon's idea of going wolf to find Misty.

What to do?

My decision was made for me by Misty herself. Her surprised look turned sad, the light in her eyes when she'd seen my wolf dimming as I didn't shift. As I didn't do anything but sit and stare. I needed to push my human ideals aside, bite the bullet, and deal with my nakedness like a man. These people were shifters—they'd understand the lack of clothes. And if not, well…at least I worked out.

A few seconds, and I was human once more. Standing before the woman who had somehow stolen my heart, whom I had an unexplainable connection to, and whom I needed more than anything else in the world. Time to get to work.

"Misty, I was so wrong."

She glanced down my body, her eyebrows rising. "I'll get you a—"

"No, wait." I grabbed her hand, needing a connection. "I was wrong. I was wrong to try to avoid you and to set this connection up as research. I was wrong when I refused to look you in the eye because it made my wolf too strong and that scared me. I was wrong to not grab you and tell you how much I felt for you the second we met. I was absolutely utterly wrong."

Misty raised an eyebrow—just one—and cocked her head. "That's why you wouldn't look at me? Because of your wolf."

"Yes. That sort of loss of control—I couldn't handle it."

"And now?"

Her being willing to at least listen had to be a good sign, so I barreled on ahead. "Now I realize how stupid I was, and I'm so sorry for that. Being mated is the most consuming thing that's ever happened to me. I believe it now, though. The mating, the fates…all of it. How could our connection not be destined? I think of you all day long and dream of you at night. I want to know what you're doing and if you're okay. I want to hang out with you and simply watch you be you. I want more than just research. I'm sorry I started our relationship that way."

She did *not* look convinced. "So *now* you want a mate?"

"Not just a mate. You. Even if the fates hadn't brought us together,

I'd want you. I need your laugh in my apartment and your hand in mine. I need you wrapped in my arms at night—every single night. I need your smile over my morning coffee and your hand in mine everywhere we go. I need *you*, Misty."

Her lips twisted as if she were holding back s mile, but she didn't give into it. Not yet. Still…I took that held back grin as a good sign. I had her. I didn't deserve her at all, but I would. I'd work to. I just needed to give her one final push.

"You're my mate," I said, letting my wolf come out to add a little growl to my voice. Appealing to her inner fox. "You're mine, and I want to earn the right to be yours. Your mate."

That grin broke free, and the tears building in her eyes looked like happy ones. I began to feel a little excitement in my blood.

Perhaps too much excitement for someone without clothes on.

"Are you sure? My family can be a little—" she looked over my shoulder, likely at all the people standing around staring at my backside "—crazy."

Before I could answer, other voices chimed in.

"Hey, what's up, skins?"

"How's it hanging?"

"You know there's grease back here? You might want to put that thing away."

I ignored them all, though Misty's cheeks reddened a bit. I'd take her family's teasing so long as she never let go of my hand.

"If I get you, the crazy will be worth it."

"Just me."

As if she couldn't believe me. I wasn't trying hard enough, apparently. "You. Not some generic mate, not some random woman—you, Misty. Your smile, your joy, your sexiness, your sweetness. Your ridiculous laugh when you've had a bottle of wine and your love for the stinky seals at the cove. All of it. I want every bit, because I love you."

Her smile fell and her eyes welled with tears. She was going to cry. Shit—had I messed up? Had I been too late? Why would she cry? I didn't know what to do to make her stop. I didn't know—

Misty jumped at me, wrapping her arms around my neck and

pressing her lips to mine. I didn't pause—didn't falter. I simply grabbed her to me and kissed her back. Thankful, grateful, and so fucking happy to have her right where I wanted her. With that one kiss, everything was perfect. I had my mate in my arms, her lips on mine as I tugged her against me. Right there, in that moment, I had every single thing I could want.

Except for a pair of pants.

"Seriously, you two," a male voice hollered. "Get a room."

Misty broke the kiss, leaning in to whisper, "You realize you're naked in front of half of my family, right?"

I did. I totally did. There was no way to deny that. "You're worth it."

She stared up at me, all sweetness and smiles. "How about I get you a cloak to cover up what's mine?"

Oh, thank the fates. "Please. I'd prefer only to be naked when we're alone."

She ran a finger down my chest, making the blood flow south. "That can be arranged."

"Can it be arranged after I have the cloak? Because standing in front of your family naked is bad enough. Getting hard with them only a few feet away might be too much for me to bear."

She nodded, looking over my shoulder. "Tilly."

"On it."

A moment later, cloth covered my shoulders, and I tugged the cloak around me. "Thank you."

"Oh no," a warm voice said, likely this Tilly. "Thank you. That's the best show I've seen in months."

A show that got me my mate. I grabbed Misty around the waist and pulled her into me, smiling. "Our reconciliation was the best show she's seen in months. That's good, right?"

"It's good, Clark. You're good."

"You're better."

"No doubt there. Let's get out of here. I'd like to get you naked again. Without an audience this time."

Sold. "Lead the way, mate. I'll follow you anywhere."

EPILOGUE

MISTY

Mated life was pretty cool. Mated life with a man like Clark—one who loved making me happy and put his impressive intellect and research experience behind doing so—was even better. Especially when he walked into a room with a box wrapped like a present. I loved presents.

"You bought me a gift."

Clark grinned and set the pretty, pink box on the table. His table, technically. Because of his job and mine, we lived in two different cities. Not apart—no, no. We'd tried being apart for a night—it had ended with Clark's wolf practically jumping through my bedroom window. Hot... but not conducive to a good night's sleep. We lived together in two different towns, shuttling back and forth depending on our schedules so I could continue working at the bakery—which I loved—and he could continue teaching. I also put in a few hours a week at my family's diner, though only when Clark was working and I had nothing better to do. My siblings were a little salty about that, but my mom had told them I needed time to be with my mate and to leave me alone. Way to go, Mom.

So, yeah—the biweekly research team had become the everyday couple living in two different towns depending on the day. It wasn't the norm or easy, but the chaos worked for us. So long as we were together, never spending a night alone, the back-and-forth was worth it.

"I saw it in the student center and thought you'd like it." He hung up his coat—ever the neat and tidy professor—then joined me at the table. "Open it."

I did as I was told, grinning while I carefully popped the tape holding the paper in place. A plain, brown cardboard box lay underneath, so I opened that as well. Inside of that…well.

"It's so pretty."

I carefully lifted the triangular object from inside the box, inspecting it. It was a beaker, one of those glass containers people used in chemistry labs. It had a lid and a wooden base, though, and inside of it was what looked like…smoke. Fiery red smoke dancing in nothing, never dissipating, never lessening.

"Shake it."

I glanced at Clark, who was watching me intently, before shaking the beaker. The smoke grew thicker, filling the entire beaker with the undulating redness.

"It's like a snow globe."

"It is, yeah. And it's you." He pushed up his glasses when I looked at him, grinning back at me. "My fiery research experiment."

Such a sweet man. "Thank you. It's lovely."

"There's one more thing." He grabbed the beaker and tilted it, showing me the bottom where a small, black button sat within the wooden circle of the stand. "Press the button."

I pressed it. Suddenly, I heard a very tinny Clark saying, "Report to detention immediately."

There was no holding back my grin, or the way I shifted in my seat. Yeah, the whole teacher-student fantasy was one of my favorites. I had myself the sexy professor, and I got to be the student he couldn't say no to. The present might as well have been porn for how that red smoke and speaker box made me feel.

"You gave me a present that is basically saying let's have sex," I said, frowning intentionally, but running my foot up his thigh to make sure he knew I was only joking around. "You are so naughty. I don't think this is right at all."

In his teacher voice—the one that made shivers creep up my spine—Clark asked, "Do you want to pass my class or not, my little fox?"

Hell yeah, I did. "Please. I can't get an F. My permanent record will never recover."

"Then I suggest you get over here and show me how much my class means to you."

Yup. I could totally do that. I rose to my feet, sauntering around the table. Dropping to my knees in front of him. "How about I show the teacher how much *he* means to me?"

His hands found their way behind my neck, tugging me closer with a gentle sort of pressure. His stare growing more intense and his expression earnest. I loved that man when he got all earnest.

"The world, my little fox. You mean the world to me."

"Ditto." I pulled his hand forward, kissing his thumb as it passed over my face. "And I want you."

"Physically or in some other way?"

Always needing to know the specifics. "Both."

"Biweekly?" His lips kicked up into a grin as I growled. "Or maybe not."

"You couldn't last two weeks without me anymore."

He yanked me up and into his lap, forcing my legs to straddle his. Pulling me close with his hands on my hips. "I couldn't the first time either."

"No?"

"No. I wound up under your bedroom window. More than once, to be honest."

That was hot. The idea of his wolf taking charge and forcing him to run over the mountain to track me down? Totally hot. "It's too cold to sleep outside now."

"Exactly, so let's not make me suffer, shall we?"

I rocked over him, sliding and pressing where he was so very hard for me. "But I like making you suffer."

"You do." He grunted, rolling his body up. Grinding back on me. "We'll make each other suffer together, though."

Dry-humping at the kitchen table was my new favorite thing, though I had a feeling having Clark fuck me across the kitchen table would soon replace that. "Together. Always. Not biweekly."

He picked me up and set my hips on the table, laying me back as he ripped at my clothes. As he rushed to bring us closer together. "Never biweekly again."

And that, my friends, was how we broke the kitchen table, though I saved my beaker present with some seriously impressive hand-eye coordination. It didn't matter, though. Nothing did—not the driving we had to do all the time, not the annoyance of being in one town when something you wanted to eat or wear or read was in another. None of that was more important than us being together. Clark was mine and I was his, and however we chose to live out our lives was exactly the way it should be.

Of course, he'd never live down being naked in my family's kitchen, but whatever. At least he looked good naked.

ESPRESSO CON EAGLE

KINSHIP COVE: CUDDLES & COFFEE

The spotlight burns brighter in a small town as does the fire between mates…no matter the age difference. Welcome to the Kinship Cove Diner, where a good cup of coffee comes with every fated mating.

I have two great loves of my life—my fox shifting family (no matter how much they drive me crazy) and being on stage. True, my acting credits are relegated to the local community playhouse, but that doesn't matter. I spend my free time learning lines and rehearsing scenes…that very few people will ever see. Dating, mating, and all that comes with it? Unimportant.

At least until a man with a sharp gaze, a little gray in his hair, and a familiar face comes walking into the diner. He's handsome, charming, and the fates say all mine.

. . .

Except he's also famous—an actor whose eagle shifter instincts have brought him stardom in the action-movie arena.

The fates aren't always kind, but giving me someone who lives his life in such a public way might just be too cruel for words. I've never really worried about finding a mate, but now that I have him? I don't want to be without him. And I've had enough sharing for one lifetime.

1

TILLY

Glitter was definitely the herpes of the crafting world.

No, really. It spread to every crevice, was totally impossible to hide, and you simply couldn't get rid of it no matter how hard you tried. Or at least, I never could. Which was what led twenty-three-year-old me to being scolded by my mother. Totally normal day at the Kinship Cove Diner.

"It's from a costume, Mom."

"Tilly Mae, only exotic dancers wear that much glitter. What have you been up to?"

My middle name, by the way, was not Mae. It was June. I guess when you have eighteen children, little details like names and birthdays get a little mixed up.

"It's for the play I'm in next week. I swear—no clothing was removed in exchange for money. I just ended up in a glittery dress that's well past its prime, and some of the silver sparkles decided to come home with me. That's all."

My mother, though, never had been one to back down from a fight. "I don't see why you do those plays anyway. It's not like they're going to get you any sort of fame. The only people who go to see them are the relatives of the people in them."

I arched a brow and folded my arms over my chest, giving her the same look she'd been giving me since about birth. "So that means you'll all come to see this one? Because I'm pretty sure you missed the last two."

"The diner is always busy. Who has time for such frivolity?" She shoved a tray of condiments and silverware sets wrapped in napkins at me and waved a hand in the air. "Go. Reset section five before the dinner rush. And don't get any of that glitter on the tables."

In other words, she wouldn't be coming but didn't want to actually admit that, so she'd rather send me off with marching orders and totally ignore my feelings on the matter. Got it.

"Yes, ma'am." Chin up and emotions locked down tight, I headed out to the dining room, tray balanced on my shoulder and—hopefully—no glitter falling from my hair and clothes. The fates forbid anyone possibly think we were hosting stripper parties at the Kinship Cove Diner.

Though that would certainly bring in some revenue.

And maybe some unmated males.

Oh, the possibilities.

"Hey, Aunt Tilly." Jackson—oldest son of my oldest brother and recent sucker to have to work at the diner—hurried my way with a bin of dirty dishes balanced in his arms.

"Hi, Jackson. Have a good day at school?"

"Yeah, though calculus is kicking my a—" he blinked and fumbled for a word that wasn't a cuss "—behind."

I chuckled, remembering being his age and trying so hard to follow the rules, while knowing I was basically an adult. An adult under the rule of one crazy fox shifter old lady who would whack you upside the head for cussing in front of her. "Well, keep it up. Not long now, and you'll graduate and be off to college."

"Yeah, that's the plan. Let me know if you need anything." He was practically right beside me when he paused and frowned. "Did you know you've got glitter in your hair?"

Might as well own it. "Yup. I sure did."

"Oh. Okay. Well, sparkle on, then." And with that, he disappeared into the kitchen while I weaved my way through the crowded tables and chairs toward section five. Having worked in the diner since I was about twelve, I didn't need anyone to tell me what needed to be done before the dinner rush, but my mom sure loved to do it anyway. Just like this whole reset of section five—of course it needed to be reset. We didn't open every section for lunch on the weekdays because we weren't busy enough, but section five—the one closest to the front door—was always open. Hence, we'd need to reset it a lot. Like before the dinner rush.

"Didn't need anyone to tell me that," I mumbled before I quickly set the silverware on the tables and refreshed the condiment stands to make sure we were ready. Once everything seemed about as perfect as I could make it—and I'd scraped a thousand pieces of glitter off the tables —I turned for the kitchen once more. There was always work to do, and if I didn't seek it out, it would be assigned to me anyway. Might as well be useful.

Something outside caught my attention, though, and I rerouted myself to the big picture windows at the front of the restaurant. Across the street, Ginger Chance—one of the owners of the Cake-ily Ever After bakery and one of my sister Misty's bosses—walked by with her handsome mate, a dragon shifter named Kingston. I really liked them both, having spent a lot of time at the bakery lately as I helped Misty and Ginger bake about a thousand loaves of bread. Not sure why they needed so much, but they did. Thankfully, the job paid pretty well, and the Chance sisters were great to hang around with. Plus, I got to spend time with my favorite sister. Newly mated, Misty didn't work in the diner much anymore. Her wolf shifter mate worked at the college on the other side of the mountain, and she spent a lot of time there to be with him. When she wasn't at their home, she was at the bakery. The diner tended to be the last place she wanted to be.

"Tilly! I see glitter on a table!"

Not that I could blame her.

"I'll get a scraper and fix it."

My mom huffed, looking as if the entire dinner service was ruined because of a little glitter.

Herpes, I'm telling you.

"Go. Go home and change." Her frown deepened as the bell rang over the door, indicating a customer had come in. "Maybe even take a shower to wash that stuff out of your hair. I can't believe you came in here looking like a stripper."

Always so much drama. "I don't look like a stripper, Mom."

"You do. Doesn't she? Tell my daughter she looks like a stripper with those sparkles all over her."

"I find sparkly things very attractive," a cool, male voice said from behind me. One that sent a shiver of something I'd never felt before sliding up my spine. I turned slowly, almost afraid of what I'd see. Of who would be standing there. Fate had set off warning bells in my head, and I couldn't ignore them.

"Go, Tilly," my mom said before I could even find out who'd been speaking. "Table for one, sir?"

I finally managed to catch a glimpse of the man in question. Tall, broad shoulders, a little gray in his dark hair, and light brown eyes that seemed to focus in on what they were looking at and not let go.

Sadly, he wasn't looking at me. He seemed completely focused on the phone in his hand.

"Yes, one, please. I'm just here for coffee, though."

"Fine. You come this way. Tilly, go home and come back when you're presentable for our guests."

"Yes, Mom."

The man's head shot up, and his eyes met mine. I'd been wrong about the color. It wasn't light brown. More amber, almost orange in tone. And the shape of them, the sharpness of his gaze—he was a bird of prey shifter for sure. Some sort of raptor—eagle or hawk, most likely. I could sense the dangerous side of him, practically feel the need to hide so as not to fall prey to such an alpha predator.

I also felt the cool hand of fate tugging me toward him.

Mate.

Definitely my mate.

Oh my stars, I had met my mate while covered in glitter and being called a stripper by my own mother.

Of all the—

"I'm sorry," the man said, taking a single step my way. "I didn't catch your—"

"Go, Tilly. Sir, come this way." My mother practically dragged the man through the restaurant toward the counter where he could enjoy a cup of coffee then head out on his way. Without me.

That's my mate.

My inner fox sat up and chattered loudly, wanting me to follow him. To sit right there on his lap and rub my scent into his skin. And I might have, except my mother was glaring and he was letting her pull him away from me, which left me with nothing to do except walk out the door. But I didn't go home. No, sir. I was not about to waste the time needed to get there, shower, dry my hair, and come back. I instead headed toward the one place where I knew I'd find someone to give me advice on what I should do.

I ran across the street and down a few blocks to the Cake-ily Ever After bakery.

"Is my sister here?" I practically yelled as soon as I rushed inside. Ginger and Kingston looked up from where they'd been enjoying a cup of coffee at one of the cute little bistro tables by the window. Thankfully, Misty came scuttling out from behind the display cases.

"What's wrong? Is it Dad? Did he finally drop dead from Mom working him half to death?"

"No. Though, that reminds me—he really does need a day off."

"We'll add that to the two-thousand-item things to do list for the diner. Speaking of which, why are you here? The dinner rush will be starting soon, and section five—"

"I already reset section five. That's not why I'm here."

"Then why *are* you here?" Kingston said, looking cool and collected as he tugged a giggling Ginger into his lap. "You seem a little worked up."

"I am. But not because of bad things, because of good ones. Or potentially good ones. Maybe. Possibly. Oh, I don't know."

"Okay, calm down." Misty came out from behind the cases and grabbed my shoulders. "Take a deep breath in and—hey, why are you covered in glitter like some sort of stripper?"

Herpes. For real.

"Can we focus, please? I have big news." I waited until Misty nodded, then grabbed her arms exactly like she held mine and leaned closer. "I just met my mate."

My sister's eyes went huge, and her mouth fell open. "Oh my fates."

"Right? Oh my fates, indeed. Now, what do I do?"

Misty choked then shook her head, her brow tightening. "What do you mean, what do you do? You go snag that man and bring him back here so I can interrogate him. Is he a shifter? Wolf, right? They're pretty common. He'd better not be a dragon. I can't handle another one—no offense, Kingston."

"None taken, but he's not a dragon. I would have sensed one of my own coming into town."

"Not a dragon," I said with an excited point in Kingston's direction... for reasons I could not explain. It wasn't as if this were some sort of game show. "He's definitely a bird of prey, though. The eyes were unmistakable."

Misty frowned. "Did he have a big nose? The only big bird shifter I know of around here is that California vulture, and he's really not attractive."

As if. "He did *not* have a big nose."

"Good. You don't deserve to be stuck with an ugly mate."

"He's handsome for sure. And his voice..." I sighed, a chill shooting up my spine at the memory. "I swear, I was ready to rub myself all over him from just a couple of words."

"That, ladies, is my cue to leave." Kingston kissed Ginger soundly then stood, smirking my way. "Perhaps I should head to the diner for another cup of coffee. Scope out this new bird shifter for myself."

"Don't you dare." I huffed and bit my lip. "What do I do, though?"

"I gave you my opinion," Misty said. "Go bring him here."

"I can't. Mom told me to go shower off the glitter—"

"She called you a stripper, didn't she?"

"Yup."

"Damn," Misty whispered. "I'm becoming our mother."

"Focus, please."

"Right. You found your mate. You should—"

"Stop," Ginger said, appearing at my side. "Don't listen to her. She met her mate and ran off like a loon. You don't want to follow her advice."

"You weren't exactly all gung ho for our mating, Sparky," Kingston chided.

"Yeah, well—you were rude. I made my amends for that incident." She blew him a kiss. "Here's what you do. Go back there, walk right up to him, and shake his hand."

"Shake his hand?"

"Yes. Shake his hand."

"But…I look like a stripper."

She looked me up and down. "Damn. Glitter. It's like herpes…you'll never wash that stuff off."

"I know, right? So, now what? Mom will be mad if I show back up all sparkly, but he said he was only at the diner for a cup of coffee. I figure I've got ten minutes, tops."

Ginger shrugged. "No problem. You strip."

That…didn't sound like good advice. "Excuse me?"

She grabbed the bottom hem of her sweater and pulled it up her body, exposing a lacy black bra. "Take your top off."

Kingston's growl exploded, practically shaking the room. "Ginger."

She simply waved him off, not even giving him a moment of her attention. I loved that bawdy chick. "We'll trade. I'll take the glitter-covered clothes, and you take mine. That way you can go back and your mom won't yell at you."

"Oh. That'll work." I grabbed the bottom of my shirt, ready to pull it off.

Kingston sighed and hurried toward the door. "I'll be outside… setting anyone who dares to look in these windows on fire. Do let me know once you're all decent again."

Ginger laughed and shook her head. "I've never been decent a day in my life. You'd think he'd have figured that out by now."

Two minutes, an exchange of sweaters, and a good hair-brushing later, Misty and Ginger were pushing me out the door of the bakery.

"Go get your man," Misty said. "Don't let Mom's perpetual bad mood spoil this for you."

"Yeah," said Ginger. "Go claim your mate. Kingston needs a buddy to fly with."

"I certainly do not," the dragon shifter said from where he leaned against the wall. "Do you need someone to walk you back to the diner, Tilly? I'd be happy to escort you."

"No thanks. I'm good." I took a deep breath and was about to set off for my destiny, but I stopped long enough to hug all three of my friends. "Thank you. I knew I'd find answers here."

"Quit talking to us, and go get your bird," Ginger said. Not bad advice at all.

I hurried off, waving to them. Running toward the diner and talking myself down from the ledge. I could do this. He was just a man. One I was expected to spend the rest of my life with. One who would be my fated mate. Just a man—and my happily ever after.

If I weren't in my twenties and therefore required to be more of an adult, I would have squeed.

I made it to the diner in record time, reaching for the door just as it opened. As if on cue, out walked the man the fates deemed perfect for me.

How could he possibly be so handsome? And calm. He looked so darn calm compared to me.

"Well, hello again," he said, a small smile turning up his lips. "I was afraid you'd left me for good."

As if. "Sorry. My mom has a thing against glitter, so I needed to change my clothes."

Those amber eyes dragged up and down my body. "Still just as lovely as before. My name is Renit."

I held out my hand, accepting his proffered one. "I'm Tilly."

"It's very nice to meet you, Tilly. Are you coming here to work, then?"

"I am. My parents own the restaurant."

He hummed, looking over my shoulder before bringing that intense gaze to mine. "I can't say I'm not disappointed that I won't be able to keep you to myself for a bit, but perhaps we can spend some time together after your shift."

Jackpot. "I'd like that."

"Good. Though if you don't mind, I'd like to exchange numbers."

"Numbers…like phone numbers?"

He shot me a million-watt smile. "Yes, phone numbers. I realize it's slightly more human than not, but I almost had a heart attack when you raced out of this diner and I didn't even know your name. I'd prefer knowing I can contact you."

How quaint. "Sure. Of course."

He handed me his phone, and I entered my number into it, sending myself a text so I'd have his before handing it back.

"There we go. Numbers exchanged." I shrugged and raised my eyebrows. "So…that's it. I guess I'll see you later."

"Yeah, later." He frowned, somehow making that expression seem far too sexy for words. "What time do you get off?"

There was a dirty joke in my answer. One I resisted making. "Eight. Maybe we can grab a drink or something afterward."

"Sounds perfect. I have to get to a business meeting but will be here to pick you up at eight."

"I might still look like a stripper." At his raised eyebrows, my face grew hot. *Ugh, brain. Work!* "I just mean I might still have glitter. In my hair. And stuff."

Renit nodded slowly, looking me up and down. Inching closer as he murmured, "I know we haven't said anything official yet so this might be jumping the gun, but considering you seem to feel the same mating pull to me that I do to you, I feel pretty confident in declaring that you shouldn't be stripping any longer. Unless it's for my eyes alone."

Oh my stars. And my heart. And my suddenly very wet panties. "Yeah. Uh…that sounds…fine. I'm not a stripper anyway—it's just glitter."

"You're beautiful with or without the added sparkle," he said before kissing the back of my hand like some man in one of those old movies. You know the ones—with gentlemen who had manners and stuff. Impressive. "I'll see you at eight."

"Eight. Yes. Right here." But I couldn't let him leave just yet, couldn't let him walk away without knowing one thing. "What are you?"

He froze, his brow pinching. "What *am* I?"

My brain really needed to catch up with my mouth. "What type of shifter? I've guessed a bird of prey, but I can't tell specifically."

"Ah. Well, my dear Tilly, the fates have thrown an eagle shifter into your path. A golden eagle, to be specific. And you're a fox shifter if my nose is correct."

My inner fox danced with glee, loving that he'd picked up on that so quickly. "Yes, that's right."

He grinned, the look blasting more heat my way than I'd been ready for. "Well, my little vixen, I look forward to getting to know you better tonight. Woman and fox."

Renit smiled again then turned and walked away, looking back over his shoulder three times before he hit the corner and disappeared around the side of the building. Meanwhile, I stood in front of the door to the diner, grinning like a maniac and watching him go.

My mate.

Mine.

I was so going to get him alone tonight and—

"Why are you standing out here all alone?" My mother grabbed my arm, having somehow opened the door without my noticing. "Get inside. We have work to do."

Yes. We did. And then…date night.

This was going to be the longest dinner rush of my life.

2

TILLY

I was still wiping down tables—not in section five—when Renit came through the door that evening. I nearly stumbled, almost fell right over. The man looked…edible. That was the only way to describe him— dark hair, a little gray at the temples, those amber eyes, and a smile that only began its ascent when he made eye contact with me.

Mine.

My fox chattered happily, running back and forth and creating havoc in my mind. She wanted to scent her mate, to rub all up and down his body to let other females know he was taken. The human side of me thought this was a horrible idea…in public.

"Maybe later," I whispered before Renit finally made it across the room. Not quietly enough, apparently.

"Later for what?" Renit reached for my hand, holding it while he leaned in to gently kiss my cheek. "You look lovely, Tilly."

Nice words, especially considering I wore a below-the-knee skirt and a Kinship Cove Diner shirt. "I look like a waitress. I'm actually going to change and get ready right now, if you don't mind. I would have done it earlier, but the dinner rush lasted a little longer than normal."

"There's no need to change." He tugged me closer, almost to the

99

point of our bodies brushing. Almost. "I happen to think you're the most beautiful woman in the world just as you are."

Swoons. There were swoons for sure. But also, I was not unaware of how not-ready for a date I was. "I happen to think I need to put on a sexy dress and some makeup to show off for my new mate."

Renit grinned. "I like the sound of that."

"Me putting on makeup?"

"Me being your mate." He settled on a counter stool and waved the waiter behind it over. "Take your time, my little fox. I'll be here, having a cup of coffee."

I definitely didn't want to keep him waiting. I rushed into the back locker room where I had an extra outfit and my makeup bag thanks to Misty. She'd brought everything to the restaurant for me so I wouldn't have to go on my first date with the man I'd be spending forever with looking—well, like I looked. Thanks be to sisters.

Ten minutes, a quick PTA bath in the sink, a little hair straightener magic, and some seriously smoky eye makeup later, I was ready. And feeling quite sassy, I had to admit.

"Whoa." My brother—Billy—stopped in the middle of the kitchen, looking me up and down. "Got a date, sis?"

A date with my mate. I loved a good rhyme. What I did not love was the gossip mill that was our family. "Just meeting with some friends."

"Have fun but be careful looking like that. Someone might try to snatch you away from us."

A girl could dream.

I didn't make it five steps into the dining room before Renit's head popped up and his eyes found me. They traveled all the way down before gliding back up the length of my body, giving me a look I could feel. I practically melted under the heat of that look, could almost taste the desire growing there. The man liked what he saw. Time well spent, apparently.

Still, I wasn't about to be rude about making him wait. "Sorry it took so long."

He was already on his feet—such a gentleman—before I reached him. He made one last once-over of me and then leaned in, brushing those wicked lips against my cheek again. "The wait was well worth it. You look stunning, Tilly."

Do not hump his leg. Do not hump his leg. "Thank you. Are you finished with your coffee?"

He hummed, those wicked lips turning up at the sides again. "I'm finished with everything except you. Come, I have a car outside."

He grabbed my hand, and a wall of sensation slammed into my body. Heat and desire, need and lust—all sending tingles straight up my spine. I shivered visibly, drawing Renit's attention.

"Are you cold?"

"No." I squeezed his hand tighter. "Just excited."

He pulled me closer, wrapping his arm around my shoulders. "I know the feeling, mate."

We headed to the Metro Lounge—a popular dance club with the tourists who came to the area. Not exactly where I usually hung out, but just fine for an evening of wine, dancing, and Renit.

At least it would have been, had my sister and her posse not been hanging out in the VIP section already.

"Tilly." Misty waved from the couch toward the back, way more than loud enough to be heard over the music. "Join us."

Renit leaned down to whisper in my ear. "Friend of yours?"

"No. That's my sister, and the other woman with her is one of the Chance sisters. They own the Cake-ily Ever After bakery."

"And the men with them?"

Was that a grumble in his voice I detected? Could Renit be…jealous? A joyous thought for sure. "Those are their mates—Clark and Kingston."

He huffed but still didn't sound too pleased, so I turned around and moved closer so I didn't have to yell over the music. But I got a little distracted because he smelled *so* good. By the fates, I could lick the man right then and there. If only I—

He set a hand on my hip, and my mind scattered.

"Renit."

"Yes, Tilly?"

What was I going to say? What were words? Why did they need to come out of my mouth?

"Tilly?" Renit asked, looking down at me in concern. "Are you okay?"

I simply could not control my response. "You smell lickable."

He blinked before letting that smile grow even wider. "As do you. I think I'd like to have your scent all over me."

My fox would have howled—if she were a howling sort of animal. Being that she definitely was not, she simply chattered about in my head. Happy and excited and wanting to get her mate naked.

I couldn't blame the little trollop for that one.

When I didn't respond, Renit chuckled. "Shall we join your friends and sister, or should I throw you over my shoulder and carry you out of here? I'm staying at a cabin in the mountains. The view is spectacular."

"My view right now is spectacular, too." I set my hands on his chest and fought to remember what it was I'd wanted to say before I'd gotten all distracted by his Renit-ness. "I like these girls and their mates, but if it makes you uncomfortable in any way, we don't have to sit with them."

Renit glanced over my shoulder toward the VIP section, likely looking at the group of people waiting for us there. "The idea of any male near you makes me uncomfortable, but so long as you stick close to me, I should be fine."

That wouldn't be a problem. "Deal."

"Then let's get this show on the road." He grabbed my hand and led us through the crowd, cutting a path to the VIP section.

Misty was, of course, the first to open her mouth. "So. This is the mate?"

Renit was as smooth as ever. "I am the lucky man gifted with the attention of such a beautiful woman, yes. Renit Threefeather. You must be the sister."

Misty raised an eyebrow at his proffered hand before taking it in a handshake. "That'd be me. This is my mate, Clark."

Her professor stood, shaking hands with Renit even as he looked the man up and down. Sizing him up. With a wolf, a dragon, and a bird-of-prey shifter in such a small space, the male posturing was about to get crazy.

I almost couldn't wait to see it.

Sadly, I didn't get the chance.

"Excuse me." A pretty blond human leaned past me, her eyes focused on…my mate. "Are you Renit James?"

Renit stiffened as she moved a few inches closer. "Yes, I am."

"Oh my gosh, I told my friends it was you. I heard you were filming nearby and…"

And suddenly there were five human women in our VIP area, all surrounding my mate as I stood on the outside of the circle. Renit… James? As in the actor? How could I have missed that particular detail?

"You okay?" Misty asked as she and Clark came up from behind me.

"I don't understand what's happening here."

It was Ginger who answered, her eyes locked on her phone screen. "I thought he looked familiar. He's famous. Like, Hollywood famous. He's landed a few good roles in action films—because, duh, of course a shifter would be in those—and has really made a name for himself the last few years. You landed yourself a movie star, Tilly."

Welp. That was…I didn't even know. Who expects to be mated to a celebrity? I'd have assumed being with a famous movie star would have been sort of exciting, but the whole fans interrupting our first date thing? Not so much.

"Want me to get rid of them?" Kingston asked, scowling toward the girls who were still completely surrounding Renit. "There's enough alcohol-based beauty products in that crowd to light them up awfully quick."

"Stop," Ginger said as she smacked him on the chest. "He can't help it that they're fans."

"They're annoying is what they are." Clark tugged Misty closer, looking almost as alpha and aggressive as Kingston. "Let's go get a drink. Tilly, why don't you come with us?"

"Yeah," I said as one of the girls laughed, her head thrown back, and moved to place her arm on Renit's. He dodged the grab, but still. The audacity. "I really don't want to watch this."

Ginger hooked her arms through mine and Misty's, dragging us across the floor toward the bar, with Kingston and Clark tagging along behind us. Renit? Still with the other girls.

"Seriously," Ginger said as Misty and Clark moved to place an order at the bar for us. "Are you okay right now? You know he's just being friendly with his fans. He's mated to *you*."

"I know, and I'm sure this isn't what he wanted to happen. I'm just disappointed. This isn't what I'd hoped for when I'd dreamed about my first date."

She blinked twice, her expression falling slack. "You've never been on a date before?"

Could my face *be* any hotter? "Nope. I was always working or at the theater, and I figured my mate would come along eventually, so I didn't put a lot of thought into it."

"Oh hell no." She grabbed Kingston and basically climbed him like a tree, whispering in his ear and gesturing wildly. His eyes met mine, a look of something close to confusion crossing his face, before he turned his attention to Renit and the girls.

"I've got this," he said, and then he was off. Blasting his way through the crowd and heading straight for my mate.

"Oh no." I rose onto the balls of my feet, trying to see over the crowds, but it was impossible. "I hope he doesn't make too much trouble."

"It's your first date and your first night out with your new mate. There is no such thing as too much trouble in that situation." She patted my arm, stretching to see what she could just as I was. "Don't worry. Kingston will get your man back."

And he did. Seconds later, the crowd parted again as a pissed-off-looking Kingston and an equally cranky Renit appeared. The scowl on my mate's face sent a ball of lead dropping into my belly and tightened my chest. I was trembling by the time he reached me.

"Renit, I—"

"Not now." He grabbed my hand and pulled me along behind him, sending Kingston one of those guy chin-nod things that could either mean what's up, thanks, or screw you. Kingston replied in the same manner, and then we were gone. Through a back door and into what looked like a service hallway of some sort, though it was hard to tell because there weren't a lot of lights on.

Just the two of us. In the dark. If my mate hadn't been growling low in his throat, this could be fun.

"Stop," I said, placing my hands against his chest. "Don't be mad at Kingston."

"Kingston? I'm thankful to the dragon and owe him a favor for getting me out of there. Those women were—" He breathed out, his hands coming to grab mine. "Never mind them. Is Kingston right? Is this your first date?"

Yup. My face could get hotter. "He didn't need to tell you that."

"Oh, my sweet Tilly. I'm so sorry." He pulled me close, wrapping his arms around me. "That happens sometimes—fans recognizing me. I can usually pull away pretty quickly, but those women were hard to discourage."

"It's okay. I understand." Sort of more lie than not, but what else could I say?

"It is far from okay." Renit dropped down to my level, our eyes even and our noses close to touching. "You deserve all of my attention. I'm so sorry I didn't handle the issue with those fans as I should have."

"And how's that? If you could do it again, what would you do differently?"

One side of his mouth kicked up in a sexy half smile, and he tugged me closer. Leaning back against the wall as he fitted me between his spread legs. "I wouldn't be here at all."

"No?"

"No." Closer still, so much of him touching so much of me. "I'd have flown you to my cabin in the woods and kept you all to myself. No loud music or interrupting fans—just you and me and a fire in the fireplace."

"That sounds nice."

He brushed his nose against mine, our lips almost touching. "Doesn't it?"

Being in the dark with him, with our bodies so close, gave me more courage than I'd ever had. Gave me ideas about what I wanted and needed from him. Gave me the balls to ask for them. "Hey, Renit?"

"Yes, my mate?"

I loved it when he called me that. I especially loved the way he gripped me just a little tighter when he said the word. "Know what else besides dating I haven't done?"

His growl deepened, growing louder. "Tilly, I swear—"

"Kiss. I've never even had a kiss." I looked up into his eyes and gave him what I hoped was a come-hither sort of look. "Want to fix that for me?"

The call of some sort of predator sounded through the hall, and then his lips were on mine. So soft, so warm. He picked me up off the ground with his hands on my rear, pressing us together as I wrapped my legs around his hips. Using his entire body to influence such a simple kiss. More. I wanted more. And then he gave it to me, licking along my bottom lip until I opened for him. Stroking his tongue against mine in a way that made my entire body tremble. By the fates, did the man taste good. Spicy and warm. Every touch intensified the burn. Every breath brought us closer. This was not a first kiss. It was a last one. My first and last first kiss because nothing…nothing…could ever be better than this.

"Renit," I gasped as he moved his mouth to my neck, sucking and biting lightly. "What are you doing to me?"

"Kissing you."

"I know that, but why does it feel so good?"

"Because you're my mate, and I want nothing more than to please you."

I rocked against him, unable not to gasp at what I felt. At the thickness of him hitting all of my right spots. "If everything you do is as good as this kiss, then I see no flaws in your plan, Renit James."

"Threefeather," he said, pausing to pull back for a moment. To look me square in the eye. "My name is Threefeather—James is just a stage name."

Not surprising. I ran a hand over his cheek, smiling up at him. "Renit Threefeather. I like that much more than James."

"Me too." He leaned in again, kissing me with the same heat and fervor as before, making me moan and gasp and rub my body against his with every stroke of his tongue.

At least until I had to break away from him…for my own sanity…

and to breathe. "Your kisses are too much. I don't even know what to do with myself right now."

"Someday," Renit said as he licked and sucked his way along my jaw, still rocking his hips into mine. Teasing me. "Oh my mate, someday I'm going to take you home with me. I'll strip you down right there in front of the fire, and I'll kiss every inch of you. I'll spend extra attention on that sweet pussy of yours, kissing it the same way I kiss your lips. I'll make you beg for me to stop before the night is done."

Okay, that might be worthwhile.

I tugged him close again, pressing my lips to his and asking for more without words. Sadly, our kiss—and whatever else we were about to do in that dark, lonely hallway—had to come to an abrupt halt as a man burst into the space.

Wait, not a man.

Kingston.

"Time to go, lovebirds."

"Huh?" I said, which was about the best response anyone was going to get from me right at that moment.

"What's the problem?" Renit asked, subtly—or maybe not so subtly—setting me back on my feet and moving his body between Kingston and me. Jealous man.

"There are humans here with cameras, and my money is on you being their target."

"Shit." Renit scowled down at me. "Let me take you home, Tilly. I don't want those vultures to get their hands on you just yet."

"Literal vultures or just paparazzi?" Because in a shifter town, that was a question that needed answering.

"Sometimes both." He kissed my nose, humming softly. "I'll take you home, give you another good night kiss, and then we can start again tomorrow with a better date. Something for just the two of us."

"I like that plan."

"I figured you would." Renit looked up at Kingston. "We'll head out the back."

"Good call. I'll tell Misty and Ginger that you're fine. You know they'll be worried."

"Thanks, Kingston."

"You're welcome. And congrats—I wish things were going to be a little easier for you."

Me too. Though Renit seemed all in on the mating, and we definitely had chemistry. What could possibly go wrong?

3

RENIT

Production meetings about script changes and filming timelines were about as droll as they sounded. Trust me, I had to live through them.

"The producers feel we need more chemistry," the director—some young hothead from New Zealand with a great accent and really bad ideas—said as he stood before us. The man had been babbling on and on about all the things wrong with the script for almost an hour, and the entire table seemed to be getting restless. Or perhaps that was just me.

There were twelve people around the table—me, my two male costars who formed our on-screen military team, our female costar, whose uniform consisted of anything that bared her breasts and abs, a literal knight from England who was playing the evil mastermind of the entire movie, and a bunch of other people with small roles or production jobs. I should have been paying attention and giving them all the respect they deserved, but I was not.

I was texting my mate.

Almost done at work?

"A romantic subplot may be woven into the story, but we haven't decided the depth of that yet."

I wish. My mother wants me to stick around and help her clean out the storage room. I don't have the energy for this.

My poor mate. She worked a hard job and needed her rest. I'd done my best to calm Tilly after we'd left the bar. I'd given her my full attention, kept my hands on her to help grow our bond, and kissed her silly on her parents' front porch before leaving like a gentleman, far too early for my liking. She'd texted me this morning that she hadn't been able to sleep, though. I hated that something—likely either the excitement of having met her fated mate or the stress from last night's failed date—had kept her awake.

Perhaps I needed to put away the gentleman and let out my inner beast. He had ideas of what would help our mate sleep—long hours of celebrating and getting to know every inch of her body. Making her come at my hands and mouth and on my cock until she was wrung out. That'd do it.

"The screenwriting team is evaluating our table-read videos and audition footage to see what may work for what the producers want."

Be strong, my beautiful girl. I'll come to you this evening as promised and take you on a date. Just us.

Just us. I liked that idea. My inner eagle loved it. We had finally found our fated mate, and we were going to treat her like a princess. A naughty princess who deserved a spanking now and again, but a princess. Definitely. Tilly had an ass that was made for the palm of my hand.

"Be prepared for changes on the fly. We'll do our best to keep you updated, but I expect a lot of last-minute adjustments and redirections."

Decades. So many decades had passed with no mate. As the rest of my eagle family—my convocation—had paired off, I'd been left alone. Searching. Wanting. I'd fallen into acting almost by accident—right place, wrong time sort of thing. They'd been filming in the woods where my convocation had nested, and I'd headed down to watch the goings-on. An agent had seen me in the crowd and approached, telling me I had an "unusual look." We'd been chatting when a widow-maker—a large branch that had broken off from a tree but gotten stuck within the canopy—fell. Shifters tend to be as fast as their animal counterpart, and my eagle always had been the quickest flier around. I saved that agent's life, and he'd promised me he'd get me work if I was interested in acting. The next thing I knew, I was in Los Angeles working with acting coaches and getting headshots, going on auditions. I'd somehow become an action star without even trying, and now my job had led me to my mate.

Fate was a wily one, for sure.

"This week, we'll be shooting a few of the more emotional scenes on set instead of outdoors. There will be children present, so please mind your language."

Children. Tilly wasn't much more than one compared to me. Never been on a date. Never been kissed by anyone but me. I also had to imagine she'd never been touched, never been with another man. Shifters weren't as prudish as humans in regard to such things, but I had to admit, being the only person to know the taste of my mate's skin made me want to take to the skies. My Tilly was so sweet and definitely inexperienced—I could tell that by the way she kissed, so sloppy but enthusiastic—but she was mine, and I could teach her. We could learn all the joys of being mated together.

Once I got out of this stupid meeting.

"Let's review tomorrow's scene."

A scene in which I barely had any lines to worry about. Wonderful.

Thankfully, I had my Tilly to distract me.

Everything okay over there? Did you save me a cup of coffee for later?

I'll brew you a fresh pot when I know you're finally on your way.

Something about that text, about the word finally, struck me as odd.

Is everything okay?

Just tired. And cranky. And having a really bad day. I could use a hug.

I was on my feet and in motion before I even thought about it, not that my decision needed any thought. My mate needed me, and I would be there for her. No matter what.

"Renit? We're not done here."

Do not growl at the man. "Yes, but I have a bit of an emergency. I'll be ready for filming tomorrow, though. No worries."

And with that, I took off at a run down the hallway of the little strip mall production had converted into offices and out into the parking lot. Flying would have been so much faster, but I'd need to carry a cloak to cover myself after my shift. Something I didn't have with me. I'd have to settle for driving like some sort of human.

Eight minutes. It took eight minutes to race down the mountain and into town. I passed the Cake-ily Ever After bakery on my way to the diner, making a mental note to order some goodies for the production team. Kingston had saved my tail last night with that heads-up about the paps. The least I could do was give his mate's business my money.

I didn't have much time to give that idea consideration, though, because I made it to the diner soon after and was up and running for the door the second I threw the car into park. As I headed inside, the scent of my mate overpowered all the others, and my eagle woke up. Ready to cherish. Ready to defend and protect. Sadly, it seemed like my job would be the latter.

"I should have called one of your brothers to help." The old woman from the day before—Tilly's mother, apparently—stormed through the dining room, an exhausted and obviously unhappy Tilly in her wake.

"None of them would have shown up. They're all busy—you get me, or you wait for the grandkids to get out of school. Take your pick." Tilly glanced my way, doing a double take when she spotted me. And then her face lit up. There was my girl. That smile soothed everything inside of me, and her making a beeline for where I was standing brought me such pride. I felt like a king all because this woman graced me with her attention.

I was so whipped already.

"What are you doing here?" she asked as soon as she stopped in front of me. Two feet in front of me. That space between us would not do.

I inched closer, keeping my voice quiet so as not to draw any undue attention. "You said you could use a hug. I'm here to provide for you."

She looked almost ready to cry, but she didn't take a step closer. "Not here, okay? I don't want my mom to see."

"Why not?" Because if Tilly was somehow embarrassed by me—

"She'll ruin it. She's so bossy and overbearing, if she finds out I have a mate, she'll want to throw a party and invite the entire skulk and likely half the town, and it will become a thing."

"And you don't want a thing?"

"My siblings are all busy with their own lives. If she decides to do a thing, all the work falls on my shoulders."

"Ah, and you don't want to deal with the labor of her thing."

"Precisely."

I sidled that much closer, letting the backs of my knuckles brush her hand. "You sure that's all?"

She gripped my hand for a second before taking a step back. "Positive. I swear, if I weren't afraid of my mom making me throw my own mating party right now when opening night of the play is just two days away, I'd be shouting it from the rooftops that you're mine."

Okay then. That worked for me, though I'd apparently neglected learning about her. "You're in a play?"

"Oh." Her cheeks flushed, and she looked away. "Yeah. It's totally silly."

"It's not. At all. I love community theaters. There's a lot of great stuff happening in them." I spotted her mother moving across the room, heading away from us, so I took a chance and tugged my mate closer. Let her feel the heat of my body. "Your mother isn't looking, so don't panic, but I definitely wanted to be the one to hug you if you needed it. And now I want to be the one to come watch you practice your play. Is that the plans you have this afternoon?"

Because we weren't supposed to meet up for another couple of hours. She'd said she had things to do to fill the time, but she had not been specific about what.

She sighed and sank into my hold, making my hands twitch with the need to touch more of her. "Yes. I was about to leave to go there when I saw you."

"Then let's go." I leaned a little closer and lowered my voice. "If we hurry, maybe we can sneak another hug on the way."

She sighed. "Just a few days. Let me get through this production, and then we can tell my mother."

"Whatever you need, Tilly. I'm here to please you." And yes. I said that last part with as much innuendo coming through the words as possible because the idea of pleasing her, getting my mate alone and naked and making her scream my name, thrilled me to no end. I needed to be patient, but I could tease.

Tilly understood exactly where I was coming from, too. Those cheeks flamed bright red, and she licked those kissable lips. "I'll just grab my coat and meet you outside, okay?"

"Don't be long."

She hurried off, disappearing through the kitchen doors just as her mother came back into the dining room. It took everything in me not to glare at the old woman. Mate the girl, mate the family and all that—I needed to be on my best behavior. Still, once she knew Tilly was my mate, there would be some rules laid down. No one talked to my mate the way her mother talked to her, and I would not allow someone to work my girl to death. Hell, Tilly never needed to work another day if she didn't want to. We could live off of what I'd earned in the past few movies easily.

Then I could have her all to myself every day, all day.

Things to consider.

Before Tilly's mom could bother coming my way, I swept outside. Anxious and ready to see my girl again. Thankfully, it didn't take long.

"Ready?" Tilly asked as she came around the corner of the diner. Not through the front door. A fact my eagle definitely noticed…and didn't like.

"Did you walk out through the alley?"

She glanced behind her as if confused by the question. "Yeah."

"Alleys are dangerous."

"Oh, quit. No one's going to bother me. This is Kinship Cove…we're safe here." She grabbed my hand and pulled me along, looking so very young and happy. "Come on. You can meet my friends. They all know not to tell my mother anything happening in my life."

And so we went, Tilly holding my hand and regaling me with stories of the plays she'd done interspersed with tidbits about the town, and me following along behind her like the love-sick fool I was.

We reached the community theater a few minutes later, the big brick building sitting back off the street and looking far too regal for such a small town.

"This is lovely," I said as we headed for the front door.

"It was built as a movie house—one of those old theater palaces, you know?"

I did. I'd lived through that time. When men wore hats and suits to take their girl out for a show and the ladies all had on stockings and heels. Perhaps I could talk my jeans-wearing mate into dressing up for me one night so I could take her out on the town. The idea definitely appealed.

"Tilly," a man said as soon as we stepped inside. "So good to see you, dear."

Others approached, all smiling and welcoming, all obviously very much enamored of my mate. We had things in common, then. And while nothing would ever fully distract me from Tilly's bright smile and sweet voice, the beauty of the theater did a damn good job trying to.

Gold columns rose from the floor to support the high ceilings, and red chairs swept downward toward the stage. A true playhouse, this building.

"Magnificent," I whispered as I caught sight of the chandelier hanging over the theater floor.

"Isn't it lovely?" Tilly sidled up beside me, bumping my arm with her shoulder. "It's one of my favorite places to be."

"I can see why. It's gorgeous." I leaned down to press a kiss to her head. "Not nearly as gorgeous as you, though."

"You're ridiculous."

And yet, her grin belied her words.

I settled into a seat toward the back of the theater as the rest of the people—Tilly included—headed for the stage. Phone in hand, I worked my way through a mountain of emails and text messages that needed answering as the person in charge—possibly the director, if that job had been assigned to someone—talked about what to expect on opening night. The excitement in the room was a palpable thing, and I enjoyed the slight drone of the voices carrying through the room as they asked questions and discussed final costume alterations.

It wasn't until the actual run-through that I put my phone away and paid attention. The play was one I hadn't heard of, and the acting was far better than I'd expected. I got swept into the story, though it helped that my mate seemed to be the female lead in the production. Smart casting people.

I was sitting on the edge of my seat at what I had to imagine was almost the ending of the play, right about where the hero's world falls apart, when one character moved close to Tilly. Way close. Too close. I wrestled my eagle into silence and watched, waiting to see what this was all about. Why this person—llama shifter, if his scent didn't lie— seemed fixated on Tilly. Why he kept inching closer with every line. Why she was looking up at him as if…as if…

And then it happened.

The llama shifter, having said some line about milk, reached out and grabbed Tilly's arm.

Pulling her toward him and leaning over her as if to press a kiss to the lips the fates had designed solely for me.

I lost control.

4

TILLY

I hadn't been expecting a night of flying over Kinship Cove in the talons of a giant bird, but that's what I got.

Renit had shifted when the kiss scene from the play had come up. In retrospect, I probably should have warned him about that, but I'd been so excited for him just to be there. He'd shown up when I'd needed him. And not like *needed him,* needed him—I'd told him I was having a bad day and needed a hug. Such a simple thing, and yet he'd dropped everything to give me what I'd wanted.

My mate was sort of amazing—and sort of pissed. And his talons were really, really sharp. Thank goodness he was also really careful with me.

Eventually, Renit descended to one of the mountains overlooking the cove. A squat little wood cabin sat among the trees, looking decidedly like something from a fairy tale. Or a murder mystery. I was going with fairy tale seeing as how I had my mate with me. And not one of those original fairy tales meant to scare children into being well-behaved adults—the Disneyfied versions. True love and animals that helped you clean.

Shifter town—that was actually a thing.

Renit landed on one foot, obviously being careful not to rattle me too hard, before uncurling his claws and releasing me. Winter in Kinship Cove never got too cold for most shifters—meerkats excluded because those little buggers froze even at the slightest breeze—but the chill in the night air still had me shivering. Or perhaps it was the rage billowing off my mate, the pure anger I felt there. His alpha power was in full effect, and my fox could do nothing but tremble in his shadow.

Renit shifted to his human form, those sharp eyes of his pinning me in place as all that warm, naked flesh appeared. I tried not to look, too afraid of what he'd do in that moment if I did. Too afraid of what I'd do, too. Another tremble racked my body.

"You're cold." He turned and stormed onto the porch, his backside and thighs flexing with every step. By the fates, I was one lucky woman. This man was pure strength, all muscles and dips and gorgeous bubble booty. I couldn't wait to get my hands on it. Once he calmed down a little.

Sadly, Renit grabbed a cloak from a basket on the porch and covered himself. He also brought me one, wrapping it around me like a coat once he'd thundered my way. I used the term thundered in an almost literal sense—the anger storming off the man was a palpable thing. It practically shook the earth as he walked.

I was in big, big trouble.

"Come inside," he demanded, pulling me onto the porch with his hand gripping my elbow. "I'll start a fire to warm you."

"I'm fine." An automatic response even as another shiver rolled over me.

My answer definitely did not make my mate happy. "You are not fine. You're cold enough to shiver. Come inside so I can get you warm before I—"

He stopped, no more words spoken, just a low growl sound that definitely caught my attention.

"Before you what? Are you going to yell at me?" My temper ignited, the fear of what was to come being pushed behind the anger of one more person trying to control my life.

"I might." He pulled, dragging me into the little cabin. Sparsely furnished, the open space still felt warm and inviting, the huge fireplace with the soft-looking rug in front of it on one side of the room giving me all sorts of ideas. Ones that certainly did not fit my current mood.

"You're not my parent."

"No, but I *am* your mate." He led me to the couch closest to the fireplace and pushed me to take a seat. "And as your mate, I *will* take care of you. That means making sure you don't develop hypothermia in my presence."

"Fine. But if you start yelling, I'm leaving."

He froze, staring back at me with the most earnest expression on his face. "You'd leave me?"

Something in his voice, in his wording, spoke to a lot more than just me removing myself from the situation if he raised his voice. "Not forever. I don't like to be yelled at—I get enough of it at home and work."

He nodded once, finally turning to start the fire he'd promised. Working hard for several minutes on the flames with his back to me and his mouth silent. Had I pushed him too far? The very thought sent my gut tumbling. This was not the way I wanted to start our relationship, but I couldn't back down. If I let him yell at me now, he'd do it forever. No way was I being subjected to that sort of nonsense.

Thankfully, Renit didn't linger over the fire once he got it burning. He joined me on the couch, still looking so very earnest. "I promise not to raise my voice at you, but I am not happy right now."

It sounded as if he wanted a discussion. Like adults were supposed to have. How novel. "Okay. Can you explain to me why?"

His eyes met mine, the anger an almost palpable thing, the flames reflecting in the amber glow. "He was going to kiss you."

Oh. The play. "Not a real kiss."

"Lips on lips is a kiss."

"It's just an act."

Jumping to his feet, Renit began to pace. Breathing hard and quite obviously struggling with this discussion. "Play or not, I can't have it. You can*not* kiss another man."

Oh, heck no. I really didn't like being bossed around. I dealt with that enough. "Is that an order?"

"Yes." He stopped and shook his head. "No, but yes. I don't want to order you not to do something, but this seems pretty intrinsic to building a strong and healthy mating bond. No kissing others."

"It's not a real kiss. It's just for the theater. It's an act."

"I still don't like it and don't want it to happen."

"That's quite hypocritical coming from you. Wasn't there a love scene in your last movie with that girl who got famous on some reality dancing show?" Yeah, I may not have recognized him right from the get-go, but I could Google. And I had. Googled, that is. I'd Googled Renit as if he were a research project. And I didn't like all that I'd found out. "And the movie before—I saw the pictures. You definitely kissed your costar."

"Past tense—kissed. Before I met you. I have no intentions of ever kissing anyone other than you for the rest of my life."

"What if it's in the script?"

"I won't do the project."

"You'll lose your clout. Moviegoers love the big, bad man falling for the woman working with him. It's practically a law."

"Then I'll stop acting."

That was…not expected. "You'd give up your career?"

He sat next to me once more, sighing. Reaching for my hands. "I have searched for you for decades, Tilly. Nothing as trivial as my career will get in the way of us being together."

Tumbling. My stomach and heart suddenly felt as if they were tumbling. "Renit—"

"I know I'm repeating myself, but I want to be clear here. I have no intentions of ever kissing anyone other than you for the rest of my life. And you'd better not, either."

I inched closer, wanting to touch him so badly. Needing to stop the world from spinning and knowing the only way to do that was through him. "You care that much?"

"More. I care that much and more. You are my world, Tilly. My new center of gravity. There's nothing I won't do for you." He tugged me into his lap, wrapping his arms around me. Grounding me the way I so needed him to. "I just hope you'll eventually feel the same way."

Oh. That. That was the issue? He felt as if I weren't as deeply committed to him or something? Silly eagle. "I *do* feel the same. You were my first kiss, and I'm thrilled that you'll be my last. Those little stage pecks and holds—they mean nothing to me. Never have."

He dropped his gaze, suddenly seeming almost...shy. "They mean something to me."

And that was it, the moment I knew my entire world had changed. This man—this strong, alpha male—was being so open with me. So honest in his feelings. How could I not give him what he needed? How could I not honor this one request?

I couldn't, which was why there was only one more thing to say to him. "I have an understudy who's doing very well. I'll ask for a lesser role in the play and let her take the lead."

"Thank you. I know it's a sacrifice, and I appreciate your making it for me."

He pulled me around, tightening his hold and breathing into my neck. Pressing us close together in a sort of side hug. That still wasn't enough for me, so I turned and wiggled until I had my legs spread around his hips. Until I sat fully on his lap, leaning into his chest.

"I'm not happy about this, just so you know."

"I know. But I can't watch you kiss another man, my little fox. My eagle and I—we can't handle it."

Renit dropped his hands to cup my backside, tugging me closer. Moving my hips until I felt it. Like...*it* it. So hard and thick and *right there*. The sensation of that between my legs suddenly made my skin prickle and my awareness of our situation light up as if we'd been hiding it somehow. We were alone, hidden away in the woods, no parents or siblings or nieces and nephews around to interrupt us. We had this beautiful cabin all to ourselves, a roaring fire, and a rug that looked made for being naked on.

Why were we wasting our time arguing?

"Renit," I whispered as I leaned in to kiss his neck, rocking my hips over his in the process. "Did you bring me to your secluded cabin in the woods to seduce me?"

"No. I wanted a quiet place to talk and to get you away from other males before I went on a killing spree." He thrust up against me, eliciting a deep moan from me as he slipped his hands inside the back of my jeans to tug me closer. "Though this does seem awfully fortuitous."

"It does. It certainly does." I dragged my lips up his neck and over his jaw, teasing him with little circles of my hips, but then he took over. Kissing me, stroking his tongue against mine as one hand stayed firmly on my backside inside of my jeans and the other slid up under my shirt. He had me in a locked hold, secured against him. And still, I wanted more. Or less—more skin, more Renit, more touching. Less clothing. "Can we get naked now?"

"Fuck, Tilly." He jumped up, shucking his cloak as if it was nothing. "Are you sure? I would never want to push you."

Ha. As if. To prove my sureness, I yanked my shirt over my head and dropped it on the ground at his feet. Game on. "Push me, twist me, position me, use me. Whatever you want. I'm ready for all of it, mate."

And then I bit him.

5

TILLY

Funny thing about shifters—biting to secure a mating was not universal. Some species exchanged mating bites, taking in the blood of the other partner as if imbibing their very essence. Some didn't. But all shifters—every breed and level of prey or predator—seemed to like being bitten by the person they were with. It was an animalistic thing, and it certainly worked with Renit.

With a growl, the man set me down on the rug, hovering over me with a wild sort of gleam in his eyes. I barely had time to take a breath before he was gone again, though. Before he sat back on his knees between my spread legs. He worked my buttons and zipper down, tugging my jeans off and tossing them away. Sliding his hands up my legs as his eyes stayed locked on mine, pushing my knees back, back, back toward my shoulders. Spreading me before him. When his fingertips curved around the fabric of my panties, my breath hitched. I couldn't help it—that look in his eyes, the intensity. It seared me all the way down to the bone.

"I'm going to kiss you here, mate." He pressed against the cotton covering me, teasing me with a light pressure that only proved how wet I already was for him. "I'm going to kiss you right here until I have your taste memorized. Do you want that?"

Such a silly question. "Yes."

"Only you," he said, before tugging the cotton fabric down my legs, exposing me to him. Baring me and pushing my knees even farther apart. "Only your lips and your taste and your scent. I will never want another female."

Good, because I was not about to share him. I reached for him, fisting my hand in his hair and tugging him closer. Needing him so much. "Make me yours, Renit. I want to be yours."

From the first touch of his flesh to mine, the first sip of his tongue along my most intimate places, I knew exactly what I'd been missing out on all this time. What I'd been waiting for. Renit teased me with soft laps and gentle nibbles, building the fire within my body slowly. There was no embarrassment or awkwardness of human first experiences—this was my mate, the man the fates deemed my perfect match. I didn't need to be worried about anything other than making sure he knew exactly what he did that I liked and what I needed more of. Which was pretty much everything.

Thankfully, the man didn't seem to be the type to tap out early. He kept up his takeover of my flesh, wrapping his arms under my hips and lifting me to get a better angle. Holding me there half suspended. All the blood rushed to my head and my legs dangled over his shoulders, but it didn't matter because his touch, his tongue, and his teeth felt so amazing.

"Renit, I can't. I don't..." I arched into his touch, the pressure building inside of me pushing down so hard I had no idea how much more I could take. Everything felt so good and right and perfect. There was no way to stop the oncoming freight train of my orgasm, no way to slow this thing down. As the crest appeared, as my body began to twitch and my muscles began to lock into place, I reached down and grabbed his hair with both hands. Tugging him closer. Rocking my hips against his face to get the perfect touch, the exact right amount of pressure. To hold him in place so he didn't miss a moment of what I was going through.

And when I finally broke, when my orgasm crashed around me like some sort of tidal wave of sensation, Renit was right there. Teasing me through it. Pushing me to experience more and better and longer. At least until he lunged up my body and settled his weight between my legs.

Right there.

"So sweet, my pretty mate." He kissed me softly, licking his way inside and sharing my taste. Making me shiver with the naughtiness of the act. "I could live on that taste. But first, I want to make this sweet pussy mine. May I, Tilly?" He rocked his hips, moving closer, almost nudging his way inside of me as I arched and panted. "Let me in, beautiful girl, and I can do even better than what I just gave you. I can make you forget your own name if you give me the chance."

"I mean…if you must." I giggled and grabbed hold of him by that delicious bubble booty, pulling him even closer. My breath catching when he slid the tip inside of me. "I'm yours. Always."

"Yes, my dear Tilly. All mine." And with that, he kissed me again, making me dizzy with the ferocity of the act. The aggressiveness of it. The kiss almost made me forget what else was happening with my body. Almost, because having someone the size of Renit push his way inside of you wasn't possible to ignore.

He kissed me through the gasp as he breached where no one had been before. Kissed me as I shook all over with the new sensations of him sliding deeper and deeper inside. He kept his lips on mine and his tongue stroking as he pressed farther, bottoming out with a groan he simply couldn't hold back.

"Ah, fuck, Tilly." He dropped his head to my shoulder and thrust into me. Softly, gently. "How did I get so lucky to be the first to experience this heaven?"

"First and last." I wrapped my arms around his shoulders, dying a little bit inside with every twinge and twitch. This would be over soon. Not the mating; that was forever. But this experience, this moment—my first time. I almost wanted to cry at how important it felt and how fleeting it would be, yet the pleasure running through my veins was too strong to let me. Such a confusing headspace to be in.

Thankfully, Renit seemed to understand.

"I can go all night," he said, grunting as he pulled almost all the way out. "You tell me when you're ready to come, my girl. I'll wait for you. And then we can start all over."

"All over?" I pushed on his shoulders, waiting until I had his eyes on mine to ask, "You mean we can do this again tonight?"

Renit chuckled and went back to thrusting into me, teasing me with slow, shallow strokes. "Of course. We can do this as much as you'd like, as many times as you'd like. I'd be happy to spend days buried inside of you."

That sounded...well, like a bad idea, but the thought behind it seemed sound. Lots of sex. Multiple orgasms per day. I was down for that.

"Now, then. Make me come now, Renit. I want to know what it feels like with you inside me."

He groaned and pressed his lips to mine again, dropping a hand between us to press his thumb against my clit. I bucked and squealed, the sudden extreme pressure taking my internal battle to the next level. I was going to come, all right—long and hard and intensely. It would only take a few more strokes, a little bit more motion from his thumb. The right angle for him to—

"Holy buckets," I yelled as my entire body locked down. Stars exploded behind my eyelids, and a chill crept across my skin. Renit, my mate, my true partner, had sent my body chasing a high I might never recover from. One I'd happily chase every day for the rest of my life. Every pulse around him, every quiver in my legs from the force of it, just reinforced how perfect we were together. This feeling was right, was meant to be. And I was the lucky girl who got to have it and him forever.

My mate didn't stop, though. Oh no, not Renit. He kept thrusting, kept pushing, kept driving his body into mine and bringing me back to the crest so I could crash again. The force of his motion dragged me along the rug until my head bumped into the couch, and still, we moved. Him grunting, me digging my nails into his back, the couch inching backward. Until finally—*finally*—with one last deep thrust, he came with a screech that would have put any mammal's howl to shame.

"Mine," he whispered, panting hard. Dropping his weight onto me and holding me close. "All mine."

"Yours. Forever."

6

RENIT

Promising my young mate that we could have sex as many times as she'd like may have been both the best and the worst thing I'd ever done. Best because being inside my mate brought me more pleasure than I ever could have imagined. Worst because she had an appetite and an endurance that surpassed mine.

I was a lucky man.

A very lucky, very tired man who should have been enjoying a lazy morning in bed but had a tablet buzzing from across the room and driving him up a wall.

I snuck out from under the blankets, doing my best not to wake my sleeping angel. It was still dark out, the gleam of the morning sun barely breaking the tree line in the distance, but dawn would be here soon. That meant leaving my mate behind to go to work. A thought that made my stomach plummet.

Things needed to change in my world, at least for a little while. As soon as I was finished with my current project. Until then, I had commitments to deal with, so I crept across the cold floor to where my tablet lay on a side table. One of many that I owned all tied together with my phone. Shifting left me without the ability to take the damn devices with me, and yet modern culture demanded I be connected at all times. I'd need to go back to the theater to see if my actual phone was still there under the seats where I'd shifted. One more thing to do, sadly without my mate at my side.

Today was going to be rough.

Fifteen text messages and a ridiculous number of email alerts decorated the lock screen of the tablet once I reached it. I dealt with the texts first, knowing they were the most important. A few from my agent —a bastard of a wolverine shifter who would quite literally take a bite of anyone who crossed him—and the rest from production. Project notes, script changes, and most importantly, schedule changes. My early-morning start time had been pushed back—I didn't need to be in makeup until noon. That meant more time with Tilly. Excellent.

And yet, I still worried. Was this too *much* time together so soon? Had I overpowered her and pushed her into something she wasn't ready for? My mate was so young, and my eagle so aggressive. The level of overprotectiveness coursing through me told me this could go badly quickly if I didn't rein him in. I needed to be conscious of her inexperience, aware that she might overreact to the simplest of offenses. I needed to treat her like a damn queen and spoil her rotten so she knew exactly what sort of mate the fates had gifted her with.

And I would. As soon as this production was over, I'd be all hers. For now, she'd have to share me with my job.

With the weight of this newfound life change heavy on my shoulders, I headed to the kitchen, needing to find something to drink. More hours with my mate could mean more sex, or it could mean talking and getting to know one another better. Either way, I needed to hydrate. The three times Tilly had woken me up for more of my body had worked me harder than I'd been worked even in training for these action films. And the four times I'd done the same hadn't helped. My muscles screamed for a chance to recover, not that I planned to give them that. It'd been a great night. One I hoped to repeat. A lot.

"Did I wear you out?" Tilly snuck up behind me as I drank from a bottle of water, pressing her warm skin against my back, bringing her hands to my chest and her lips to my shoulder blade. Then her teeth. The little vixen.

"If you keep biting me like that, I'll show you worn out." Water forgotten, I spun around and captured her in my arms, needing more of her already. "You should be asleep."

She shrugged as she cuddled against me, practically purring when our skin met. "I woke up alone and a little cold."

I needed to buy more blankets and start charging my tablet on the nightstand instead of across the room. That way, I wouldn't have to leave her side until it was time to go to work. "I'm sorry. I had to check my texts for today's schedule."

"It's okay." She shrugged against me, softening her voice as she murmured, "I just missed you."

My heart. It grew. As did other parts of me. Gripping her ass tightly, I leaned down to place a wet kiss on her neck and breathe in her delectable scent. "I missed you too, mate." And I would even more if we had to separate later. Which got me to thinking… "How about you come to the set with me today?"

She jerked back, excitement lighting up her beautiful face. "Really?"

"Of course. I don't want to spend hours away from you. But only if you don't have anything else planned." I tugged her closer, my eagle thankful that we'd get to spend more time with our mate. Even if it was with other people around.

"I'll call and ask my sister to work for me. She owes me a few favors."

A day without that frown on her face when her mother bossed her around? I'd take it. "Perfect. I need to be in makeup by noon."

"What time is it now?"

I glanced at the clock. "Half past five."

The mischievous smile that crept across her face told me exactly what she had planned for the morning. And that I'd need more water… and perhaps a protein bar.

"That gives us a couple of hours."

"It does," I said, trying my hardest to look innocent and unaffected by her as I asked, "Should we try to sleep some more?"

She tapped her chin, adorably thoughtful in a playful sort of way. "I think there might be something I need more than sleep."

Clueless. I pretended to be absolutely clueless even as my cock filled with blood and my hands tugged her closer of their own volition. "Like what?"

Brazen as all get-out, she reached between us, palming me and rubbing her thumb across the tip. Sending sparks of pleasure shooting up my spine. "I need this."

Lucky fucking eagle. Without comment, I grabbed her, throwing her over my shoulder and stalking to the bed. "I think I can take care of that need."

She laughed as I tossed her on the mattress, creeping toward the headboard as she gave me quite the naughty little temptress look. "I know you can. So come, Renit. Make me scream your name again."

More than lucky. Blessed. I covered her body with mine, tucking my hips between her legs and lining us up even as I bent to take a sweet nipple into my mouth. Whispering once I popped off the hard tip, "I prefer when you yell about buckets."

Holy buckets, to be exact.

Tilly practically glared. "Are you going to tease me forever about that?"

"Yes. Forever." I pressed inside, groaning at the heat and tightness of her. At the way our bodies fit so well together. At the way her eyes fluttered closed and she sighed when I filled her. Forever? Not nearly long enough. "I will tease you and please you and fuck you forever. Every day of forever."

And I would. I'd sworn an oath by accepting this mating, and I'd do anything in my power to keep her happy.

TILLY

Movie sets were exciting and fascinating to be on. All the energy and activity, all the people who—I assumed—were famous. The Hollywood stars. Renit had the coolest job on the planet. The problem with actually filming movies? It seemed to take forever, and in the chill of a winter evening in Kinship Cove, the time spent was at best uncomfortable and at worst painful.

"How are you not done yet?" I leaned into Renit's hold, tugging the blanket he'd covered me with a little tighter around my shoulders. "I swear, you've filmed half the movie today."

Renit chuckled, moving in to kiss my neck. "This is the last scene on the call sheet. Once the director says we've got this, I'll take you home."

Well, that wasn't any better. "I'd rather stay with you at the cabin."

He growled softly, nipping my earlobe as if in rebuke. "When I said home, I meant my home, mate."

Ah, I'd upset his eagle with the idea of my leaving his side. I'd always known mated males could be territorial and aggressive—I'd seen my father and brothers and neighbors practically lose their minds at times over their mates—but not like Renit. He took protectiveness to the next level. If he wasn't in front of the camera, he was wrapped around me. And the fates forbid another male even look my way. I didn't mind, though. It was nice to be so obviously cared for, to be wanted. Renit protecting me made me feel valued.

"I'd been hoping this would end sooner," Renit said, sounding far more tired than I liked. "We need to stop at the theater once we're done here."

"For what?"

"To look for my phone."

Oh. "Because you shifted so fast."

"Exactly."

"I'm sure someone collected your clothes and phone and set them aside. You're not the first shifter in town to go animal over a little jealousy."

He nipped my neck. "I'll give you a little jealousy."

Sadly, he had no time to.

"Okay, folks," the director yelled as he scrolled on his tablet, his eyes never leaving the screen. "Let's try this again. Renit and Jen, I need a little more chemistry between you two. We're not getting that juicy sort of romance moment we need."

"It's an action movie," Renit grumbled, tugging the blanket around me once more. "Are you warm enough?"

Not even close, but that was only because I would be losing his body heat. Something he couldn't stop from happening. "I'm fine."

His frown told me he knew I wasn't fine, but he didn't push. "Stay right here, okay?"

See? Overprotective. "Right here. I wouldn't miss your big romantic moment for anything."

He stared at me for a long moment, his face still. Those amber eyes I already loved so much capturing me and making all the air around me disappear. One look, and I couldn't breathe. How did he do that?

"You and me last night in the cabin?" He stepped closer, lowering his voice. "That was my big romantic moment, Tilly. This all means nothing in comparison."

Sweet talker.

"I know that." I ran my hand down his chest to grab hold of his belt, using it to yank him closer. "And I hope to have another big romantic moment tonight."

"Anything for you."

A quick kiss, a simple peck, really, and then he was jogging away. What's that human saying? I hated to see him leave, but I loved watching him walk away? Yeah…Renit's ass in those military pants was a thing of beauty. He needed to wear pants like those more often. If it wouldn't have distracted him, I'd have pulled my phone out right then to see if I could get them on Amazon. Next-day delivery would have been worth the added fee.

"Do you need another blanket, honey?"

The hair lady slipped in beside me as she'd been doing all night. Her hands almost immediately moved to my hair, combing out tangles with her fingers.

"No, thank you."

"This hair," she said. "It's just so lovely. I don't think I've ever felt hair this soft."

Yeah, she kept saying that, and every time, I got more uncomfortable. Of course my hair was soft—I was a fox shifter. And humans like her? They still used our fur for coats.

"I work in a diner. Must be all the grease in the air." I took a step to the side, moving away from her. Not too far, though. I didn't want Renit being distracted by my not standing exactly where he'd left me. Overprotective—remember?

They filmed the same scene five times, the director always saying he needed more chemistry. I could have told him more chemistry wouldn't be happening—every time the female lead flirted, Renit locked down. Well, more likely, Renit's eagle. A mated male wasn't about to accept the come-ons of a woman who wasn't his mate. It simply wasn't done. The director could ask for more chemistry all he wanted, but if that woman kept pushing Renit, the chemistry he got would be the turbulent kind instead of the romantic variety.

"Jen, how about you go ahead and ad-lib a little like we talked about," the director yelled, catching my attention. "Let's see if we can amp this up."

"Sounds good," the woman playing opposite Renit said back. She smiled at my mate, chatting easily with him. Renit seemed comfortable enough, though a stiffness remained in his shoulders. He darted looks my way throughout their conversation, never once making me feel forgotten. I loved that about him, and I'd show him exactly how much once I got him alone again. So many hours without being able to touch him as I wanted to felt almost torturous. I could see why some newly mated couples disappeared for a few weeks. Maybe I could talk Renit into doing that once his filming was over. A little trip with just him and me? That sounded like heaven.

I was running down my list of siblings, nieces, and nephews to ask to cover my shifts—completely ignoring what was happening in front of the camera as I'd seen this play out fifteen times already—when something inside of me lurched. The bond to Renit almost vibrated, the shift inside so startling, I stumbled backward. When I had found my footing once more, I looked up. Hoping everything was okay. Wondering what on earth could have caused such an extreme reaction in our connection.

The answer to that?

Renit and his costar in a serious lip-lock.

"Huh," I said, unable not to.

"Maybe now the director will be happy. That's some chemistry, all right." The hair lady chuckled, but I did not. In fact, laughing was about the furthest thing from my mind at that point. I was closer to the rage side of the spectrum.

"Can you do me a favor?" I asked her. "Tell Renit I wasn't feeling well and needed to go home."

Mine, not his.

She frowned, glancing from me to where my mate was kissing another woman. "Is there anything I can do?"

Not unless she happened to make eagle-feather jewelry on the side. "Just tell him that. I'll be fine."

And I would be. And Renit and I would be. Eventually. But right then? Less than twenty-four hours after that man had yanked me from my play practice and told me I couldn't have a stage kiss with my costar?

I was far from fine. If I couldn't act in a kissing scene, then neither could he, and while I consciously understood that my acting was just for fun and his was a true career, that distinction didn't help. What was it he'd said? Not kissing others seemed pretty intrinsic to building a strong and healthy mating bond.

Guess he'd changed his mind on that.

I hurried through the crowded set, dodging all the people running around, and weaving in and out of the equipment. I caught the eye of a couple of shifters along the way—all of them gave me concerned looks. Of course, because Renit—the newly mated eagle shifter—had just kissed another woman right in front of his female. And I was running.

This would be all over the shifter gossip stations by morning.

Wonderful.

Thankfully, I had Renit's car keys in my pocket, so I actually had a way home. Well…not home. That was the last place I wanted to be. Plus, Renit would find me there because no way was he not going to follow me. No, I didn't want to go home. I wanted to go somewhere where I could catch my breath, hide out for a few hours, and decide how I wanted to deal with this problem. Somewhere other people wouldn't try to overpower my emotions or tell me what to do.

I needed a safe space to think, and I knew just where to find one.

8

TILLY

You must be kidding me."

I shrugged, somewhat intimidated by the cranky dragon shifter standing on the staircase—in nothing but some boxer briefs and a T-shirt, mind you—but trusting Ginger had not been lying when she'd texted me that it was fine to come over.

"Stop it," Ginger said, waving him off. "Ignore Sir Cranky-Pantless. He's just upset because his weekly schedule has to be adjusted."

"It's Taco Tuesday," Kingston replied with a growl. "I'm pretty sure you'll be the one upset when we miss this particular scheduled event."

Oh. I'd interrupted their meal. "I didn't realize you'd be eating dinner so late. I can just go."

Ginger grabbed my arm with a sharp no as Kingston said fine.

"He's not talking about a meal, and you're not going anywhere," Ginger said, shooting her mate an exasperated look. "Honey, why don't you go find some clothes and something to do? Let me deal with Tilly."

"Oh no," Kingston said, settling into the chair just inside the living room. "I'm all in on this now. What seems to be the problem, young one?"

Another shrug, my confidence in the place I'd chosen to hide out slowly shrinking inside of me. "Renit and I had a disagreement."

"You fought?" Ginger asked, moving to sit on Kingston's lap as I took a seat on the couch.

"Not really, no."

Ginger frowned. "But you're here, so…something happened."

Something, yes. Something big. "He kissed another woman."

Kingston jumped to his feet, a low growl reverberating through the room as he placed Ginger delicately back in the chair. "I can handle this."

"Hang on." Ginger grabbed his arm but focused on me. "What do you mean, he kissed another woman?"

"I mean lips on lips. Kissed. You know…" I puckered up and smacked my lips together. "Kissed."

"I didn't think that was possible." She frowned up at Kingston. "You told me mated males would never have an interest in another woman."

"They don't." Kingston shot his predator gaze my way. "Who did he kiss?"

"His costar."

"Oh." Ginger laughed. "Like, on camera? I mean, I'm sure that was uncomfortable for you, but it's his job."

"He promised me, though. He doesn't want me to be in the play at the community theater because it involves kissing a costar. And that's a very chaste kiss. This—" I shivered as the picture of Renit and Jen pressed so tightly together shot through my mind "—this was *not* chaste."

"Okay, so you need a break." Ginger smiled my way. "A day or so to get your head on straight and figure out how to deal with your mate."

"Exactly."

"I remember you taking a break from me," Kingston said, looking even crankier than before. "And how desperate I was to find you."

His words hit me like a sucker punch. Renit would worry—he was probably searching all of the cove looking for me. And yet, I couldn't find it in me to care. Much.

"I'll text him to let him know that I'm safe but need a little time alone to process what happened." Except he didn't have his phone on him—we were supposed to go to the theater to grab it. Apparently, I'd just skip the text and let him worry.

Mean? Yes. Necessary? Probably. I needed to make a point, and that seemed like a good way to do it.

"If that's what you feel you need," Kingston said, as if reading my very scattered and unhappy thoughts. The dragon leaned over to kiss the top of his mate's head. "I'm going to run out for some ice cream for you ladies. I'll be back in a few."

Ginger grinned up at him, looking so happy and in love. So much how I'd always hoped to look once I'd found my mate. I probably looked the opposite—miserable, with tear-streaked cheeks and bloodshot eyes. Maybe it was best that Renit couldn't see me right now.

Kingston walked out without a lot of fanfare, which left me alone with Ginger. She settled deeper into her chair, frowning my way and giving me a solid stare.

"You know he's an actor, right?"

One who was supposed to be filming an action movie, not an erotic one. "I do, and it wouldn't have bothered me as much if we hadn't just had this fight over my acting."

"But—and I mean this with total respect—your acting is for fun. This is his *job*."

"I know that, too, but it's the point of the matter. I don't like my feelings being dismissed." I sighed and shook my head, trying so hard to find reason through all the chaos inside of me. "I don't want to feel less important than my mate."

Ginger stood and hurried over to me, grabbing my hand and taking the spot next to me. "You shouldn't feel less important than anyone. You love to act."

"I do."

"And you're good at it. I enjoyed your Mary Poppins role very much."

"You saw that one?"

She nodded. "I did."

"Even my mom didn't come to that play."

"Well, I did. And you were great. Renit may need a little time to adjust to being mated—and to know how to handle situations like this, though. And he may also need to lay new ground rules at his job. They might not understand the shift that's happened with him."

Humans were so much more level-headed than shifters sometimes. "He likely does. I thought I'd made myself clear, though."

"Men tend to be a little slow at times."

That made me laugh. "You're mated to a dragon shifter—he's faster than just about any earthbound shifter out here."

She winked and grinned. "I meant mentally."

"Oh." I had brothers—I knew what she meant. "Yeah, that I can see."

Ginger sat with me for a few minutes, being quiet but staying there. Giving me time to process everything. At least until she said softly, "Running away won't help. Trust me on that one."

Because she'd run from Kingston, just as her sister Coco had run from her mate, Magnus. Just as their other sister had run from Jericho. And mine from Clark.

Goodness, we were a group of running women for sure.

"I know I need to talk to him," I said, suddenly so darn tired. "I'll do that tomorrow. I just need a few hours to get over the sharp sting of what I saw."

"That I can understand. C'mon, you can help me get the guest room ready. We can have a girls' night in. Ooh." She jumped up and down, dragging me toward the stairs. "We can do face masks. I have these awesome unicorn ones I've been wanting to try."

That sounded awesome, but still...I missed my mate.

Tomorrow. I'll talk to him tomorrow.

9

RENIT

Another woman's taste was on my lips, and I wasn't happy about it.

If I hadn't been at work—hadn't been trapped in front of my insanely ignorant costar and director—I would have shifted on the spot as soon as that woman had touched me. The fact that I hadn't, that I'd been trapped in my human form and forced to keep my eagle under control as I shoved some human woman away from me and stormed off to find my mate, really turned up the fire on my temper.

I swooped lower, circling the bakery, hoping to spot Tilly somewhere. Failing and feeling the rage inside of me climb a notch higher. I had a lot of things to be raging about tonight. First, the trickery of my costar and director—deciding behind my back to add a kiss should our *chemistry* not improve. Then, Tilly running from me because of that kiss. Instead of giving me the chance to talk things over, she'd disappeared. Such an immature reaction, and yet one I likely deserved. I'd argued hard against her kissing that llama in her play—how could seeing that woman's lips on mine not upset her? But to run when she had to know I'd be concerned—that I'd worry about her safety, that I'd spend hours hunting her just to make sure she was alive and not in danger—was a reaction I hadn't been expecting.

143

My worry for her didn't improve my mood one bit.

But as the minutes flew past, as I searched and searched for any sign or feeling of the girl, my anger turned further inward. I was furious with myself. I should have seen this coming, should have known my being so much older than my new mate would cause me to make mistakes. Should have realized how devious the people around me were —people who had hurt my mate with their carelessness. If Tilly would just talk to me, we could work out her feelings about what she must have seen. Together. Hell, I'd take her little hand slapping me in the face right now if it meant I got to see her. To know she wasn't at risk somewhere down below me.

I made another loop, fighting hard to focus on our bond. It twinged now and again, a sharp, almost painful sensation, before settling into a low hum. Not enough strength or pull for me to follow, though. Not enough for me to find my girl. I was searching for a needle in a haystack, and the stack was the size of a mountain.

As I turned away from the water, a shadow passed over me and headed toward the foothills. Something larger than I was, flying awfully close. It took me a moment to get a good look at the creature in the moonlight, but when I did, I cawed and gave chase.

A dragon.

Kingston.

I followed him over the foothills and up to an outcropping of stone that ran deep into the mountain front, landing right after he did. Kingston shifted first, fully clothed and carrying a cloak. I would forever be jealous of that particular trick.

"You're going to need this," Kingston said, holding out the plain, brown fabric. I shifted human as well, taking the cloak from him. Speaking before I even had it tied into place.

"Thank you. Have you—"

"Tilly's fine."

A segment of the anger I felt, of the tension in my body, left at his words. She was fine—*safe*. I could relax about one thing that I had been obsessing over since my world had decided to tip sideways.

Thank the fates for small miracles and big dragons.

"You've seen her?" I asked, stepping closer. Wanting so badly to lay my eyes on my mate. My hands, too. Just to make sure she wasn't hurt. "Where is she?"

"She's at my house." He held up a hand as I opened my mouth, stopping me. "And no, I won't take you there. She says she needs time to figure out her thoughts."

I couldn't hold back the low growl as I said, "She's my mate."

Kingston's sharp eyes homed in on mine, his stare one of force and power. Likely finding my own look just as hard and alpha. Predator-to-predator, even when fighting on the same side. "I am well aware of what she is to you, and trust me, I know exactly how your mate running from you makes you feel. When my Ginger disappeared on me for an entire day—" he shook his head, pausing to take a breath "—I was a mess. And she was human, so delicate and fragile, that species. You've been missing Tilly for what…an hour? Try multiples of that all stacked up, and you'll begin to understand how hard that day was for me."

I couldn't imagine losing my mate for a full day now that she was mine—didn't want to. It hurt too much. "Tilly is my heart. I'd do anything for her."

"Then give her the space she needs. She'll come around quickly enough, and I'll keep my eye on her until she's ready to deal with you." He put a hand over his heart and half bowed, making me a promise. Swearing an oath, really. "Nothing will happen to her while she's in my care. I give you my word."

My eagle, and me by proxy, didn't like the idea of another man watching over our girl—hated it, in fact—but I needed to respect Tilly's wishes. If she wanted time, I'd give it to her. Kingston said he'd keep an eye on her—that was the best I could do to protect her considering the situation.

The one that, at its base, was entirely my fault.

And I hated that.

"Thank you, Kingston. There aren't enough words to express my gratitude. At least I can rest my mind that she's not in danger."

"Definitely not—I'll keep her as safe as I do my Ginger." Kingston gave me a hand, shaking mine like some sort of human businessman. "I know this is painful, Renit. I know the exact depth and spread of the ache this will cause you, but I'll do my best to minimize it."

Handshake over, I took a step back. Blowing out a breath. "I appreciate that. I wish I could fix this tonight, but I respect her needs and will give her the time she desires. Even if it kills me."

"It won't, but it'll hurt like hell." He smacked me on the shoulder, huffing a laugh as he said, "These women will be the death of us, Renit. We fliers, we need to stick together, especially with how rare we are. You're only the second golden eagle shifter I've ever met."

Not surprising. "You're the fourth dragon in my life."

"Really?"

"They like Hollywood."

"That actually makes sense to me." Kingston walked to the edge of the outcropping, looking ready to shift, ready to fly home.

I wasn't ready to lose my link to Tilly just yet, though. "Tell her I'm sorry and that I'll fix this. That I never meant for her to be hurt, and that it won't happen again."

Kingston cocked his head, his eyes appearing to stretch longer. His dragon coming closer to the surface. "You shouldn't have hurt her in the first place. These young ones—they're sensitive. They need confirmation of their place as the most important thing in your life. They need time to truly accept the mating is as deep and permanent as it is."

"I'll give her that."

"Good. Because if not, I'll roast you. Flying shifter or not. Those fox shifters are family to my mate, and nothing will ever come to harm them while I'm alive."

And with that, he shifted from human to dragon in the blink of an eye, screaming into the night as he took off for what I had to assume was his home. Where my girl sat. I didn't follow him, respecting him too much and Tilly's own wishes that I leave her alone. Instead, I sat down on the edge of the ledge, wrapped my cloak around my shoulders, and I waited.

She'd come back to me.

She had to.

1 0

TILLY

Hangovers were the worst.

I'd woken up hungover. Not because of alcohol—Ginger and I hadn't been drinking at all. No, I was hungover on ice cream and tears. I'd missed my mate something fierce, had worried and fretted and spent far too many hours focused on the low hum of our mating bond to rest. As soon as the sun had come up, I'd wanted to run to the little cabin in the woods to track Renit down, but I'd screwed up. Big-time.

I had no way to reach him.

I had no idea where his cabin was. And unless Renit had gone to the theater without me, he didn't have his phone on him. I was stuck without a way to reach him. When I'd mentioned that to Kingston over breakfast, he'd smirked.

"You won't need to text him, fair Tilly. He'll track you down."

I'd hoped he was right, but as the hours had passed, I'd grown more and more worried. I missed my mate, but as they said in the theater— the show must go on.

Literally. I had a final run-through before opening night.

"Tilly," yelled Katherine, one of the older women in the show and a very cantankerous owl shifter who happened to be quite fond of me. "Is everything okay? I was worried about you after last rehearsal."

"Yeah. I'm fine." I kept my phone in my hand where it had been all morning, waiting to hear from Renit. Hoping.

"Good." She pulled me closer, lowering her voice as she led us away from the rest of the people. "Now, your eagle friend's clothes and phone are in the will-call booth. I tucked them aside myself."

His phone was still here? "He didn't come pick them up?"

Her big eyes widened. "Well…no, dear. They were still there this morning when I came in. Is everything okay?"

"Yeah. Sure." Everything was not okay, not even close. How would I be able to track down Renit? The bond wasn't strong enough to actually follow, and without a phone, I had no way to contact him. Maybe I could pay Kingston to fly around the mountain until he found the cabin. The cranky dragon wouldn't like it, but he'd hate losing out on another night alone with his mate. I could make that happen. I could be a major cockblocker to get what I wanted.

That plan actually had merit.

"Okay, folks. Let's take our starting positions." The director plopped into one of the seats about halfway up, a clipboard in hand. "We're going to do a straight run-through and see if we're ready for opening night."

The lights dimmed as I hurried backstage, most of my thoughts of Renit shelved for the moment. Time to do my thing. And if my mate truly missed me as much as I missed him? He'd find me. Of that, I had no doubt.

"Alas, there can be no chocolate without spilled milk." The llama shifter stepped closer, the part of the play I'd been dreading upon me. It was *the* scene. The kiss. The moment that had thrown my mate into such a rage, he'd shifted on the spot and had carried me to his secret lair to have his wicked way with me. Or his cabin in the woods. Same thing.

"But the milk," I said, waving my arm in an arc and fighting back the feeling of nausea rolling through me. "It needs to be cleaned."

"To hell with the milk." Llama shifter—whose name was Greg and who happened to work at city hall in the finance department—grabbed me around the waist and pulled me closer.

I practically fell over backward trying to get away from him.

"Cut," yelled the director, as if anyone needed that particular order. The entire cast had already stopped and stood staring at me. "Are you okay, Tilly?"

"Yes. No. I don't..." I took a deep breath, my eyes burning. My heart breaking even more. "I can't do the kiss scene."

"Why not?"

Because I didn't want to. The rightness of that decision was like a glass of ginger ale for my churning stomach. Renit hadn't wanted me to kiss Greg the llama shifter, but in that moment, as Greg had moved in for the romantic climax of the show, I hadn't wanted to go through with it either. This was my decision, and I was saying no.

"Because I found my mate, and it feels wrong to share affection with anyone else."

I wasn't sure what I'd expected, but what I got was a standing ovation. Every one of the people I'd been acting with for the past few years suddenly wanted to congratulate me, though not with hugs. They all kept a respectable distance, which was something I appreciated. I was already on edge from missing my mate and Greg's attempted kiss—I didn't need more to push me over the edge.

"I thought maybe that was the case after your eagle swooped across the stage the other day, but I didn't want to jump to any conclusions and make you uncomfortable with a bunch of questions," Greg said with a chuckle. "Congratulations, Tilly. It seems we have something to celebrate."

"Celebrate?" I practically squawked. "I've screwed up the whole play. I can't kiss you."

Greg just shrugged. "Your understudy can handle that part for you, or we can fudge our way through the scene. This play means so little in comparison to a lifetime with the one the fates deemed your perfect match."

"Yes," the director said, Katherine grinning at his side. "Your partner is much more important than a stage kiss. We'll work something out."

My heart practically exploded in my chest, but then it dropped as the mating bond between Renit and me practically sizzled. The doors swung open, and Renit—all tall, broad, handsome man that he was—came strolling into the theater.

"I apologize for interrupting," he said, those eagle eyes locked on mine. "But I really need to talk to my mate."

The whispers grew, people on the stage recognizing him. Star struck. My entire cast would be star struck and hogging his time if I didn't stop this. I wanted to be the one to hog his time.

"You guys keep going," I said, hurrying toward my mate. "I'll be right back."

Renit grabbed my hand as soon as I reached him and changed course, dragging me out of the theater and into the projection room at the top of the stairs. Dark and private, the space had always seemed creepy, but right then, it was perfect. All because Renit was there with me.

By the fates, I had missed him. "I'm sorry—"

"Don't you dare apologize," he said, interrupting me and tugging me against his chest. "I'm the one who's sorry. The director wanted a pure reaction, so they didn't tell me that the plans to ramp up the chemistry included a kiss. I wouldn't have approved that."

Deep down, I knew that. But that scene had played through my mind all night, and there was still something that bugged me about it. "You didn't pull away, though."

Renit sighed, rubbing his hands up and down my back. "I'll admit, I was quite shocked. It took all I had not to shift—my eagle wanted to claw her eyes out for touching me."

"She'd have deserved it."

"Jen was just doing what she'd been told to do. I can't fault her. Much." He leaned in, breathing across my lips. So close and yet not kissing me. "When I said only you, I meant it. Only your lips on mine. Only your body touching me. I don't want anyone else."

"Me too." I rose onto the balls of my feet, unable to resist him a moment more. Needing to reacquaint myself with his lips and taste. "I only want you, Renit."

He gave me a kiss, a small one, before pulling away. "Am I forgiven, then?"

"Yes."

"Thank the fates."

And then he was kissing me for real, his hands finding their way down to grip my butt and his body pressing hard into mine. Securing me to him. I dissolved into sensation, needing him so much, wanting more than a kiss. Wanting everything.

What I got was a sharp smack on my ass.

"Hey," I said, jumping and reaching to cover his hand. "What was that for?"

"That was for running." He smacked me again, grinning when I moaned at the sensation. "And that was because this ass was made for my palm."

"But I—"

He smacked me again, and I trembled. How could something so sharp and stinging feel so good?

"Don't tell me you don't like it, mate," Renit said, his voice low and filled with an aggression that made me so very wet. "I can smell your arousal. You like my spankings."

Yeah, I guess I did. "I do, just… I don't want the others to hear."

"Then I suppose you should try to stay quiet." He didn't smack me again, though. Choosing instead to kiss me senseless as he rubbed the soreness out of my rear cheeks. As he tugged me even closer and rocked his hips into mine, trapping his hardness between us.

"Renit," I said on a whisper as he moved to nibble along my neck.

"I've got you." He rotated us around until my hips ran into what I assumed had to be a table. I climbed up on it, spreading my legs so he could step between them. Wishing I'd been smart enough to wear a skirt. "Lean back."

"My jeans—"

"Are in the way, yes. But I'm not going to fuck you here."

My little snarl of annoyance only made him chuckle. Not what I was going for. "Renit, please."

He leaned over me, smiling. Slipping his hand into my pants as he said, "You were the one who reminded me that there are people on the other side of this door. The sounds you make when I'm inside you are mine alone. I'll take care of you, though. I'll always take care of you."

And he did. He slipped his hand into my pants, rubbing his thumb over my clit as he plunged two fingers inside of me. There was nothing gentle or slow about his actions—the man was on a mission. A mission to get me off. Thank the fates for that level of dedication and skill because he certainly accomplished his goal. Within minutes, I came with a squeak and with my fingernails practically embedded in his shoulders, my name on his lips as I gave in to his ministrations.

My mate had skills, and I would be forever grateful to the fates for that particular gift.

"I missed you so much," I whispered as I came down from my high. As I curled into his arms, Renit's hand still in my panties. "I'm so sorry I ran from you."

"I understand why you did, but please don't do that again. If Kingston hadn't found me and told me—"

"Kingston?" I sat up, forcing his hand out of my pants. "You saw Kingston?"

"Yes, last night. He tracked me down to let me know he had you and that you were safe. If he hadn't, I would have torn up the entire town looking for you."

Maybe Kingston wasn't so cranky after all. Or maybe he'd just wanted to get his mate alone. Probably the latter. "I'm glad you weren't worried."

"Oh, I was worried, all right." He helped me to my feet, pulling me in close for a deep kiss. "I will never not be worried unless you're at my side where I can protect you."

"Then I'll do my best to stay at your side." I breathed out, cuddling into him. Rocking back and forth as my mind spun in an entirely new direction. One I hated to voice but had to. "We need to tell my mother we're mated. Before she finds out through the rumor mill, seeing as how my entire cast now knows who you are and who you are to me."

"Finish practice, then we'll go."

Ugh. Practice. "I don't think there's any need for me to be here. I can give my spot to someone else since I can't complete the role."

"But I thought the llama said—"

"That we can skip the kiss? You heard that?" I sighed when Renit nodded. "He did, but we'd have to adjust the entire scene. It might just be easier to hand the role to my understudy and let her deal with it. I can take on a lesser part or skip the play entirely."

Renit frowned, staring down at me. Looking so serious. "You really love acting, don't you?"

"I do. I never expect to be famous or anything, but this theater and this little group mean a lot to me."

He sighed. "Fine. One kiss."

"Sorry?"

"One kiss—none in practice, but during the actual show, one kiss. I'll...do my best not to kill the llama."

"Greg. The llama is Greg."

"I don't need to know his name—he's the llama. A prey animal. Leave it at that."

Oh, my sweet, overprotective—and obviously quite proud of his predator status—eagle. "Renit, you'll—"

"Hate every fucking second of it, yes. But this is your love, and you've been working hard. I won't take that away from you."

I threw my arms around his neck, pulling him down for a deep, thorough kiss before smiling up at him. "Thank you."

"Yes, well—you can thank me once I get you home and naked."

And I would. Lots of times. All day and night and...

"But first," he said, interrupting my lovely train of thought. "We go see your mother."

Hell. "Fine, but let's make it quick. I've got lost time to make up for."

"We both do." He picked me up, carrying me out of the projection room as I laughed. "Now, where might my phone be from the other night?"

"Will-call room."

"Another private little hideaway in the theater you love so much? I'm beginning to like this place even more."

"There's a soundproof recording studio in the basement. Just in case you had any ideas."

"I always have ideas, mate. Ideas and fantasies and pictures of what I want to do to this sinful body of yours once I get you alone."

Thank the fates for that, too.

TILLY

Three shows. Months of work had come down to three shows. The first two had gone off without a hitch, save for the screech of an eagle on opening night when Greg had put his arm around my shoulders and bent me backward to fake a kiss. Thankfully, Kingston had come along for the show—whether that meant the play itself or Renit losing his mind over another man touching me, I might never know—so he'd held my mate back. No shifting and carting me off during a production.

For the second show, Kingston and Jericho—Madeleine's big, bear shifter of a mate and the town alpha—had dragged Renit into the hallway before the kiss scene had even started. That had seemed like a better plan and far less of an interruption, but I'd felt Renit's stress through our bond. I'd worried. And after the show, I'd run to find him, jumping into his arms and apologizing for torturing him. He'd calmed me down and taken me home to spend hours claiming me as his own, something I couldn't complain about. Well, unless you counted the muscle strains from so much…activity. It was hard to walk the next day and even harder to sit. Renit had been exceptionally pleased with himself at that.

Oh, and I also had gotten an education on what Taco Tuesday meant even though it hadn't been a Tuesday. Mexican food would never be the same to me.

Tonight was show number three—the last one of this production. My final stage kiss. I was nervous as always, but even more so because Renit wasn't in the audience. At least, I couldn't see him. The bond told me he was close but not there. Not watching me. These three plays had been a stress on him, as had his dealing with his director and costar over his own ill-fated on-screen kiss. I'd be happy once we were both done with our projects and had extra time alone together.

"You'll be fine," my mother said as she fluffed my hair. "Stop looking so nervous."

"He's not out there."

She huffed. "Your mate is here. He'll be watching."

Of course he would, but I wanted to see him. "Thank you for being here."

"I know I'm harsh at times, but I'm so very proud of you." Mom leaned down and kissed my cheek. "Now, finish up this silly acting thing and go make some babies."

My eye roll—it was large. And exaggerated because, babies with Renit? Yeah. I wouldn't say no to that.

"Places everyone." The director rushed through backstage, ever-present clipboard in hand. "You ready, Tilly?"

"She's ready," my mom said, sounding like her fierce, diner-running self. "You had better make sure everyone else is able to match her skills, though. That llama slipped on a few words last time."

The director blinked, looking surprised and slightly scared. I couldn't blame him. "Yes, ma'am. We all try our best."

"Your best is not my Tilly's best. Now, go. Get them ready."

I giggled as the director hurried off. "That was mean, Mom."

"It was the truth. Now, you get ready to go on stage. I'm going to track down that handsome mate of yours and make sure he's okay."

I grabbed her hand, needing one more minute. "Thank you."

She smiled at me, truly smiled, and tapped my cheek with a single finger. "You are a gift, Tilly. Never forget that."

And then she was gone, and I was headed out on stage for the final production of our play.

Everything went fine, even though I was completely distracted by the lack of Renit in the audience. Greg played his part well, not slipping this time, and the rest of the cast seemed extremely hyped up and excited for some reason. We were almost done—just two scenes left, including the dreaded kissing scene—when my world went sideways. Again.

"Why is there milk on the floor?"

The line was so familiar to me, I almost reacted simply out of habit. But the man saying it, the voice behind it, was not what I'd expected. Instead of Greg the llama shifter, I had Renit. My mate. The eagle shifter and Hollywood movie star. On stage with me.

Be still my heart.

Renit stared at me as the air grew thick and heavy, as the silence pressed on my body and brought every nerve ending to life.

Silence. Oops.

"I was making chocolate for the children, my Lord. It seems I'm a bit clumsy today."

Renit swept across the stage, moving closer to me, almost circling me like an animal on the hunt. "Alas, there can be no chocolate without spilled milk."

Oh my. He was going to kiss me. Right there, on that stage, in front of the whole town.

Well, not the whole town—it was still just a community play. But the point remained. He was going to kiss me in front of others. I almost couldn't wait.

"But the milk," I said, moving my arm in an arc and fighting back the grin that tugged at my lips. Soon. I'd have his lips on mine soon. "It needs to be cleaned."

"To hell with the milk." Renit's voice had dropped, his words infused with an air of sex and need that I couldn't resist. And when he yanked me into his arms, when he held me close and moved in for the kill, I knew this would be one hell of a kiss.

"You," he whispered just before his lips landed on my own. "Only you. Forever."

And then he kissed me, bending me backward and making the world around us fall away. There was no stage, no audience, no smelly costumes or bright lights. It was just the two of us alone, as we preferred to be.

At least until the applause began.

Renit—the ultimate professional—topped off the kiss with a quick smack to my behind before releasing me and moving on to the rest of his lines. We finished the play quietly, Renit playing out Greg's role and me fighting back my grin at every line he said, every exaggerated movement. He was a great actor and handsome to boot.

And he was all mine.

"So," he said, once the play was over and we were lining up for our curtain call. "How'd I do?"

I shrugged, keeping my eyes on the closed curtain before me. "Could have been better."

"Excuse me?"

"It could have been better." I turned toward him and winked. "I think we should practice more. Especially the kiss—we should practice that a lot."

Renit smirked and yanked me into his arms, leaning over me. "I agree. Kissing practice should definitely become part of our daily routine." He kissed me, slicking his tongue against mine as the curtain rose, as the applause began again and the lights shone in my eyes.

I tried to pull out of his hold, but he held strong. Kept looking down at me, kept giving me that arrogant, predator smile. And then he went in for the kill.

"Especially if that kissing practice includes all parts of your body. Taco Tuesday should be every day in the Threefeathers household."

My face heated, but Renit just laughed and let me go, leaving me aroused, embarrassed, but ready to face the crowded theater. With my mate at my side.

Not that I could let him get away with that Taco Tuesday remark.

"When we get home," I whispered, playing his game. "I intend to practice my own kissing skills on your body. I think my lips need to spend some serious time wrapped around your cock, don't you? We can call it Sausage Saturday or something."

I ignored the choked sound he made, waving instead to the friends and family in the audience. Even Renit's agent had shown up, a cranky wolverine shifter who seemed to have taken quite the liking to one of the shyest bunny shifters I'd ever met. No clue how that would work out...if at all.

"Perhaps we should skip the after party," Renit said, pulling me from my thoughts of how wrong wolverine-rabbit matings could go, his hand finding mine and hanging on tightly. "To give us more time to practice."

As the curtain fell, as the last show of the play season went dark, I turned to my mate and grinned. "Patience, my love. We have forever to practice our kissing and only one after party to go to." I rose onto the balls of my feet and gave him a sweet, soft kiss to the lips. "Besides, you can't rush the ending."

He grinned, grabbing me close and pulling me in. Onlookers be damned.

"We definitely can't do that. In fact, I think we should slow things down. Find a better pace for ourselves."

What the... "Why?"

He shrugged, so damn arrogant. "Because I've rented another cabin. This one on a secluded island not far from the Philippines. And I was thinking you and I could spend some long, leisurely weeks there. Alone."

My mate was a genius. "Will there be swimming?"

"Definitely."

I rose to whisper into his ear. "Will there be skinny-dipping?"

He grabbed my backside, gripping me tight and tugging me closer. "So long as no one else gets to see what's mine."

"Then I say, let's do it." I plopped a quick kiss on his lips and shot him a grin. "Beaches and naked swimming and spankings. It's like a dream come true."

Renit laughed, the sound so very loud and pleasure-filled, it suffused me with joy.

"Oh, my mate. You're the dream come true."

Yeah, he was mine, too.

"Then let's do it. Real life can wait. We need to spend some time working on our happily ever after."

And we would. On a beach. Together. Hopefully naked.

My life post-mating…it would not suck.

CAFFÉ WOLVERINO

KINSHIP COVE: CUDDLES & COFFEE

The fates definitely love their version of Beauty and the Beast, especially when their beast comes with a record. Welcome to the Kinship Cove Diner, where a good cup of coffee comes with every fated mating.

I haven't spent much time thinking about dating or mating or any of that sort of stuff. I'm more of a good girl, waiting for the fates to bring me my perfect match and working hard to help my family in any way possible. That's how I ended up in Kinship Cove in the first place—my aunt needed help at her diner, so here I am. Staying in an old bed-and-breakfast, trying to avoid being yelled at by my loving—if not constantly frazzled—auntie, and avoiding winking shifters like the plague. Men? Not on my radar.

At least not until a beast of a man comes strolling through the door. Literally. He's not what I expected—gray hair, deep, dark eyes, and a temper known throughout the town...including by local law enforcement.

The fates definitely want us together, but when his past comes fighting its way into our present, the fates may not be enough.

Love behind bars is a thing, right?

1

LUCY

Tilly! Section five needs to be reset before dinner tonight. Don't forget."

My cousin—the Tilly who'd just been yelled at from across the room —rolled her eyes in my direction. The only direction where her mom— the one who'd done the yelling—couldn't see her.

"Yes, ma'am. I know. Lucy and I will get it done." Tilly shook her head, continuing to fill sugar containers with little packets of various colors—white, yellow, pink, blue, green. The tables were a virtual rainbow of sweeteners.

"Is that a big deal?" I asked, still feeling out this new job working at my aunt's diner in Kinship Cove. "Resetting section five?"

Tilly laughed. "Not really. We reset every section between services to be ready for the rushes. It's what we've always done. She just likes to ride us about section five."

I glanced to where I knew section five to be. At least, I was pretty sure that one was five. "What's the big deal about five?"

"It's the closest to the door so the one that's always open. It gets reset a lot. Three and two are already set for dinner because they won't be used until then unless we get some sort of mad rush for breakfast or lunch. Five has to be reset for every meal."

"And it's been that way since—"

"Since long before I started working here, which was when I turned twelve. Seriously, it's just my mom being cranky."

She wasn't kidding. My aunt was a wonderful woman and someone I'd always loved being around, but her soft attitude turned rock hard the second she walked through the front doors of her diner. She was a beast in the restaurant, running everything with an iron fist and a harsh voice. At least where her own kids were concerned.

"Why is it that she yells at you like that but not me? Is she going to start on me eventually? What can I do to not have that happen? She seems awfully—" I glanced toward the kitchen where I could hear my aunt yelling at someone, likely her grandson Jackson "—angry. I really don't want that turned on me."

Tilly shrugged. "She may yell at you eventually, but you should take it as a sign of love."

That did not compute. "What do you mean?"

"If she yells at you, she considers you more than just a niece—you're a daughter to her."

"Still not understanding that one."

"She's not your mom and, therefore, not responsible for you. She won't yell…much. But when she feels invested in your future? The voice gets louder. Take it as a compliment when it happens." She grabbed the box of sweeteners and moved to the next table. "Besides, the woman had eighteen children, who are pretty much all having litters of their own and bringing a lot of babies and chaos into her life. With a skulk that large, you'd be cranky too."

Of that, I had no doubt. I came from a family of five—me, my mom, my dad, and my two brothers. Between sports and school and games and just getting on one another's nerves, it had been hectic and loud in our house for a while. I couldn't imagine a home life with eighteen kids running around.

Well-deserved crankiness. "Are you going to follow in her footsteps?"

Tilly—newly mated and really only working at the diner to train me since she was soon moving to live on location with her movie star husband—looked up, her cheeks pink and her eyes wide. "You mean with a skulk so large, I could field a baseball team with just my own kids?"

"That really was cool when your mom did that."

"It was—we had fun. But I have no intentions of heading down that same road. Renit and I want a family, not a clown car."

"Yeah, eighteen seems a bit…"

"Crazy?"

"Totally." I nodded toward the counter where a man in work boots and a heavy flannel shirt had just taken a seat. "We've got a customer."

"Perfect. I'll let you take the lead and just…hang around in case you need me."

"Okay." I took a deep breath and pasted on a big smile before striding across the room to my first potential tip of the day. "Hi, welcome to the Kinship Cover Diner. What can I get you this morning?"

The man glanced up, his posture straightening when he caught my eye. My inner fox chattered in my head, not liking the look in his eyes. Not happy about feeling like prey all of a sudden.

And then he smiled.

Uh oh.

"Good morning, sunshine. How are you doing today?"

"Fine, thanks. And you? Having a good morning so far?"

"It's better now."

Double uh oh. "Can I get you some coffee?"

"Please."

I hurried to grab the pot, not missing the fact that his eyes had to bounce up—way up—once I spun back around. So he was going to be *that* sort of customer. Just what I needed. Still, I poured his coffee and kept my smile on. No sense making waves and all.

Besides, I had a job to do. One I wanted to be good at. "Do you know what you want to order, or do you need some time with the menu?"

"I'm in here almost every day—I know what I want." He leaned across the counter, coffee in hand. Eyes locked on mine. "Though, I haven't seen you here before. I'd have remembered that."

"I'm new—the owner is family, and I'm helping out while Tilly heads off to spend more time with her mate."

"So I guess Tilly meeting that movie star worked in *my* favor, too." He took a sip of his coffee, winking at me over the cup.

My smile dropped, the effort becoming too much. He winked? Who did that? Creepy guys, that was who. "Looks like you've got a little problem with your eye—you might want to get that looked at. Now, what can I get you?"

His expression soured, my answer obviously not to his liking. "English muffin sandwich with two eggs and Monterey Jack cheese, plus a side of bacon."

I nodded, ready to get out of there. "You got it."

I left him at the counter, heading for the POS machine to enter the order that would be sent to the kitchen. He didn't try to stop me or flirt anymore, just sat there drinking his coffee and staring. A lot. But hey... he wasn't winking anymore. Bonus.

"New friend?" Tilly said with a smile as she sidled up beside me.

I huffed. "He's flirty."

"He is. His name's Jacob, and he's a tiger shifter. You don't want to get messed up in his world. They're not exactly known for their loyalty."

Jacob was also a winker. Automatic no from me. There was always something that was a no, though. "I don't want to get messed up in anyone's world."

"Not a big dater?"

I felt my face heat, felt my neck go hot too. "I'd prefer to wait."

"To wait...for your mate?" She smiled when I nodded. "I did the same thing—I never really dated until I met Renit."

I hadn't known that about her, but it made sense. At least to me. "Do you regret it now?"

"Not in the least. He was my first kiss...and everything else. I don't regret waiting for him at all." She glanced toward the guy at the counter. "Though I didn't really have to wait too long for him to show up."

Truth. The girl was still relatively young in terms of shifters. Renit, though, was a little older. The two made a gorgeous couple, but mostly, he was sweet to her. So sweet. I craved that same sort of care and connection. Wanted it like nothing else.

But I would have to wait for the fates to provide it. "Well, here's to hoping I don't have to wait long either."

"In Kinship Cove? The waiting period is much shorter than elsewhere. Everyone seems to be finding their mates."

Good. Because that was definitely one of the reasons I'd agreed to spend a few months helping at the diner. The cove was a shifter town, and that meant lots of options for finding a mate. Hopefully one who didn't leer at me from across the room.

Customers. They weren't always fun to deal with. "I'm going to check on that guy's order."

Tilly nodded. "Good call. And, hey. If he gets too flirty, sic my mom on him. She'll set him straight."

Yeah, of that, I had no doubt.

"Order up," Jackson said just as I made it to the kitchen doors. He carried a tray with a single plate on it—English muffin sandwich and bacon on the side.

"I've got it."

Jackson shook his head, balancing the tray perfectly. "Counter guy?"

"Yeah. Want me to—"

The ringing of the buzzer indicating someone was at the delivery door interrupted me, making Jackson smile.

"How about I take this to him? You handle Nijel."

"Who's Nijel?"

"Delivery driver. Cranky old man—he never says more than a few words to me. But I doubt that he's a winker."

So he'd seen and was rescuing me. I liked him so much. I could handle cranky old men just fine—better than flirty younger ones. "You've got yourself a deal. Don't forget to ask if he wants a warmer."

"I'm on it. But hey—be careful. Don't piss off Nijel, okay?"

"Why not?"

He blanched, looking as if he had something to say but didn't want to. Jackson never had been one to gossip. "He's been in some trouble in the past—nasty temper, that one. Just...be polite."

"I'm always polite."

"I know, even when some jerk is winking at you. So, go—let Nijel bring in the supply order before my grandmother starts yelling again." And with that, Jackson rushed off to deliver the food while I strode through the doors into the kitchen, heading for the back. The delivery entrance sat down a long, dark hallway lined with metal shelving, where boxes and containers were stacked to the ceiling. It was very claustrophobic. And dark. Creepy, even. Or maybe I'd been listening to too many true crime podcasts.

The buzzer rang again, the sound impatient and demanding. My heart pounded and my breaths came faster as I moved through the shadows. *It's just a hallway.* My internal reminder didn't help anything, especially as I stumbled over the edge of something that could have been a box or a dead body. Because, of course.

Did I mention it was dark?

I rushed the last few feet, lunging for the door and squinting as soon as I pushed it open.

"Sorry," I said, unable to see the person at the door for more than just a shadow against blinding light. "I was in the dining room when you buzzed."

The man stepped forward, the door ajar just enough to fill the hallway with light. I still couldn't see anything, too many spots before my eyes as I blinked. But I could smile up at the...huge, hulking shadow. That was the impression I got. Size. Mass. The man had to be almost a foot taller than me and three times as wide. Ginormous.

And I was alone with Mr. Bad Temper in a still-somewhat-dark hallway that happened to be about as far away from all the other people in the restaurant as one could get. Wonderful.

"Uh, my aunt is in the kitchen. I'm sure you'll need her to sign things." I tried to back up but tripped over the dead-body-box again, stumbling. A large, strong hand grabbed my elbow, supporting me. Keeping me from falling flat on my behind. His skin was hot against mine, burning, really, and rough. So rough. I could hardly breathe, could barely figure out what I was seeing. The man...he was...

"Are you okay?" he asked, his deep, rich voice sending chills up and down my spine. My eyes finally cleared enough for me to get more than just an impression of him. Dark hair slightly grayed across the top and temples, with a decent curl to it, shoulders so broad and muscular they seemed to take up the entire width of the hall, and a chest made for lying on. Thick. The man was thick. That was the only word I could think of to describe him. At least until I looked in his eyes—then a new word reverberated through my mind.

Mate.

Those dark brown eyes locked on mine, and I was a goner. Lights out. Heart no longer my own. The fates didn't just bring us together—they locked me to him in an instant. Threw me headfirst into the sea of fated mates without a life preserver in sight. Just me and this man.

"Oh," I whispered, leaning closer out of pure instinct. Wanting more touch and smell, wanting to get to know every inch of him. "So this is what that feels like."

I reached out, ran a finger over his bicep, my eyes following the path. At least until he grabbed my hand...and pushed it away.

"What are you doing here?"

I had no idea how to answer that. Not really. So, I went with the obvious. "Opening the door for you."

He huffed, those dark eyes leaving mine, those heavy hands clenching at his sides. "I wasn't ready for this today."

"Is anyone ever ready to meet their mate?"

He darted a look my way, then shook his head. "I need to make this delivery."

Everything inside me—every hope for love and happiness and a happily ever after—deflated. I was a husk, empty and dry. Worthless. At least to my mate, it seemed.

"Of course," I said, refusing to look directly at him again. "Do what you need to do."

I turned and strode back into the kitchen, fighting the urge to cry. Trying to catch my breath as the man—Nijel, if Jackson had been accurate—brought in stacks of boxes and plastic containers. My aunt soon shuffled over from the office, inspecting the delivery. Mumbling to herself about produce quality and the people of the Cove's obsession with ranch dressing.

"They put it on everything, Lucy. Meatloaf—they coat their meatloaf in it. Blech."

She continued to check the shipment while I stood behind her, trying really hard not to watch every move Nijel made. Not to give him a single bit of my attention. Not that I *could* stop—the man was just so big. He stole the show, lording over the kitchen on nothing but size.

And he was ignoring me.

"That's everything, Ms. Fitzgerald."

My aunt nodded, looking over the paperwork with her reading glasses perched on the end of her nose. "Thank you, Nijel. I appreciate your quickness unloading all of this."

"No problem." He seemed to turn, to look my way, but I was still refusing to make eye contact, so I couldn't be sure. "Well…you all have a nice rest of your day."

"You do the same. Lucy, go check on the customers. Make sure they have enough coffee."

"Yes, ma'am." I paused for just a moment, long enough to give this Nijel a chance to say something. Anything. But when he stayed silent— nothing more than a statue in the corner of the room—I knew there was no point in waiting. So, I took a deep breath, and I looked up just in time to get kicked in the gut by his dark eyes meeting mine.

And I walked out of the kitchen.

Alone.

Nijel didn't follow me.

2

LUCY

Men are so stupid." Ginger, one of the Chance sisters, set a mug of hot cocoa in front of me. Right next to the chocolate croissant her sister Coco had already put there. I was apparently in a chocolate emergency.

"They are." I clutched the mug, the Cake-ily Ever After logo shining brightly on the side. Tilly had brought me over right after I'd told her about Nijel. About meeting my mate…and having him walk out on me. About the hours of waiting for him to come back, of watching the world pass by as I hoped and prayed he'd walk in the door. About watching the sun set and still no Nijel.

Yeah, chocolate was a must.

I picked up the croissant and took a small bite. The flakiness didn't soothe my broken heart, but it certainly made me want to groan in delight. These Chance sisters were magicians in the kitchen.

"I just don't understand why he'd walk out like that," Misty—my cousin and sister to Tilly—said as she paced across the kitchen. "He's your mate. Who does that?"

Ginger shrugged. "Me, you, Jericho…it seems to be a trend in our group."

171

"Shut up." Misty glowered at her friend, a smile tugging at her lips. "I didn't run. I just…removed myself from the situation."

Ginger's grin turned downright wicked. "Yeah. The one where your mate admitted to buying my sister's panties."

I choked on my hot cocoa. "What's that?"

"Long story," Misty said as she waved a hand. "I still think he messed up somehow. Do we know anyone who knows him?"

"Knows whom?" Kingston, the dragon shifter mated to Ginger and an all-around badass in my eyes, strolled in from the back door, making a beeline for his mate. "You look ravishing this evening."

Ginger rolled her eyes but her smile was huge, and she walked right into Kingston's arms. "You said that all those hours ago when I was leaving the house."

No snark was going to stop the dragon, though. "I'll try to be more original in the future."

"Hey, Kingston. Do you know Nijel?" Misty asked, leaning against the counter. "Delivery guy. Probably drops stuff here as well as at my mom's."

Kingston took a moment to answer, his lips a little busy on Ginger's. But when he finished giving her a kiss that could have sent steam shooting into the sky, he turned toward my cousin and frowned. "Wolverine shifter, right? Surname Carr, like the football coach. Big guy, quiet."

Misty shrugged. "You say quiet, I say grumpy."

"Grumpy isn't allowed at this bakery," Kingston replied with an almost evil smirk. "I make damn sure of it."

"So overprotective," Ginger said with an eye roll. "What else do you know about him? We need all the details."

"Why?"

The others in the room all looked to me, so I lifted a shoulder at the dragon shifter. "Apparently, he's my mate."

Kingston blinked. Again. Then opened his mouth as if to speak, but closed it once more.

"Yeah," I said. "That's about how I feel right now. Especially after he left me at the restaurant without a word. Guess wolverines and foxes don't mix."

"Perhaps he needs a day or two to work out the mating instincts," Kingston said, sounding far too diplomatic. "It can be an adjustment for some people, and wolverines are particularly private."

"What else do you know?" Ginger asked as she hopped up on a counter and swung her legs. "About him or wolverines in general. Tell us everything."

Kingston sighed. "Well, wolverines are tough fighters—their animals can take down prey two or three times their size. That's likely why his human form is so large—he's carrying some serious muscle for his animal form."

Misty inched closer. "What else you got?"

"I know Nijel Carr to be very much in sync with his inner beast. He's quiet and lives quite the isolated life, but a good fighter. Very tough to beat." He looked my way, seeming almost worried about his next sentence. "And he's been in trouble with the law a bit."

Of course he had.

Misty scrunched her nose and looked over the dragon. "You're afraid of him?"

It was Kingston's turn to roll his eyes. "I wouldn't say that at all."

"So you're convinced you're bad enough to beat him?" Misty shook her head, her voice turning playful. "I don't know, smoky. Even dragons get beat occasionally."

"Not this dragon," he said. "Honestly? I wouldn't want to meet him in a dark alley, but I'm not afraid of him. It would be a rough fight…that I would eventually win."

I nodded, taking everything in. Still feeling a little heartbroken and letdown but knowing there was nothing else I could do about it tonight. It was time to let the ladies who'd picked up the broken parts and helped put me back together go about their lives.

"I'm exhausted. I think I'm going to head home for the night."

Ginger whipped around, looking me over. "Are you sure? I hate the thought of you being all alone tonight."

"You can come hang out with Clark and me," Misty said as she grabbed her coat. Obviously ready to go, that one. "We're just going to be sitting around watching some documentary about how math makes cool things."

Thrilling. "Yeah, I think I'll just head home. I've got a few episodes of the *Bachelor* on the DVR and some ice cream."

Ginger came up behind me, giving me a hug. "Your night sounds way better than hers."

But Misty wasn't one to go down easily. "Except mine will end with sex. So, I win."

"Pretty sure my sweet mate will be the winner tonight," Kingston said, pulling Ginger along behind him as he ushered us toward the door. "I'll make damn sure of it."

"Okay, you all are beginning to make me sick to my stomach," I said, stepping out into the cold, dark parking lot behind the building. "Can we stop talking about all the sex I'm apparently the only one not getting?"

"There's always the tiger shifter in town," Misty said. "He's got one hell of a wink going on."

Ah, so my friend was a well-known winker. Wonderful. I laughed and went to turn to reply, but something hard and solid blocked my path. Something that smelled like vanilla bean ice cream and was warm to the touch. Something that grunted when I hit it.

I screamed and jumped back as Kingston slid between me and the thing.

Or rather…the man.

Nijel.

Kingston had said he wouldn't want to meet Nijel in a dark alley. A dark parking lot wasn't much better.

"We really need cameras out here," Ginger whispered, watching her mate and mine with a worried expression. "This is getting ridiculous."

"What are you doing here?" Kingston asked, his voice low and growly.

Nijel didn't move forward, didn't threaten any of us intentionally. He simply stood there, flicking glances at me, silent. Until he wasn't.

"I came to see her."

I had to admit, my heart fluttered. Just a little. Okay…a lot. "Me?"

Nijel's eyes finally locked on mine, and my stomach knotted up in a way that was both nauseating and quite pleasurable, if that were possible.

"Yeah, you."

Visions of an old movie I'd watched—of a girl in an ugly dress and the high school boy she was in love with showing up and saying that same line—flew through my head. There he was. My very own Jake Ryan. On steroids.

Not literally.

"I'm Lucy," I said, having no idea what else to do.

Nijel nodded, glancing again at the people crowded around me. Kingston had said wolverines were solitary creatures—this was not a solitary moment. At all. How hard must it have been for him to track me down here, to wait for me in the parking lot, knowing I wouldn't be alone? I had a feeling him showing up was a much bigger deal than anyone would assume.

Kingston relaxed a little, still keeping himself as a dragon-shifter shield, though. "Hanging around dark parking lots isn't the way to win her over, my friend."

Nijel grunted, tossing a fleeting look his way. "Not my fault there are no lights back here. You really need some floodlights installed. They make those ones that run on solar and have a camera. Those are good."

"Yeah. I'll get right on that." Ginger grabbed Kingston's elbow, looking a little nervous still. "Can we go?"

But I couldn't leave—not yet. Not without knowing why Nijel had shown up in the parking lot in the first place.

"Is there something you need?" I asked, edging around Kingston's arm. Fate or need or desire or just plain old curiosity drawing me closer to the wall of muscle that made up my mate. "Something you wanted?"

He grunted again, flinching as if the sound irritated him. Fidgeting a bit with the seam of his jeans as he stood there watching me.

"I was hoping I could talk to you." Nijel looked over the three people with me. "Alone."

It was Kingston's turn to growl. "I know she's your mate, but she's young and a little too sweet for this world. I'd prefer to stick around, if you don't mind."

Nijel frowned, looking from Kingston to me and back. "Whatever makes Lucy comfortable."

Oh, he said my name. A shiver raced up my spine, and I suddenly wanted to jump him. To climb up that large, tall body and plant kisses all over the lips that had caressed the syllables of my name. I wanted to rip the clothes from his body and explore every inch, touching him all over and letting him touch me too. I wanted—

To not be dreaming of getting naked in a dark parking lot with so many other people around us.

"We could go to the diner," I said, nodding toward the assembled group. "That way, Nijel and I can talk privately, but Kingston can stay close."

Nijel frowned. "The diner's closed."

"Not for me." Misty held up a key ring and started around the building, leading our little party in the direction of the diner. I walked beside Kingston, with Nijel a step behind me. Close but not close enough. This was what I'd wanted—a little interest. A little opportunity to get to know each other. A little sign of some sort that my mate wasn't repulsed by me. I wanted what Ginger and Misty and Tilly had already found—a man to show me some attention.

I had apparently gotten that in Nijel; it had just taken him a bit to be willing to interact with me.

Score one for Lucy.

When we reached the diner, Misty opened the doors, locking them behind us once more as soon as we were inside. She didn't turn on any extra lights, simply led us all toward the counter before jogging into the kitchen. A few minutes of awkward silence later, and she returned with glasses, straws, and bowls of snack foods.

"You two can use the kitchen," she said, setting the food down in front of Kingston and Ginger, who'd taken seats at the counter. "We'll be right here."

"What about Clark?" I asked, suddenly nervous. So very nervous.

Misty shrugged. "He can watch his math movie alone. If he misses me too much, he'll come down here. I'm not worried about Clark right now."

The pointed look she threw Nijel's way spoke volumes—she wasn't worried about Clark. She was worried about Nijel. The wolverine shifter. The wall of muscle. The criminal?

Honesty time—I was a little worried too.

Nijel stepped back, allowing me room to move past him and lead the way into the kitchen. Misty had turned on those lights and left out a bowl of pretzels and two glasses of ice water. She'd also dropped a couple of chocolate-mint candies on the counter. I loved my cousin.

I grabbed a candy, bringing it to my lips but not slipping it between them. Holding it there until I had Nijel's attention. Until his eyes locked on my fingers and his breath caught. Then I dove in.

"Are you disappointed that the fates picked a mate for you?" I slid the candy onto my tongue, letting the cool sensation of it keep me calm. Letting the weight of it be a distraction from an answer I very well might hate hearing.

Thankfully, Nijel didn't keep me waiting. "Disappointed?" He looked me up and down, his eyes growing darker, his look almost a physical touch. "Not in the least. Surprised, though."

"Why?"

"My kind...we don't often end up with a mate. Not a real one, at least."

There were fake ones? "You're going to have to explain that."

He sighed and looked around, hurrying across the kitchen to where three metal stools were stacked against the wall. He grabbed two of them and brought them back to our section, setting one down for me before making himself comfortable.

"So..." he started, still looking completely uncomfortable. "You know I'm a wolverine shifter, yeah?"

"Yeah."

"We're pretty...solitary."

"That's what Kingston told me. Solitary and good in a fight."

"Very much so. Whether we don't mingle enough with other shifters to find mates or it's something else, I don't know, but wolverine shifters rarely end up in mated pairs. Especially not with someone who isn't another wolverine."

Oh. Oooooohhhhhh. "You're disappointed I'm a fox."

I rose to my feet, that candy turning my stomach. I couldn't change who I was, wouldn't hide it either. My fox was as big a part of me as his wolverine was of him. There was no way to adjust, no possible compromise. No—

Nijel grabbed my elbow, his hand rough but gentle and so very hot against my skin. "Don't take me the wrong way, Lucy. I'm not disappointed in the least. Surprised, shocked even...but not disappointed."

"But you left without a word."

"I did, and I'm sorry. The mating pull took me by surprise, and I..." He sighed again, that uncomfortable expression back on his face. His hand still on my arm. "Solitary, remember? I'm not good at social stuff."

I reclaimed my seat, inching closer to him. Covering his hand with mine and bringing it to my lap. "I like social stuff. I can help you figure it out."

"Yeah?"

"Absolutely. I mean...you're my mate." If I weren't sure the knowledge would embarrass him to no end, I'd have called out the fact that the man blushed at my words. Blushed. How cute.

"I am. Or rather, I'd like to try to be." Nijel scooted his seat closer, towering over me even as we both sat. Allowing me to hold his hand and even weaving his fingers through mine. The moment felt heavy, weighted down by some sort of anticipation. Especially when he gave up moving his own body and simply tugged me toward him—stool and all.

"I'm not good at this stuff," he said, his voice a husky whisper that sent sparks up my spine. "I don't know how to make you happy, but I'd like to try."

And what more could I have ever asked for? "Why don't we start slow?"

He nodded, his eyes on my lips again. His body leaning toward me. "Slow is good. What's slow?"

I shrugged, suddenly uncomfortable. Not sure I was ready to be the one driving this car. "Maybe a date?"

"Okay. Yeah. Maybe a date."

But he didn't continue. In fact, he went silent, watching me with those dark eyes but not making a move. Not asking me out. I waited for what felt like hours for him to take that first step, but he refused to budge. An immovable mountain of a man was my mate. This whole situation was going to test my patience for sure.

Finally, I broke. "You have to ask me, you know."

"I do?"

"Yes. You have to ask if I'd like to go out with you. On a date. That's how this works."

He brought us even closer together, our faces mere inches apart, his legs spread so there was nothing in our way.

"Hey, Lucy?"

"Yeah?"

"Will you go on a date with me?"

My grin was unstoppable. "I'd love to."

He smiled, and my world went a little wobbly. Goodness, the man was handsome. Rugged and beastly, but so very handsome. And mine. All mine. I was going on a date with the man the fates deemed my perfect partner.

And I wanted to reward him for that. "Hey, Nijel?"

"Yeah?"

Mimicking each other was going to be so much fun. "I think this should count as a date."

He frowned, glancing around the kitchen. "This? Talking in the diner?"

I slipped off my stool, standing between his legs. Bringing my hands to his shoulders. "Definitely. This is our first date. Do you know what happens at the end of a date if it's a good one?"

His eyes dropped to my lips, but he shook his head. "Not in the least."

"The couple shares a goodnight kiss."

He slid a hand around my waist, his touch hesitant. "Do they really?"

I nodded, closer still. My nose almost brushing his. "They do. So… goodnight, date."

"Goodnight." He leaned that much closer, brushing his lips against mine in the softest, sweetest kiss I'd ever imagined. It was a quick kiss—no open mouths or anything, more affection than anything else—but it was one I'd never forget. And when it was over, when I broke the kiss, Nijel placed his forehead against mine and held on to me. Bringing us together. Making my heart sing.

"So," I said, smiling. Excited for new opportunities and the chance to get to know this man. "When is our next date?"

3

NIJEL

I *am so screwed.*

    I paced my little cabin, running a hand through my hair and breathing hard. I'd been doing the same thing for approximately twenty hours. Ever since I'd arrived home after my evening at the diner with Lucy. My Lucy. My fated mate.

Screwed, screwed, screwed, screwed, screwed.

A knock at my door yanked me from my thoughts, and I hurried across the floor to throw the wooden slab open.

"What took you so long?"

Bennett—my neighbor, another driver at the restaurant supply company, and my only friend, even if I'd never admit that to him—came prancing inside, looking far too pleased with himself. "You called me exactly three minutes ago. If you had wanted to see me without pants—"

"Nope."

"Well, that's how long it took me to find pants, put them on, cry about having to wear them, then hike it over here. Now…what's going on?"

But I had gotten caught up on one thing. "Did you really cry about having to put on pants?"

Bennett shot me a look that was far more earnest than the

181

conversation required. "It's Saturday. Yes—I cried about having to wear pants. This was supposed to be a pantsless weekend for me."

Okay, then. "Fine. Sorry I screwed up your weekend."

"You're forgiven. Care to explain why you look like the sky is falling on your head?"

I took a deep breath, trying to calm myself, before whispering, "I met my mate."

Bennett stared at me, silent. Blinking. Those big eyes of his—courtesy of his being a reindeer shifter and all—were wider than usual. A darker green, too. I may have sent him into shock.

"Bennett?" I stepped closer and waved my hand in his face. "You in there, buddy?"

He shook his head, pinning me with a gaze. "What do you mean, you met your mate?"

I shrugged, suddenly uncomfortable talking about Lucy for some reason. "I met her. At the diner in town."

"Oh my Santa, is it the old cranky lady with the hundreds of children?"

"No," I said, nearly insulted. "It's some new waitress there—Lucy. Young thing."

"How young?"

"She looks about seventeen, so under fifty for sure."

"You're not under fifty."

No, I wasn't. I was far older than that, as was Bennett. Neither of us looked our age—even for shifters who stayed youthful far longer than humans—but we were showing signs of it. My dark hair had been more salt-and-pepper for a few decades, and Bennett was nearly all white. Old men.

And I'd just been handed a young, sweet mate to make mine.

Yep, still screwed.

"Never mind the age thing," I said, not needing one more brick to pile on my load. "I need to take her on a date. In town. With people around me."

"You hate people."

"Exactly. What am I going to do?"

Bennett shrugged, the picture of ease. "Take her someplace quieter."

I...hadn't thought of that. "Just the two of us."

"Sure. Then you can relax, she can get to know you, you can find out her favorite memory of the big man—"

"I'm not asking her about Santa Claus."

"You're no fun. But still—keep her away from people, and hopefully, you can try to control your constant foul mood so she doesn't decide to leave your ass and go find someone more chipper." He grinned widely. "Like me."

"Gee...thanks for offering to steal my girl. You're getting coal in your stocking this year."

"Santa loves my hairy ass. Now, how about a picnic? What have you got in your kitchen?"

Two hours, more cooking than I'd done in years—thank you, my reindeer friend—and far too much discussion of the right shirt to wear, and I was headed into town to pick up my mate for an afternoon of getting to know each other. At least I was trying to.

"Get off the fucking road if you don't know how to drive!"

I huffed and glared at the car in front of me. The one being driven by someone who obviously couldn't decide if they needed to turn left or not. Being that there was only one lane heading into town, this decision ended up affecting everyone behind them. Namely me.

I was going to be late.

I slammed a fist into the horn, letting it sound long and loud to get the jackass's attention. "Let's go. Make a damn decision."

A blond-haired woman leaned out the driver's side window, looking back at me with large, round sunglasses covering about half her face. And then she smiled. "Sorry—I'm a bit lost at the moment. You wouldn't happen to know where I can find a place to stop and grab a cup of coffee, would you?"

A woman lost. In need of assistance. Of course. Even I wasn't asshole enough to curse her out. Though I wanted to. There were signs pointing toward town. Big signs saying *Kinship Cove, home of the Kinship Cove Diner* with an arrow pointing to the left. They were *right there*. It was like that movie Bennett made me watch with the guy in New York and the hot dog and…something about the Hoover Dam. Whatever. *There are signs everywhere!*

Apparently, she'd missed them.

"Yeah," I said, taking a breath and doing my best to tamp down my rage. "I'm heading to the diner in town. You can follow me."

"Great. That'd be perfect." The woman slipped into her seat and pulled forward enough for me to drive around her, then followed me after the turn. She kept with me the rest of the way, not that I was paying that much attention to her. I'd just get pissed off if I did. *Signs. Everywhere.*

We pulled into the diner parking lot at the same time, her taking the spot right next to mine. I didn't wait for her—I had someone inside I wanted to see—though I still couldn't be a total jerk.

"Diner's here," I hollered to her as I hurried across the lot. "There's a bakery down the road a bit that also has coffee and some really good donuts. There's more—just look around. Good luck."

With that, I forgot the blonde with the big sunglasses and closed the distance between me and my future. My mate. The woman the fates deemed perfect for me. I sure hoped I wasn't too late. Two minutes— that was all it was. Just two minutes past our scheduled time. She could forgive me for two minutes, right? I'd never be late again if she did.

Worried and stressing and trying really hard not to want to turn around and yell at the blonde for making me late to such an important event, I raced to the entrance of the diner The chime banged against the glass as I yanked the door open, the cold air and scent of delicious food slapping me in the face. I took a quick look around, hoping against hope that I hadn't screwed up by being two minutes late. And then I died.

I mean, not literally, but it was a close call.

Shoulders. Soft, pale shoulders with freckles dancing across the skin. That was the very first thing I noticed when I spotted Lucy at the counter across the way. Shoulders and long, bare legs peeking out from under some frilly pink thing and the biggest, brightest smile. And that smile was directed *at me*. I felt like a damn king being able to pull that smile from her. An old, cradle-robbing king because that woman was so young. Too young for someone as cranky and jaded as I, and yet… Fate.

"Oh, excuse me."

A woman—the blonde, of course—sidled up beside me, making Lucy's smile falter and my skin crawl as she reached out as if to grab my arm.

"I just wanted to say tha—"

"No problem." I strode away from her, heading straight for my mate. My very young, very beautiful mate. The woman whose smile grew once more with every step. I wanted to keep it right there on her pretty face. Would do anything for that. Forever.

But first, we had to get through this date. "Hi."

She ducked her head, suddenly looking shy. "Hi."

"I'm really sorry I was late—that woman who walked in behind me caused a bit of a traffic backup because she was lost."

Lucy looked over my shoulder, her brow furrowing as she took in the blonde with the sunglasses. "There are signs all over, mostly for this place. How on earth did she get lost?"

Fated for sure. "No clue, but she's not important. You are, and you look lovely. Thank you for waiting for me."

She shrugged those bare shoulders. "It was only a few minutes."

"It won't happen again." I offered her my arm, which she took without a single second of hesitation. Her skin on mine might as well have been a brand—a tattoo of sorts. She set me on fire and claimed me as hers with a single touch. I'd always remember where her hand had first made contact.

"So," Lucy said as we passed through the door and out onto the sidewalk. "Where are we going?"

All my plans—all the plotting and deciding I'd done—suddenly seemed wrong. As if I'd made all bad choices. As if I'd failed.

I blew out a breath, shifting my weight from one foot to another. Wishing I'd chosen a backup plan in case she hated this idea.

"Well, I planned to take you to the overlook for a picnic dinner, but now that seems ridiculous—"

"I've never had a picnic or been to the overlook. Is there a view?" Lucy grinned again, looking excited.

"You can see the whole town and to the cove beyond it from up there."

"Oh yes. Let's go there. I want to see."

"Are you sure? I can try to get us a table at the restaurant at the hotel or something. That's so much classier."

"I'm not really a high-class sort of girl. Besides, I want to see what you put together for this picnic."

Picnic it was, then.

I opened the door to my truck for her, making sure she was settled in the front seat before running around to take the wheel. Being in such a small space with her nearly undid me, but I held it together. I may have warped the steering wheel, but I didn't reach out to take something she wasn't freely giving. No way.

Lucy, meanwhile, seemed unfazed by the proximity to me. She chattered away, telling me all about how she was new in town and didn't know a lot of places. I listened intently, trying to collect every piece of info about her. Trying to make sure to show interest at all the right points so she never lost that bubbly tone in her voice. She had a lot to say, and I was going to prove to her that I'd be a good listener.

Eventually, we pulled off the mountain road into a wooded area. There wasn't a lot or even an official trail, but I knew these mountains like the back of my hand. Knew every turn and dip of the path leading to the best overlook of Kinship Cove up here. I'd keep Lucy safe.

"Let me help you." I grabbed her hand and assisted her out of the truck, making sure she didn't wobble when her feet hit the ground. I knew my truck was big, but I hadn't really thought about that when I'd bought it. Lucy was a bit short—I'd need to get her a better running board so she could climb in and out easily.

Or trade in my beast for a smaller model.

Decisions, decisions. All before dinner.

"Can I help you carry something?"

"Nope—I've got it." I grabbed the basket we'd put all the picnic supplies in and then reached for Lucy's hand. "Don't be nervous, but we have to walk through this patch of woods."

"Will you keep me safe?"

"Of course."

"Then let's go."

No hesitation. No fear. Motherfucking king.

Her hand in mine felt more right than just about anything in the world and made me want to toss her pretty butt back into the truck and kiss her senseless. Not yet, though. Someday. Because I wanted to give her the view I'd promised and treat her well, be the gentleman I hoped I could be—the one she deserved.

I led the way through the woods, holding back branches so she could pass and making sure she never stumbled along the route. Once we made it through the pines, once we stood on the rocky cliff looking over a sunset-painted Kinship Cove, I knew it was worth the drive and the time. Lucy made sure I did.

"This is..." She stared out across the view, taking in the pinks and oranges lighting up the sky, the glow of the businesses in town, and the beauty of the world we lived in. The world she outshone.

"Beautiful." I felt my neck heat when she looked up at me, when that smile turned knowing and her cheeks flushed pink. Time to get down to business. "Give me just a minute, and I'll get everything set up."

"I can help."

I shook my head, already pulling out the blanket. "I can handle it."

And I could. Did. In three minutes, I had the blanket on the ground and all the food Bennett had helped me prepare laid out. We even had a bottle of wine. And real silverware. That had to score me some points.

"This is perfect," Lucy said as she sank onto the blanket and reached for an olive. "You put a lot of effort into this."

"I figured I made a really bad first impression. I needed to recover from that."

Lucy laughed softly, her cheeks once again reddening. "It wasn't that bad."

The fuck it wasn't. "You don't need to soften the blow—I was an asshole. A huge, ornery asshole who really should have handled things differently."

"Fine," she said once she'd finished eating a handful of grapes. "You were an asshole."

I doled out the chicken salad, making sure to sprinkle it with the dried cranberries as Bennett had demanded. I added a few crackers to Lucy's plate, then handed it off to her. "Thank you. I promise to try not to be that way again."

She took the plate, her eyes serious. "I have a feeling I'll see that side again."

Likely, but with one caveat. "Not directed at you. Never at you."

And that seemed to be enough for her. "Okay, then."

We sat under the fading sun and nibbled on our dinner of finger foods and chicken salad. Drank a bottle of wine too. The conversation stayed calm and easy, the two of us keeping things casual. Meanwhile, the beast inside me was anything but casual. As Lucy told me about growing up cousins to the fox clan who owned the diner in town, my wolverine scampered back and forth. Needing Lucy closer, wanting to touch her, wanting to kill anyone who tried to come between us. Finding our mate had kicked his protective instincts into high gear, and the rage he felt—and therefore I experienced—wasn't going to help me be less of an asshole. At least that attitude wasn't directed at Lucy, but still—it needed to be tempered a bit.

The beast and I were going to have to have a long mental talk. And at some point, I was going to have to tell Lucy about my temper. About how it had nearly destroyed me. About the fights, the arrests. Jail time.

Not today, though.

"I do need to get back," Lucy said, having just finished a story about working in the diner and all the ketchup they went through. Who were these ketchup-loving neighbors of mine? And why?

But that really wasn't important. "Of course. Give me a minute to clean this up, and I'll get you back."

"I can help."

"No. I've—"

"Got this...I know," she said, grinning once more. Softer this time, sweeter. I wanted to learn all her different smiles so I could mentally catalog them. Keep record of them to brighten up my darker days. To help hold back the anger and rage from my inner beast. I didn't smile much, but Lucy…she was made of happiness and sunshine and smiles.

And she was mine. "So then why don't you let me handle this?"

"Because I *can* help, and I'm going to. Just tell me what to do."

She stood so tall and strong, making her presence known. Deciding what she wanted to do and setting down a rule. Who was I to disobey her?

"If you can put the lids on the last of the food containers, I'll handle the garbage."

"Perfect."

Yeah, she was.

It took us no time to clean up our mess so we could leave the forest the way we'd found it. Once all the food had been put away and the empty wine bottle was tucked back into the basket, I held out my hand. Lucy took it without fear or hesitation. Without a single pause. My heart soared and my body burned. This was my mate. Mine. And I would do anything to keep her safe.

We clung to each other through the now-dark woods, me leading the way and her seeming a bit more nervous than she needed to be. That was okay—she'd learn soon enough that I would never let anything happen to her. Wolverines were fierce and protective—solitary, but good fighters. She had nothing to fear anymore. Especially not when I had a solid hold on her.

"All set," I said once we'd made it back to the truck and I'd secured the picnic basket in the bed. I hurried to her side, ready to help her up into the truck. But Lucy stopped me with a look, her body not moving the way I thought it should. Not heading for the truck.

She was leaning into me instead. "Hey, Nijel?"

"Yeah?"

She inched closer. "I didn't get to hear much about you tonight."

I grunted, feeling like an ass because I'd kept my mouth shut on purpose. I wasn't ready to tell her everything about me. Not yet, but soon. "I wanted to know more about you. Plus, I love to hear your voice."

"I like your voice too." She slipped a step toward me, closing the distance between us. Pressing her chest against mine as much as she could considering the height difference. My hands dropped of their own volition to rest on her hips, my head ducking lower so I could get a good scent of her. My god, this woman was so very perfect. And mine. How did that happen? What had I done for the fates to bless me so? Why was she—

"Nijel?" she asked, yanking me from my stupor.

"What do you need, Lucy?"

"We're alone out here—no nosy neighbors to worry about or people to see us, right?"

Damn straight. "Of course."

"Well, see… I've been thinking about our goodnight kiss, since we're on a date and all."

Welp. I was dead. Dying. Killed by the bluntness of my young mate. "Okay."

"I think I'd rather have it alone instead of at the B&B where I'm staying."

Definitely dead. "Alone is good. But we don't have to kiss if you don't want to. There're no rules."

Those bright eyes met mine, that shyness gone. "Oh, I want to. I just don't want to share my very first real kiss with anyone but my mate."

"Real?"

Her cheeks flushed, her shoulder rising in a shy sort of shrug. "You know…more than just a closed-mouth one. I mean, I'd never even had a closed-mouth one before, and it was nice. But I was thinking we might try a little…more."

Her words didn't make sense. My brain had gone completely sideways…until the wheels finally caught and jerked me back to reality. Holy shit. The woman had never been kissed other than the little peck we'd shared at the diner. My heart thumped loud and strong in my chest, every inch of my body in tune with hers. I tugged her closer, leaning over her. Running my nose along the length of hers to give her a tease. No fucking way was this going to be a simple kiss. I'd give her a first kiss to remember, for sure. I had to.

"You've never been kissed, my mate?"

She sighed, her sweet breath fanning across my face. "No. This is all very new to me."

I bumped her nose to lift her face a little, cupping her cheek in my hand. Damn near coming in my pants at the sight of my big, rough fingers against her creamy, smooth skin. Beauty and the beast, indeed.

"I'll take care of you," I said, and then I dropped just a bit more and pressed my lips to hers. Soft at first, giving her a moment to adjust. A second to push me away if this was too much. She didn't, though. Instead, she pulled me in closer. Tugged me until our bodies were touching from knees to shoulders. She rose up on the balls of her feet too, as if trying to climb me. Trying to bring herself to my level. She wasn't tall enough for that, but I could help.

I grabbed her by the hips and lifted, pressing her back against the truck as I slipped my tongue between those cherry-red lips. She gasped but dove right in, those long legs of hers coming around my hips and her arms tightening against my neck. Clinging to me. Making me hers. And her taste. By the fates, there was nothing better. Sweet, my mate. Like sugar on the tongue. I kissed her long and deep, rocked my hips into hers a bit as well. Teased her. She was so responsive, so damn needy and wild. She took everything I gave her and basically demanded more. I could smell her desire, could feel the need pouring off her. This girl was so ready for more. For everything I had to give her.

But this wasn't the time or the place, and I wouldn't disrespect her by putting her in a position where she could be seen by other men. Already, my wolverine was on edge, worried someone could sneak up behind us. Ready to destroy anyone who got too close.

As much as I hated stopping, it was time to get my mate to safety.

Another deep kiss, slower this time, and then I pulled away. Keeping my hand against her cheek. Working to catch my breath. "I should get you back to town."

The little fox kissed my thumb, smiling. "Yeah. That's probably a good idea. We can't get naked in the woods."

I nearly whimpered. My wolverine definitely did. "Not here, but the ones by my house…"

She chuckled, letting me set her back on her feet, still clinging to my arms. "We should have picnicked there."

I leaned down to kiss her one last time. A single, soft press of my lips. A repeat of how this all got started. "We'll get there, little one. There's no rush."

Her grin grew, and she threw herself into my arms. I hadn't been hugged in…well, I had no idea. But I liked it. From her. The warmth, the connection, the way she breathed against me before pulling back. Perfection.

"Help me up into your truck, please."

"Of course." I gave her my hand, lifting her a little so she could settle in on the seat. "I'll install new running boards so this isn't such a strain on you."

She grinned down at me, one eyebrow raised. "You mean you don't like manhandling me and showing off how strong you are? Because I figured that was part of why you drove this giant beast of a vehicle. To impress the ladies."

I was up and leaning into the cab of the truck in a breath, shoving her against the back of the seat in the next. Gently, of course. Always gently.

"The only lady I want to impress is you. And just so you know, you're the only woman who's ever even been in this truck. So no, I didn't buy this so I could impress anyone. But I'd sell it and buy you whatever you wanted if you asked me to. You're my priority, Lucy. My sexy vixen, my sweet mate—from here on out, it's all about you."

She caught her breath, staring at me with wide eyes before raising her hand to caress my cheek. "The fates chose well for me."

I didn't believe that—Lucy was sweet and kind, beautiful and young. I was…not. But I'd give her the world if she asked for it. I'd do my best to spoil her and show her I could be a good mate. I wasn't perfect in any way, but I was a worker. I'd get the job done. And the job was taking care of the fox shifter before me.

"Let's get you back," I said with a rough voice, not wanting to leave her side for even a second. Already panicking about having to leave her at her place for the night.

She kissed my cheek before I hopped down, gifting me with her softness once more. "Thank you for an amazing night, Nijel."

"You're welcome. Now, let me get you home and safe."

"Okay."

The drive to town was quick—too quick. There wasn't much between us in the way of conversation, but she clung to my hand the whole way. I saw that as a plus. Of course, when we made it back to the B&B she'd been staying in, my overprotective senses flared.

"You're staying here?"

She looked up at the old house on the lonely stretch of road just outside of town. There weren't even streetlights. "Yeah—my family didn't have room for me and my cousins have recently mated, so I didn't want to bother them. My aunt found me this place instead."

My wolverine practically roared, the need to protect her making me want to explode. "How many people are staying here?"

"It changes every night." She led me through a little gate—not exactly great security there—and up to the front porch. "I'm the only guest tonight, but someone is coming tomorrow."

"What about the owner?"

"He lives in a cottage out back—says he doesn't like staying with a bunch of strangers." She stopped, giving me a patronizing type of smile. "We're in the middle of nowhere with no one around. No one will bother me. It's fine."

It was a long fucking way from fine, but I couldn't say that. I couldn't let her see just how crazy I could be when her safety was threatened in any possible way.

"Are you at least in a room upstairs?"

She giggled as if she knew how much this whole thing was bothering me and thought it cute. "No—I'm in a room at the back of the house. It had the best bathroom."

Of course. And the main floor windows were all open to catch the night breeze. Open and easily accessible.

"Stop worrying," Lucy said as she rose onto the balls of her feet and tugged me down. "Give me one more little kiss, then go home and get some rest. You can get all cranky about my living situation tomorrow."

I did as asked—the kiss, at least. But when she turned and walked inside the door—unlocked, of course—my wolverine put his paw down hard, and I agreed. No fucking way were we leaving her. So, I moved my truck out onto the road—mostly so Lucy wouldn't see it—and stripped down. Clothes and shifting didn't go together, and I'd need something to wear in the morning. Once ready, I shifted and rushed through the trees until I'd reached the house. It only took me a minute of sniffing around to figure out exactly which room she'd been staying in, her scent strong around the window. I could even hear her moving around in there, which settled me just a little. She was safe...for the moment.

Because I couldn't just assume everything was fine inside, I circled the entire house, making sure she was alone. Checking for signs of peeping toms and intruders. I didn't find any. I also didn't scent or hear anyone else inside the building. That was good—Lucy was alone in the very open, very unlocked house. But she had me to watch over her, so she'd be fine.

I settled in under her window, and I waited. Watching and listening. Not sleeping.

Let someone try to come for my mate.

I'd show them why wolverines were such a feared predator.

Then I'd cart Lucy's scrumptious ass back to my cabin in the woods —the one with the doors I kept locked—and make sure she was never threatened again.

Overprotectiveness—activated.

4

LUCY

Lucy! I need you to clean up that eight-top and break it apart. Now!"

"Yes, Auntie." I rushed over to the big table, a dish tub on my hip. The morning had been absolutely brutal. From crowds to rude customers, screaming babies to a bossy aunt—there had been no stopping. You'd have thought I'd be in a bad mood with all that going on.

Not so, my friends. Not so. Why? Because I had a mate. A mate who took me on picnics. A mate who was actually sweet and kind, even if he had made a horrible first impression. I had a mate, and I couldn't wait to see him again.

Thankfully, I didn't have to wait too long. I was in the kitchen after cleaning and breaking up the eight-top when the delivery buzzer rang. My heart jumped and my throat got tight. It had to be Nijel. I hurried to the door, patting down my hair along the way and wishing for even just a touch of lip gloss. I'd been running through the restaurant so much that I'd been a little sweaty earlier. A brush, some lip gloss, and deodorant. My kingdom for those three.

But when I reached the door, I had nothing but my smile, so I made sure it was bright and wide and aimed right at—

195

"Nijel." My voice came out breathy, my heart practically fluttering. I'd never really been attracted to a man. I mean, I'd thought men were handsome or boys in school were cute. But attracted…as in my entire body heating for him? As in needing Nijel's big, rough hands on me? Wanting to experience things I never had before…yeah. Attracted was an understatement and something totally new to me.

He stepped inside, and my heart about leaped out of my chest. My goodness, he was such a big man. Thick and strong and beastly. I wanted to climb him like a tree. Wanted to know how all those muscles felt holding me up. I wanted—and I was really hoping I wouldn't have to wait too long to get.

"Good morning, beauty." He smiled at me, which only increased the attraction. He was handsome when he smiled. He was handsome no matter what, but him looking happy was the best. He definitely looked happy, but not well rested.

The door closed behind him as he stepped into the back hall, the darkness making the space feel far more intimate than it should have. Still, he seemed a little pale, a little too dark around the eyes. A little…

"You look tired," I said, drawing a finger over his cheek. "Are you okay?"

He leaned into my touch and sighed. "I'm fine. I just didn't get a lot of sleep last night."

"Oh." My heart sank a bit, my excitement dampened.

But Nijel saw. He knew, and he slipped that big, broad finger under my chin to make me look at him. "What's that tone? Why the sad little *oh*?"

"It's fine. I'd just thought… I mean, I was going to see if maybe you wanted to—"

"Yes."

His curt answer and the way he tugged me closer made me think he was just as happy to see me as I was him. "You don't even know what I was going to ask."

"Doesn't matter." He dropped down to place a quick kiss to the corner of my mouth before whispering, "Whatever it is, whatever you were about to ask me, the answer is yes. It's time spent with you. The answer will always be yes."

And that was the moment I completely lost my heart to the big lug. Without thought to time or place or appropriateness, I rose onto the balls of my feet, wrapped my arms around his neck, and planted my lips against his. Lip gloss be damned, the man deserved a kiss. A big one.

Nijel nearly froze for about one-point-four seconds, but he recovered well. Wrapping his arm around my waist and lifting me right off my feet. Holding me in midair against his body as if I weighed nothing as he deepened the kiss. As he gripped and grabbed at my body, those big hands making me wish for fewer clothes and more privacy and…more. Just more.

The man made me greedy.

"Lucy! Where is that child?"

My aunt's voice doused me in cold water, and I broke the kiss to look over my shoulder. Nijel stiffened, a low growl reverberating through his chest. Hot, but not helpful. No way should he be anywhere near my aunt if he couldn't handle her…loudness. I patted his shoulder and wiggled my feet until he let me down, hoping against hope that my aunt wouldn't appear at the end of the hall. She didn't, thankfully, but my time was limited.

"I'm sorry," I said, keeping my voice down. "She probably needs me in the dining room. We've been busy."

"That doesn't mean she needs to yell so much," he said, sounding ready to fight. Looking ready to kill. For me.

Bless my feminist heart, but that was hotter than anything else could have been.

"It's okay. I'm used to her."

"Why is she always so cranky?"

"If you had eighteen kids and a business to run, you'd be cranky too."

He stiffened again, his hand on my arm tightening, his gaze turning molten hot even in the dim light of the hall. Oh, that look. That energy. He didn't need words to communicate what was going through his mind. It was going through mine as well—babies. You needed to have sex to make babies. And we were going to…well, have the sex. Hopefully not make the babies just yet. But the sex? Yes. Practice makes perfect and all.

"Lucy! Child, I need you," my aunt yelled from farther out in the kitchen, cooling my arousal and reminding me where we were and what needed to be done before we could get to anything more fun.

"I should go," I whispered, tucking my head against his chest.

"Fine. But you let me know if you need me to step in. I don't like that lady yelling at you."

I chuckled, taking one more deep breath of his mouthwatering scent before stepping back and offering him a smile. "So, tonight...say six?"

"Sounds good. I'll pick you up."

"Perfect." One more quick kiss to the cheek, and I was ready to go. Nijel wasn't ready to let me, though. He grabbed my arm and yanked me back, making me bump into his thick, hard chest. Slipping his arms around me and enveloping me in his warmth and his scent and his comfort. I swooned so hard, and that was before he planted a kiss on me that made my toes curl. Deep and wet, overpowering. He kissed me as if he'd been dying to. Kissed me like it was a way for him to breathe. Like I was a meal and he'd been starving for so long. He kissed me, and the room began to spin.

Later. Much more of this later.

"Go," he said once we broke apart, his voice rough and his hands still holding on to me. "Before I pick you up and cart you back to my house."

"Is that supposed to be meant as a deterrent? Because it's not working."

He chuckled and kissed the top of my head. "Don't tempt me, beauty. We both have work to do."

"Fine." I ran my hands over my hair and made sure my dress was perfectly in place. No sense attracting negative attention from my aunt. "See you tonight."

"Damn straight, you will."

With that, I headed toward the kitchen, my steps wobbly and my heart pounding. This day was going to absolutely drag now that I had Nijel to look forward to. There simply wasn't—

"Where have you been?" My aunt turned the corner, those sharp eyes pinning me in place.

I didn't even falter, though. "There's a delivery. I had to answer the door to let him in."

"Ah, good. I was wondering when he'd get here. Go take care of your customers, and I'll handle him."

I nodded and went to move past her, but her cold hand landed on my arm, those dark eyes growing more intense, more investigative. More...concerned.

"Your cheeks are flushed. Are you feeling okay?"

"I'm fine."

"You sure?" She placed the back of her hand against my forehead, and there it was. The mother in her. The softer side. I rarely got to see it, but I always knew it was in there.

I grabbed her hand and kissed the back of it, giving her a smile. "I'm fine, I swear. It's just warm outside, and I had that door open. Now, go— I'll handle the customers."

She tsked and patted my cheek, shaking her head and mumbling to herself as she scurried across the kitchen toward where I knew Nijel would be unloading his truck.

Nijel.

My mate.

Being all strong and muscular and...him.

Yup, this was going to be a long, long day.

5

LUCY

A few hours of working at the diner, a few text messages with Nijel to set up the evening, and a whole lot of lady prep later, I was ready. Ready for a night out on the town with my man and my cousins. Misty had been the one to suggest the dance club—her mate was a college professor in a town on the other side of the mountain, but they were in town for a few days and available. Her sister Tilly was also up for a night out, though that could end up cut short if we weren't careful. Her mate was a literal movie star and tended to attract attention. Mostly from the female persuasion, to Tilly's dismay.

Whatever. We were going out. And while I wasn't really one for those loud club scenes and drinking to excess, I wanted to dance with my big, strong mate. I wanted to be in a public place and feel his body up against mine. I wanted to do a lot of things that weren't acceptable for those public places, too.

"All in good time." I puckered my lips—coated in lip gloss finally—and double-checked that my makeup was on point. A knock on the door sent my heart rate through the roof, and I hurried over. The owner of the B&B stood on the other side.

"Good evening, Lucy. You have a visitor in the parlor."

Parlor. So quaint. "Thank you, Max."

I grabbed my purse and rushed out the door, passing Max as he headed for the kitchen. My steps were quick and long, my excitement nearly palpable. A night with Nijel…I couldn't wait.

But when I turned the corner into the parlor, all thoughts of anything other than *hhhoootttt* flew right out of my head. I was going to get into a fight with any woman who made the mistake of looking at my man the way I was. And I was looking. I was looking hard.

Nijel stood before the fireplace, his elbow up on the mantel and his ankles crossed. He'd combed his graying hair into a controlled wave and even had some scruff on his face as if he'd skipped shaving. Perfect, arousing, and totally lickable. He looked like he should have been in an advertisement for something super masculine. Some sort of English hunting lodge or men's clothing company. He looked—

"Gorgeous." He smiled and sidled toward me, the hunter stalking his prey. His eyes ran up and down my body. Down again. Locking on the hem of my dress. "You're absolutely stunning."

But he still wasn't looking at my face. "What's wrong?"

He jerked his head up, and his eyes finally stayed on mine. "Nothing."

Lies. "You're staring at my dress."

He looked down again. "I'm staring at your legs."

"Why?"

"Because I can see so much of them."

I had no idea what that meant. My dress wasn't that much shorter than my diner uniform. One hit my knees and the other…didn't. At all. Not even close. Okay, fine—the dress was short. No way would I be bending over tonight. But I had great legs, and my momma had always said to work your assets. My legs were at work.

I took a step closer, forcing Nijel to look right at me once more. Pouting my bottom lip just a bit. "You don't like the dress?"

"I like the dress." Nijel huffed and tugged me closer, running a couple fingers up the back of my thigh all the way to the hem that was only just below the curve of my ass. "I like your legs even more. This dress is a delicious tease for me, but the first man who makes the mistake of thinking you're on display for him is going to regret it. My temper is…short."

Silly man. I rose up to give him a peck on the lips. "The show is just for you."

His growl had my body heating, made my panties wet and my heart pound. This was going to be such a long night.

Nijel led me outside to his truck, taking the time to help me climb inside. He hadn't been kidding—there were new running boards installed that made the climb a lot easier. My dress didn't, and I was pretty sure I flashed the man my panties at one point if his whispered curse was any indication. Whoopsie. Still, he drove us across town to the Metro Lounge, where Tilly and Misty would be meeting us, holding my hand the entire way. Once parked, he again hurried around the truck to help me down, watching carefully as I descended the running boards and made it safely to the concrete.

"That was much easier."

He grunted. "Good, though don't go trying to get in or out without me. Especially not in those shoes."

I glanced down at my heels. Sure, they were a little high, but they weren't extreme. "What's wrong with my shoes?"

"Absolutely fucking nothing. They don't look especially supportive, though."

I giggled, clinging to his arm as we headed inside. "They're not meant to be supportive—they're meant to make my legs look longer."

"Well then, they're working just fine. You ready for this?"

The air around the club practically vibrated with the bass from the music, and already people were everywhere. The noise, the commotion...was I ready? No. But that wasn't going to stop me.

"Ready if you are."

Nijel took a breath then reached out, holding open the door for me, keeping his hand on my lower back as we headed inside. There was something about that move—about him wanting to touch me, wanting to keep me in front of him but needing that physical connection—that was just so swoony.

But falling deeper into my feelings about my new mate was going to have to wait. The bar was packed, and I was already drowning in the sea of energy and sound and light. Thankfully, I spotted Tilly's actor mate,

Renit, in about two-point-five seconds. He stood toward the back in the VIP section, looking out over the crowd.

"There," I said, leaning closer to Nijel so he could hear me. "See that tall, dark-haired guy in the back."

Nijel stiffened. "Yeah?"

"That's my cousin's mate. That's where we're headed."

Nijel looked over the dance floor we'd need to pass through, frowning. "Got it."

He grabbed my hand and tugged me close into his side, leading the way to the far edge of the floor before beelining it toward Renit. Heads turned along the way, and people seemed to almost stumble over themselves to get out of his path. Not that I could blame them. Nijel had a serious frown on his face—a determined sort of expression that screamed he wasn't stopping for anyone. He was also more than a head taller than just about every man around him. I'd have been jumping out of the way too. At least, if I hadn't known him. If he hadn't been my mate. At that moment, I actually wanted to be closer to him. The other people had no idea what they were missing out on.

"There you are." Tilly hurried over, pulling us with her into the little structure carving out the VIP area. No security, no real walls, but just enough definition to make it clear that section was off-limits. I felt awfully fancy.

"Hi." I gave my cousin a hug, still holding on to Nijel's hand. "Tilly, this is Nijel. Nijel, this is Tilly and her mate, Renit."

"Hi," Tilly said, looking him over with curious eyes. "We've met before at the diner."

"Good to meet you," Renit said, offering Nijel his hand, the two practically dripping testosterone. Renit was smaller than Nijel, but he looked strong enough to hold his own. Misty's professor mate...did not.

"Nice to meet you. I'm Clark." The professor leaned in, eyeing Nijel hard. Okay, fine—he may have been smaller than either man, but the wolf shifter wasn't one to be dismissed. I had a feeling he was sneaky enough to hold his own in a fight. Not that the men would be fighting. Ever.

"For fuck's sake, it took you long enough." Misty came barreling into the space, a tray of drinks in her hand. "Here—have some champagne. We're celebrating."

I grabbed a glass, handing it to Nijel before snagging another one for me. "What are we celebrating?"

"Your mating, of course. Congratulations to the latest fox to fall into fated bliss with a not-fox. May you live every day as if it's your last." She grinned, winking toward Nijel. "And every night as if it's your first."

My face heated, my mind going directly to firsts. Firsts we still needed to accomplish. We'd only kissed; anything else was still upcoming. And I couldn't wait.

If the way Nijel gripped my elbow and softly pulled me until my body was flush with his was any indication, he felt the same. "Thank you, Misty. And it's great you all could join us tonight. These sorts of places aren't my usual hangouts, but I wanted Lucy to have fun."

Misty cocked her head. "I have to admit, I was surprised when Lucy agreed to this place. You wolverines are usually so…isolated."

Nijel sort of shrugged, looking uncomfortable. Whether because of the question or the crowd, I didn't know. What I did know was that the guilt of dragging him out to a place where he never would have wanted to go, where he likely wouldn't have a good time, and where others would comment on his being there hit me like a ton of bricks. My mood sank, my smile falling. I hadn't been a good partner to my mate by making him come here with me.

"You okay?" Tilly frowned my way, her brow furrowed and her eyes locked on my face. Okay was not the word I'd have used to describe myself, but I did my best to pull myself together.

"Yeah. Of course. I'm just…really tired."

That got Misty's attention. "Is it my mom? Is she working you too hard? I tell her all the time to stop with the yelling and the ordering around, but after so many years with so many kids, it's like she can't help herself. Of course, now that you're mated, you'll likely stop working there, right? We all did. Are you moving here permanently, or is Nijel heading to your town?"

The man himself stiffened, his grip on my elbow releasing. We hadn't gotten that far yet—hadn't discussed the options of how we were going to move forward as a couple. We hadn't done anything but have a picnic and show up at the most wrong venue in the history of the world for us.

My chest grew tight, my breaths coming fast and my body heating. It was all so much. Too much.

Tilly again seemed to be the one to notice. "Lucy, you look a little flushed."

I waved a hand in my face, pasting on the fakest smile known to human or shifter. I didn't even have to see it to know how fake it was—I felt it. "I'm fine. It's just really warm in here. Can you get me an ice water when the waitress comes around? I'm going to run to the restroom."

"Sure. Okay." Tilly glanced over my shoulder. "Want me to come with you?"

I was about to say no, but Nijel's deep voice overrode that one. "Yes, please. Stay with her."

Tilly looked back at me and smiled softly. "No problem. I'll be right back, Renit."

Her eagle-eyed mate looked me up and down, taking in the situation. Making me feel oddly like prey. "Hurry back."

And with that, we were off. It took almost no time to work our way to the back where the restrooms were tucked away, and once there, I took advantage of the sinks to run cold water over my wrists. My body cooled again, and my chest loosened. Panic subsided. For now.

"It's overwhelming, isn't it?"

I caught Tilly's eyes in the mirror. "What's overwhelming?"

"A new mating. All the questions, the getting to know each other, the pull to be together, to mate…it's a lot."

I shut off the water and turned around, taking the paper towel she offered to dry my hands. "It's way too much, and I already feel as if I'm screwing up."

"Why's that?"

"Because we're here. We should be alone someplace quiet, learning about each other and stuff. Instead, I dragged him into a place he'd never go because I wasn't focused on his…"

Thankfully, when the word refused to come to me, Tilly knew what I meant. "His wolverine-ness."

"Yes. That."

"Lucy, if he hadn't wanted to come, he wouldn't be here."

"But—"

"No buts. This is called compromise. Would he have picked this place to spend his time? No. But you wanted to go because your family invited you, so he's here. He'll want to do things you don't want to as well and go places you'd rather not, but you'll go because you love him and want to see him happy. Compromise—give-and-take."

"What does Renit make you do that you don't like to."

She cocked her head, keeping her voice deadpan flat. "I have now seen every single kung fu movie ever made. Twice. With commentary on fighting styles and stunts."

I winced. "Yeah. That's...not you."

"Not me at all, but he loves them and I love him. So, quit feeling guilty, get out there with your man, and shake your little booty for him. That will make it all better."

That...I could do.

We left the bathroom laughing, heading straight for the VIP area. I definitely felt better after that little break—more centered and sure of what I was doing. More tolerant of the tornado of sound around me. Nijel and I had only been mated for a couple days, mere hours, really. All the things that went along with that would come with time, including knowing when to turn down an invitation because my mate would be uncomfortable. I'd get there.

I made it through a crowd of people and spotted the man himself. He was standing with Renit, both looking handsome and huge and slightly worried. As if Tilly and I couldn't handle a bathroom trip alone. I was about to take her arm to point them out when someone grabbed my elbow. Tilly didn't stop and I was pretty sure Nijel hadn't seen me yet, but someone had. Someone who yanked me against their body and leaned over my shoulder to whisper in my ear.

"Hey, baby. I really like that dress. How about—"

"No." I pulled away, nearly elbowing the man in the gut to get him to release me. Sadly, recognizing him as well. Winker McWinkerson, mayor of Never-Gonna-Happen town. "Jacob, right? From the diner?"

"You remember." His grin was positively…smarmy.

"Yeah, I do. But I'm not interested."

My words didn't seem to deter him. "You sure about that?"

"One hundred percent."

His smile fell, and a malicious sort of glint shone in his eyes. Every one of my instincts was screaming *fuck politeness* and making me want to run away from him. My fox chattered loudly in my head, not liking this situation. Wanting her mate. She was ready to bite this guy's nose off if she had to. And from his glazed-over eyes, the wide pupils, and the obvious slur, she might have to. Drunk tiger shifters were the worst.

And the most likely not to give up. "You don't have to be a bitch, you know. I was just trying to—"

"Trying to put your hands on what's not yours? Trust me, I know. And again, I'm not interested."

His face turned mean, his smile twisting into a scowl. Before he could spit out whatever hateful words he felt like spewing, another hand grabbed my elbow. But this one, I knew—it sent electricity zinging through my body and made my inner fox relax. This one belonged.

"The lady said no. Leave her alone." Nijel stood with Renit beside him, both men looking as if they were about to rage. About to shift and cause some serious damage.

The guy obviously didn't seem to understand the trouble he was in. "I was talking with the lady."

"I was a bitch a second ago," I said, crossing my arms over my chest. "Now I'm a lady?"

Nijel's growl deafened the music, and the crowd around us miraculously found somewhere else to be, leaving a large circle of space.

"You called her a bitch?" Nijel asked, his voice nothing more than a rumble

The man didn't answer. Didn't give Nijel any respect either. Instead, he made a mistake—a big one. It wasn't the roll of his eyes or the burst of sarcastic laughter at Nijel's words. No, I had a feeling my mate could have brushed those off just fine. The mistake was worse. He reached out to grab me once more. He actually sidestepped the two males and snatched my wrist, yanking me toward him. Putting his arm around my hip and sliding his hand over my ass as if I were someone he knew. Someone who was his.

Nijel exploded.

He jumped forward, his arm swinging wide, his fist connecting with the man's jaw. I nearly fell forward with the guy, but Nijel grabbed me and held me up. He protected me.

From the man who was nothing more than a limp noodle on the floor

Good.

"All you had to do was let the lady make her own choices." Nijel stepped forward, lording over the smaller man. Grumbling as he said, "You don't touch her, don't talk to her. You don't even bother looking at her. And if you ever make the mistake of calling her a bitch again, you'd better run your ass straight out of town because I'll be taking a chunk of it. You hear me, son?"

"Yeah," the guy said as he clutched the side of his face. "I hear you."

Something in his words, in his speech, didn't sound right, but I was too angry to care. He'd gotten what he deserved. You didn't threaten a man's mate. Not in Kinship Cove.

"Good." Nijel still looked just as furious as before, but his eyes were on mine this time. Angry eyes. "It's time to go."

Uh oh.

"Nijel, I—"

"I won't force you to leave, but I'm asking you to. Now. With me." He huffed a breath and ran a hand through his hair. "Please."

Renit stepped forward, looking worried. "I think that might be a good idea. Security is on their way over."

Nijel didn't need to deal with them—not after what had just happened. So I agreed, nodding, hearing the strain in his voice. Knowing how hard this night had been on him. Compromise, Tilly had said. He'd come to this place with me. I'd leave it with him. No matter what.

"That's fine. Take me home."

Nijel didn't grab my arm or lead me toward the door. Oh no. The man swooped me up into his arms and carried me out of the club. He didn't pause all the way across the floor, simply used his mass to intimidate people out of his way. Even the bouncers knew the trouble blowing through—they held the doors open to let us outside, disappearing back into the bar as quickly as possible.

And then we were alone. In a dark parking lot.

"Nijel, I—"

"Not yet."

"What?"

"If I try to talk to you right now, you're going to think I'm mad at you because I'm so fucking furious. So, please—not yet. We can talk when we get to the B&B."

The B&B. He was taking me to where I was staying. The isolated, solitary wolverine was not inviting me to his den, instead joining me in a public house with other people. That was not what I wanted.

The B&B. He was taking me to where I was staying. The isolated, solitary wolverine was not inviting me to his den, instead joining me in a public house with other people. Compromise again.

"Fine. When we get to the B&B."

Nijel lifted me up into the truck, breathing a sigh of what sounded like relief once I was buckled in. "Thank you."

I leaned down to press a kiss to his jaw. "No, thank you. Now, take me home, mate. I want to be alone with you."

A muscle in his jaw ticked, and those dark, fiery eyes locked on mine. He knew what I meant. We both knew what was likely going to happen when we got to my place. It was time to complete the mating. To physically bond and ease the ache inside us. It was time.

And I was more than ready.

6

NIJEL

I'd never felt like more of a jerk. Not for hitting the tiger shifter at the bar—and he was definitely a tiger. I could smell that on him. But no, not for that. Even a breed as disloyal as a tiger should have known better than to treat a woman the way he had. No, I felt like a jerk because Lucy had wanted to go to that bar—to drink and dance and have a good time.

I'd ruined her evening.

I simply couldn't have allowed that man to treat her so poorly—to disrespect her wishes and put his hands on her when she hadn't wanted him to. He'd grabbed her ass after she'd clearly told him she wasn't interested. The tiger was lucky he still had teeth. Still, I hadn't been in a fight—been in the kind of trouble losing my temper like that could bring—in a long time. A very long time.

I was way too old for that sort of shit.

I pulled up at the B&B and killed the engine, hurrying out to help Lucy down. I had yet to say a word to her, had yet to try to explain myself. I needed to, though. Especially if this was us saying goodnight. I wanted to take her back to my place, tuck her into my bed, and wrap her body in my scent. I wanted that badly, but I also didn't want to push her or assume. Especially not after the scare at the club. She could be in a fragile state. I'd drop her off and leave her alone if that was what she wanted.

And then I'd sleep under her window again.

"Lucy," I said once we reached the porch, knowing it was time to apologize. "That guy totally deserved the punch I threw at him, but I'm so sorry for ruining your night."

"You didn't ruin anything." She didn't rise up to offer me a kiss, though. Just turned and opened the door. My heart sank and my body went cold as I stared at the floor. This was it. The moment she told me to go away. That she decided I wasn't—

"Would you like to come inside?"

My eyes flew up to meet hers, to catch the fact that she was smiling at me with her hand out. Inviting me in. My mate was…needing an answer.

"Yes, I would." I followed her inside, excitement brewing in my belly. Heat, too. I couldn't help but glance down as she walked, eyeing the curve of her ass in that dress. Staring at all that skin revealed below the hem. Yeah, the guy at the bar had seen the best-looking girl and gone after her. I couldn't blame him for trying when Lucy looked the way she did. He just shouldn't have manhandled her or called her a bitch when she rejected him.

"This is me," she said, opening a door inside the house and stepping through it, holding it open for me to pass her. The room was cute…neat and tidy, decorated well…but not her. At all.

Temporary.

The space was exceptionally temporary.

"Nice place," I said, wishing I could see where she really lived.

"It's a stopping point," she said as she slipped her shoes off and tucked them away. "I was only supposed to be here for a few months to help my aunt."

"The one who yells at you."

"She yells at everyone. Can you unzip this, please?" She turned her back to me, holding up her hair. Giving me a smile over her shoulder that told me she knew exactly what she was doing. I was about to unzip that magical dress—see the skin that lay beneath. Know the fabric could fall at any moment. My mate was seducing me.

I was the luckiest man on earth.

I slipped in behind her, tracing the curve of her neck with my fingers. Planting a slight kiss there before slowly tugging the zipper down. Very down. Lots of down. And so much skin. Sweet merciful heaven, the bare skin.

"Thanks," she whispered, those eyes of hers smoldering. "And my aunt yells at everyone. I'm not special in that regard."

Right. Aunt. Conversation. *Skin.* "I don't like people yelling at my mate."

She turned slowly to face me, that damn fabric draping low. Showing me more skin. Teasing me like nothing else could have. "You don't like people touching your mate either."

My growl couldn't have been stopped, the way my hand flew out and gripped her arm impossible to change. My breath came faster, my other hand somehow finding its way to her hip. Holding her against me. Needing more. I wanted to strip her naked and touch her all over. Rub my body all along hers to rid her of anyone else's scent and bathe her in mine. I wanted so much.

"I'm the only one who should be touching my mate. Ever."

Her smile turned positively wicked. "Agreed."

One second, she was a tease in draping red fabric. The next, she was practically naked. That dress seemed to drop of its own volition, that fabric falling to the floor in a pile I could only barely notice because my mate was standing before me in nothing but a scrap of red lace around her hips. So flimsy, that lace covering what I wanted to touch and taste and get to know. So, so flimsy.

I'd buy her a million pairs of those if she'd just let me destroy this one.

"So, touch me," Lucy said, giving me permission. Granting all my wishes with three words.

I was not a man who needed to be told twice.

I picked her up, choosing to place her beautiful body on the couch. The bed looked lovely, but I wanted to get up close and personal with the pussy I knew to be under that red lace. For that, I needed a different position. True, I could hold her up and wrap her legs around my neck. I could let her ride my face too. Good possibilities and things we could play with later, but for now, I wanted her comfortable. And I wanted full access.

Without a word, I spread her legs and dropped to my knees, letting a low growl do my speaking for me. Running my rough hands up her thighs and lifting one leg over my shoulder. Open. Spread wide open. Just for me.

"That dress was the devil," I said as I began my long, slow journey from her knee upward. Dragging my lips all along that bare skin. "Pure evil. It made you temptation personified."

"That's why I wore it."

I jerked up, coming to kiss her lips. Needing a taste of her sweetness to calm me down so I didn't dive headfirst into things. "You don't need such a dress to tempt me, mate."

She smiled, sliding her fingers softly over my cheek. "I know, but I like to play."

I was going to come in my pants. To distract myself, I gripped her thighs tighter, massaging the flesh. Forcing them just a little wider. "You're naughty."

"Only with you."

Damn straight. I didn't answer her, though. Instead, I slipped a finger under that last bit of red lace, and I tugged. The fabric gave way, blessing me with the vision of her pussy on display just for me. Soft and pink and so beautiful. A gift for me—one I didn't deserve. One I would treasure and care for always.

I ran a thumb over the side, teasing her the same way she'd been teasing me. Letting her know what was coming. Warming her up. Not that I needed to.

"You're wet already," I said, licking my lips as I stared at the glistening flesh before me. "Are you that ready for my touch, mate?"

She arched back as I teased her opening, groaning softly. "Yes. So ready."

Again, being told once was plenty.

I rose to meet her lips once more, kissing her deeply. Letting her warm up to me. I couldn't thrust inside her just yet. Not without prep. I was a large man—just the bulk of my body and the breadth of my hips between hers would be something new to her. I needed to give her time to get used to me. To become comfortable with the way I felt against her bare skin. So I yanked off my shirt, pressing my chest to hers. Letting her feel my heat, the hair on my body, the muscles that had always been a part of me. She gasped and tugged me closer, moaning as I rocked against her just so. As I pulled back and waited for her to open her eyes again, making sure she got a good look at me. That she truly saw what a wolverine shifter in human form looked like.

Lucy smiled, biting into that plump bottom lip and making my dick jerk in my pants. "I always thought wolverines were smaller animals."

Hah. "They are." I dropped back to my knees, rubbing my face up her thighs as I held her gaze. Slipping a hand along the outside of her thigh in preparation for what was coming. "They're not big at all."

"But you're huge."

"My animal form isn't big, but he's strong. He can take down beasts three times his size without missing a trick. My human form ends up like this because of all that strength."

"I had no idea. I'd never met a wolverine shifter before."

I grabbed her leg and pulled it over my shoulder, kissing up her thigh. Biting now and again as well. Softly. Gently. "You're going to meet all of me tonight. Are you ready for that?"

She started to reply, but I planted a kiss right over the mound of her pussy, so her words turned into nothing more than a gasp. Her thighs shook, and she reached down to grab me by my hair. To tug me closer. So responsive, my little mate.

"That dress tonight was a show," I said just before I licked up her entrance. Before I sent her squealing. She even grabbed a pillow and covered her pretty face. Silly girl. "I wanted to be alone with you so badly. I wanted the full effect instead of small peeks and little glimpses of skin that should have been hidden. I saw more of you every time you moved around me." I licked her again, growling at the taste of her.

Unable to hold back. "Next time, wear it when it's just us so I can play more."

Her whispered yes became a chant as I slipped a finger inside her and flicked my tongue against her clit. She was so sweet, so warm and soft and willing. Not ready, though. Not for all of me. Not for me to pump my dick inside her and break her wide open. No, no, no. That needed more wetness, more softness. That needed her to have come a time or two before I could even contemplate sliding inside the heat of her.

Besides, I wanted to taste her first orgasm with me. To own that little piece of it.

I never let up—fucking her with my finger as I flicked and licked and sucked on her clit. As I pushed her body toward the breaking point. There was no pausing, no taking a break, no slowing down. I needed to be inside her, which meant I had to make her come. And I would—but every second spent with my face buried in her pussy, every taste of her on my tongue as I teased her toward her orgasm, was a gift in and of itself. I was all about giving tonight.

"Nijel," she gasped, wrapping her fingers in my hair again and holding my face against her. I loved it—loved that she had the confidence to drive. To direct me. I hoped she'd keep it up once I moved us to the bed because that surety made my balls positively ache.

"More?" I pressed my tongue flat against her clit, giving her additional pressure as I slipped a second finger inside her. "I'll give you more. I'll give you all of me. I want you to come first, though. Need it."

"Nijel, I...I..."

Yeah, I knew. She was going to come. I could feel it in the way her legs shook and her breaths were coming in pants. I could practically taste her arousal in the moisture all over her pussy. She'd soaked me, and she was ready for her reward. I just had to give it to her.

A third finger joined the party as I began to growl against her. I couldn't tell if it was the fullness or the vibration that finally sent her flying. Either way, my mate came on my hand with my mouth on her pussy, writhing against me and full on yelling *my* name. It was the greatest moment of my life.

I was ready for even greater, though.

"So sweet when you come," I whispered against her, letting one finger slip out, then the next. Teasing her through her orgasm. Placing soft kisses over her clit as she shook and pulsed before me. "I could lick you this way for days, you know. Tie you to my bed and torture you with my tongue. You'd like that, wouldn't you?"

"More," she said, her voice hoarse and her words breathy. "Need more."

"So greedy, my girl. Good thing your mate has the stamina to give you what you need." Without even wiping her arousal from my face, I picked her up and carried her to the bed. This was it—time for us to bond completely as mates. For me to thrust inside her and make her mine.

I didn't want to wait another second.

But I'd make damn sure she was ready first.

So, I laid her down, and I knelt over her. My pants undone and my dick in my hand. My body ready to claim hers. "Are you sure about this, Lucy? Once we bond, there's no going back. You'll be mine forever. Stuck with me for all your days."

She smiled sleepily, reaching for me. "And you'll be mine—stuck with me just the same. I want that—give yourself to me so I can be yours."

Fuck yeah. Those words were music to my ears, a balm to my weary soul. They were the start of a brand-new life, one filled with joy and companionship. One not shadowed by past troubles. The fates had given me the greatest possible gift, and I would never take it for granted.

So I nodded to my mate, slipping off the bed to remove my pants. Crawling back over once I was naked. Ready. As was my mate...who could not tear her hungry eyes from my dick.

The vixen.

"If you keep looking at me like that, I'm going to come before I even make it inside you."

Her eyes shot to mine. "Like what?"

"Like you're hungry for my cock."

That bottom lip pursed out, a pout dancing on her pretty face. "I am. I'm hungry for it, but I've never done this. I'm afraid I won't please you."

Motherfucker, this girl. "You please me just by breathing."

I lay on top of her, kissing her deeply once more. Letting her taste herself on my lips. Letting her feel the weight of me. She bent her knees and brought her legs around my hips. Pulling me in. Being greedy once more.

"Lucy, I—"

"It's my first time." She wrapped those arms around my neck, running her hands over my back. Soothing me. "I saved myself for my mate."

She had, and there was something so sweet about that. Unnecessary, but sweet. I'd take care of her. Make sure she never regretted that decision. Make sure she understood how honored I was by her restraint.

I'd make sure she never wondered what else might be out there. "I promise I'll be gentle this first time."

Her own growl overpowered mine, her fingers digging into my flesh as she practically yanked me down on top of her. "Don't be."

7

LUCY

I loved him. Already, Nijel and our connection had destroyed any reservations I could have had regarding my new mating. I loved everything about him—his gruffness and grumpy attitude, his sweet side, his rough hands, his gentle smile. All of it. I loved him…and I wanted him.

"Please, Nijel." I arched forward, rising up to meet his lips when he tried to retreat. To bite that pouty bottom one simply because I could. "Please be inside me. I want to feel you."

"Ah fuck. My little vixen." He grabbed my hands and held them over my head, pinning me in place. "You're making this so damn hard."

I lifted my thigh against that hardness. "I know. I can feel it."

He chuckled. "Not my cock, sweetheart. Resisting you. You're making that difficult."

I moaned as he rocked into me, not sliding inside yet but teasing me. Pressing where I wanted him most. Trying to distract me. "Why would you want to resist me?"

"Because I don't want to scare you or do something you won't like."

"I'll like it all." I tugged on my arms, trying to free myself. Puffing out a breath when he wouldn't let me. "Fine. I might not. But I'll tell you in

219

the moment if you do something I don't like or if I think you might be heading in that direction."

"Are you sure?" he asked, leaning close. Locking his eyes with mine even as his cock continued to nudge my delicate flesh. "Once we mate, the bond between us is permanent."

"You already reminded me of that." Multiple times. The man was truly worried about me being unsure, apparently. If only I could prove to him just how sure I was.

Maybe I could.

I lifted my hips and twisted slightly, angling myself against him. Letting the tip of that glorious cock slip inside. Trying hard for more. Wanting him to truly trust that I was ready for everything. "I want you to be mine, and I want to be yours."

He sighed, rocking into me. Obviously still holding back. "You'll be stuck with me forever."

My silly wolverine. "Sounds perfect."

"You might end up hating me."

"Never."

He stopped moving, his face growing serious. His hands loosening their hold. "You might end up afraid of me."

Oh. So *that* was the issue. My big, strong predator worried he was too much for me. Too mean and direct, too strong. Silly man. Those were some of the traits I adored about him—the way he made me feel safe and protected, how he cared for me in even the simplest of situations. He was a gentleman with me, but knowing he could—and would—go full wolverine on others if they bothered me? That was hot.

And I needed to make sure he knew that.

I flipped my hands over his, clinging to his wrists as he'd done to mine. Not letting him pull away as I stared up at him. As I refused to break eye contact. "I will never be afraid of you, my mate. You are sweet and kind—" I shushed him when he tried to speak. "No, no. It's my turn."

Without thinking, I pushed him. Thankfully, he went along with what I wanted because no way could I have moved him on my own. So, I pushed, and he rolled onto his back, allowing me to settle on his hips.

On his cock. Oh, that feeling was delicious and made me want to lift up and slide him inside of me, but I couldn't. The conversation was too serious.

I just needed two minutes of clearheadedness.

"You, Nijel Carr, have a caring soul. You're fierce and possessive, but only because you want what's yours to be safe. I see your protective side. I also know your gruffness isn't because you're mean-spirited but more that you're wary of others. You want to protect me—let me protect you too. From the cruelty of the world. From being disappointed. From loneliness. Give me the chance, and I'll make you happy, mate. I promise."

With a growl, he rolled me underneath him, sliding inside me before he had me on my back. Filling me with himself. Holding me down once more. "Mine. You're all mine. I'll keep you safe, my vixen. I promise."

So thick. I could barely breathe, I was so filled. Could barely find the presence of mind to mutter, "And I'll make you happy."

"You already do." He kissed my lips, gasping and breathing hard as his hips began to move in earnest. As he pumped and pumped and pumped into me. Slowly at first, staring down at me with obvious concern. Watching my reactions closely. So very closely. I nodded, biting my lip, begging for more with every movement when I couldn't find the words. Because I did want more—of him, of us, of this. Of everything. But man, words were so hard.

The headboard began to hit the wall, the thumping rhythmic and distinctive to anyone in the vicinity, but I didn't care. Let the other guests at the B&B hear us—my mate and I were doing exactly what we were supposed to do. Bonding. And we were doing it well.

"Nijel," I gasped, my brain gaining traction for about three seconds before everything scattered again. "More. I need more."

Nijel grunted and rose slightly onto his knees, lifting my hips and hitting a new place inside me that made stars appear behind my eyes. I might have cried out—I likely screamed, to be honest—but I didn't care. My mate was making me feel cherished and full of electric energy.

Every thrust of his hips drove him deeper inside me, every grunt and groan telling me how good this was for him. And as we moved in tandem, as we climbed that hill of pleasure together, I had a true moment of clarity. There was no pain for my first time, no fear or nervousness. This was fated, meant to be. Perfect. His big, heavy body on mine. His cock buried inside me. Stretching me. Filling me. Perfection in every sense.

I had never been so filled with joy.

Especially once he pulled both my legs over his arms and tugged my hips right up off the mattress.

"Oh fuck," I gasped, trying hard not to scream again. Not that he seemed to mind my loudness.

"There you go, vixen. I'm getting so deep inside your heat. All the way deep." And he was. He was hitting good places inside me. Such good places.

Places that made me tremble and clench as the inevitable crest appeared. "I want to come. I need to."

He tugged me higher, rising onto his knees. "I've got you. I promise."

He soooooo did. It wasn't long before the tension and pressure of what he was doing broke something inside me. I came with a full, guttural yell—calling his name to the heavens as my entire body seized up. Bliss. That was the only way to describe the sensations—pure, unadulterated bliss.

The way I squeezed him seemed to bring out the animal in my mate. He began to thrust harder, to growl and snarl through every move. To lose his rhythm but pick up his pace. I knew what was coming and couldn't wait to see it.

I didn't have to wait long.

"Fuck, Lucy. I'm coming." And he did, holding me tight and stilling for a long moment while he released a howl that shook the walls. While he emptied inside me. While he filled me up again and again as he trembled in my arms. There were things to worry about, of course—problems and blessings that might come up since I wasn't on any sort of birth control—but I didn't care. Let the fates choose our path once more —they'd done a phenomenal job so far for me.

He finally collapsed on top of me, rolling slightly to the side to keep his weight off my body. Which was not what I wanted.

"Come here," I whispered, tugging on him. He curled into my side, resting his head on my shoulder and his thigh across my legs as I wrapped my body around his. As I cuddled him and ran my fingers through his hair. As I surrendered to the happiness coursing through my veins. "That was amazing."

"It'll only get better." He kissed my breast, letting his tongue swipe the nipple and chuckling when I jumped. "Are you okay?"

Okay? That word no longer fit in my vocabulary, especially not when it came to Nijel. "I'm amazing."

"Fuck yeah, you are." Another kiss, and then he tugged me tighter. "And mine. You're totally mine now."

I was. And I couldn't wait to figure out all the ins and outs of what that meant.

But first, I needed to close my eyes for a second. Needed to snuggle deeper into his hold and let the darkness envelop me.

Sex was amazing…and exhausting.

I needed to rest.

8

LUCY

There was nothing as joyous as waking up warm and rested with my big mountain of a man behind me. He'd thrown an arm over my hip during the night and curled his body around mine. Protecting me even in his sleep. His breath tickled my hair, and his soft snores rumbled against me. Bliss, I tell you.

I would never get enough of Nijel Carr.

The sun had brightened the space, and the sounds of life beyond the walls of my rented room reached my ears. It was far past time to wake up, and yet there we lay. Exhausted. Sated. Together.

Still, the fact that we were in my room, my little rented space, bothered me. Like the seam of a shirt that wouldn't lie flat or the tag on a pair of pants that scratched just so…it irritated. This wasn't truly my space. This wasn't where I wanted to be either. I wanted the comfort of someplace permanent—the knowledge that came from investigating the space where someone truly lived. All the little trinkets they collected, the things they saw as important. I wanted all of that information about my solitary wolverine.

Which meant it was time for him to wake up and take me to his home.

I rolled over slowly, trying hard not to wake him just yet. Knowing I was going to soon enough anyway. Nijel slept on with his heavy arm over me. So handsome, my mate. So rough and rugged. I could see how his size might intimidate people, but he had a soft side to him. A caring one. I didn't fear him for a single second.

Itching to touch him, I brought my hand up. Ran my fingers through the hair on his chest and up to his shoulder. Down his arm to his wrist and back again. So strong. So much muscle. I was one lucky little fox.

"Are you trying to wake me, mate?" Nijel opened one eye, staring at me. Smiling softly. "Or just exploring?"

"Both." I placed a hand flat against his chest and pushed him over until he lay on his back. Then I leaned over so I was angled above his chest. "It's time to get up and go home."

He blinked, his smile falling. "Oh."

The words I'd said reverberated through my head, that *oh* telling me he'd taken them wrong. Very wrong. Evidenced by the way he started to rise from the bed as if to leave.

"Not alone." I practically climbed on top of him to hold him in place. "I said that all wrong. It's time for both of us to get up and go to your home. Together."

He frowned, hanging on to my thighs with both hands as he settled back into the pillows. "You want to come to my house?"

"Yes. This place isn't me. It's temporary. Your place is permanent. I want to see it. I want to investigate it."

He huffed a breath, wiggling a little underneath me as if to get comfortable. He was thick and hard beneath me. Obviously ready for more than a conversation. Something I hadn't considered until he was right there. And he was…*right there*. So I rocked my hips a little. Teased him just a bit.

His growl told me he knew exactly what I was doing. "I'll take you there, of course. But I don't want you to think of my place as permanent."

"Why not?"

"Are you sore, sweet Lucy?" He massaged my thighs, making his want clear. "Should I stop?"

"No. Never."

"Sweet angel fox." He grabbed my hips and lifted me, nudging the head of himself inside me. Tugging me down onto him with a groan that had me shaking all over. "Fuck. You feel so good."

He did as well. So good and thick. And deep. My goodness, being in this position made him slide right into the deepest parts of me. I liked it.

"I love how you fill me up." I dropped my head, enjoying that initial stretch of him sliding inside. Rolling my hips to help bring him all the way in. Already, this just felt right. Everything with my Nijel felt right. Except his words. "Why is your place not permanent?"

"My little vixen—riding my cock but still wanting to have an actual conversation." He chuckled, those rough hands of his squeezing my hips and moving me on him. His breaths coming faster as we worked to find the right pace for us. "It's not permanent because you might not like it. I'll move, my mate. Whatever you want." Another groan and he lifted his hips right off the mattress, taking me with him. "Oh fuck. I'm so deep inside you like this."

His groan turned into a deep growl, his body working harder as he thrust up into me. Words were too hard, so I shook my head instead. Riding him as my body took over. As I chased the breaking point he'd taught me the night before. And when he added his thumb into the mix —pressing against my clit with a solid pressure as he continued to fill me—I broke. Shattered, really. Chanting his name as I came all over him. As my body shook and convulsed on his. As he followed me over that edge with an arch of his back and another impossible roar that likely shook the windows of the B&B. Not that I cared that morning any more than I had the night before about what others heard. I was with my mate—they could all be jealous.

"Fuck, Lucy. I can't get enough of you," Nijel said before pulling me down to snuggle against his chest. "If I take you home with me, I might not let you leave for days."

"Not seeing a negative here."

"True. Sounds pretty damn good to me." He slid his hand along my back to cup my ass, squeezing the flesh before flicking up and down again. Giving me a quick yet solid smack. One that made me quiver all over. "Oh, you like that."

Yeah, I did. But… "Don't get any ideas."

"Oh, I've got ideas." He brushed the hair away from my face as I rose over him. Staring up at me with a softness and joy in his eyes that filled me with so much happiness. The man truly liked me, maybe even loved. Beyond the mating and the fated part, he was happy with *me*. Knowing that—seeing it in his expression—was priceless.

"I'm so glad the fates chose you for me," I whispered, unable to hold in my emotions.

Nijel's smile softened, his hand coming to cup my cheek. "There's no one else more perfect for me. I am truly blessed, and that's not something I'll ever forget. Now, let's get ready to go."

A quick kiss—closed-mouthed because morning breath wasn't a good look on me—and another smack to my ass, and we were up. Dancing around the room as we threw on clothes for the day and laughing over how we kept tripping over each other. Sex brought out the ridiculous in me. Who knew?

"Come on, my love," Nijel said as we were walking out the door. "I'm taking you to breakfast."

"At the diner?"

"It's the only good breakfast spot in town." He helped me into his truck, keeping his hand on my leg as I got settled. "Why? Would you rather not go there?"

"Oh no. It's fine. I just…we'll likely see my aunt." And he was obviously wearing clothing that didn't speak to a casual morning breakfast.

He stepped up onto the running board, bringing his face even with mine. "You afraid to tell her I'm your mate?"

I kissed his lips. Shushing him. "Don't be ridiculous. I just know that how she sees you will change once she knows. You'll be family—she'll yell."

"Let her. I can take it. Besides, if she's yelling at me, that means she's not yelling at you."

I laughed, knowing that wasn't how my aunt worked but letting him have his silly daydream.

The drive took almost no time whatsoever, and then we were at the scene of the crime. The diner—where I'd first laid eyes on my new mate. Where he'd left me behind without a word. Where I'd thought the fates had chosen wrong. Instead of pouting over that bad moment, I took a deep breath and enjoyed the good one I was in. The feel of Nijel's hands on me as he helped me out of his truck, the look in his eyes as he set me on the ground, the hum of his soft growl as he slipped a hand down to my ass and pulled me closer.

"I'm going to feed you, and then I'm taking you home and not letting you out of my bed for the rest of the day."

Yup. Enjoying the good. "Promise?"

Nijel's laugh nearly stopped traffic, but I didn't care. He was happy, I was happy, and we were about to get some pancakes. This day couldn't get any better.

We walked inside holding hands, standing at the hostess station for only a moment before my aunt came bustling over. She glanced at Nijel, noted our joined hands, then pinned me with her steely gaze.

"What's this?"

Direct. The woman always had been direct. "Good morning, Auntie. You know Nijel."

"Yes, of course I do. What I don't know is why he has his hand on you."

I squeezed the hand that was technically not on me but in mine. "Because he's my mate."

She blinked. Again. Jerked her head to look at Nijel, back at me. At him, at me. And then—finally—she grinned. "Oh, my dear child. How very joyous for you and the family."

I was swept into a hug, those strong arms tugging me close. When she released me, she went straight for Nijel.

"Get down here, you big lug. We're family now."

Nijel acquiesced, leaning over so she could grab his face and kiss his cheeks. Looking adorably shocked at the affection.

"Now, you'd better treat her right," my aunt said, growing more serious. "I want this girl to be happy and healthy for all the rest of her days. Do you hear me?"

"Yes, ma'am. Happy and healthy." He shot me a wink. "I'll get right on that."

"Good." She grabbed a couple menus and led us to a quiet table in the back section. "You'll have enough privacy to chat back here. Much better than section five."

"Thank you, Auntie."

"Oh, my dear, you're welcome." She leaned in close, whispering, "You got yourself a good one. But maybe don't have too many kids. Three is nice. Four might be pushing it. A small family would be just fine."

I was still trying to come to grips with her words—considering the woman had eighteen kids, she'd know for sure how many were too many—when she strolled over to Nijel and smacked him upside the head.

"And you—don't take her from me too soon. All my help is being stolen by fate's blessings. I need her."

Nijel sat back, looking contemplative. "If she wants to stay working here, I won't stop her."

"Good. Now, take a look at the menu. Breakfast is on me." And with that, she was off. Rushing across the restaurant and greeting the customers she'd been feeding for more years than I'd been alive.

Nijel chuckled. "That woman is a ball of energy."

"She is. And she makes the best meatloaf in the history of the world."

"Really? I've never had it."

"We'll come back for dinner one night." I shot him a smile. "Once you let me out of your bed."

He picked up the menu all casual-like, looking at it as he said, "So then, maybe next week."

Yup, sounded about right.

Breakfast came and went as things did between us—with lots of talking and laughs. Longing looks and a little footsie under the table, too. But all things had to come to an end, and we left the diner stuffed and happy and ready to keep the day going.

"Your house?"

Nijel started the truck and began backing out of his parking spot. "Yeah, I think it's time to go to my house."

"Good."

He waited until he'd navigated through the crowded lot to the highway leading out of town before he reached for my hand. "So, it's small, and it's pretty deep in the woods. It's not scary, though, and I do have a neighbor—a reindeer shifter named Bennett."

"Reindeer shifter...I didn't even know there were any in Kinship Cove."

"Just him, apparently. They're super rare and apparently only mate within their breed. They have a convention every year to try to find their mates—but so far, no luck for Bennett."

"A convention of reindeer shifters?"

"Yup. Up in Alaska. Bennett likes to joke that it's at the North Pole, but I'm pretty sure he's full of shit."

Reindeers at the North Pole. That definitely piqued my interest. "I need to know more about this."

Nijel turned down a wooded drive that had been almost hidden by the trees surrounding it. "I'll invite him over one of these days. He's a great guy."

"Just not today," I said, grabbing his thigh and squeezing. "I want you to myself today."

His growl vibrated through the cab of the truck, and he stopped a little short as he threw the thing into park. "Inside. Now."

We tumbled out of the truck, Nijel rushing over to help me down like normal. I let him, of course, practically falling into his arms simply because he was there to catch me. And catch me, he did—he actually swooped me right up off my feet and kissed me too. The man somehow managed to do that all without tripping, making it to his own door in seconds and opening it without breaking the kiss. Talent—he had it.

He also had what I could only describe as one of the coziest wood cabins I'd ever seen.

"Oh, Nijel. It's—"

"Dark, I know. And I'm not really a decorator or anything."

I slipped out of his arms, unable to stop looking around. Such a strong, masculine space. So him. And just like him, there was a softness built in—squishy pillows and flannel blankets laid across the arms of couches, books lining the walls, and little touches that told me so much about him.

Just like our mating, the place was perfect.

"I love it," I said, dancing through the open space.

"You do?"

"How could I not? This place is pure you."

Suddenly, his hands were yanking me into his hold and his lips were on mine again. I bent backward, the force of his kiss something I hadn't been expecting. The strength of his grip not unwelcome.

"You," he gasped as soon as he broke the kiss. "You take me by surprise at every turn."

"Good. Now take me to bed, my mate. I need a nap and some serious alone time with you."

"You never have to ask me twice." He picked me up again—I was beginning to think he liked having me in his arms—and headed toward a hallway just past the kitchen space, but a knock at the door stopped him in his tracks.

"I swear to the fates, if that's Bennett, I'll kill him."

"No killing reindeer." I tapped him on the nose. "Santa needs them."

Nijel put me down, grumbling something about what Santa really needed, before heading for the door. It wasn't a reindeer shifter on the other side, though. It was two police officers.

"Nijel Carr," the one on the left said. Not a question—a statement. They knew who he was.

Nijel stiffened, his brow furrowing. "You know who I am, Carl."

The officer—Carl, apparently— simply nodded. "I'm afraid I'm going to have to bring you in. You're under arrest for the assault and battery of Jacob Edwards."

Nijel didn't fight them, but he didn't exactly look pleased. And he certainly didn't take a step in their direction. "I have no idea who that is."

Not-Carl yanked off his sunglasses, his glare firm and strong. "He was at the Metro Lounge last night and ended up with a broken jaw. Ring a bell? Or are you back to fighting your way through town and can't remember all your victims?"

Nijel's eyes met mine, and his face paled. This was bad. This was very, very bad.

And my mate knew it. "I want a lawyer."

Carl nodded. "I figured as much. Let's get you Mirandized and into the car. You can call for your attorney at the station."

No goodbye, no explanation, no nothing…from any of them. I'd never felt more alone and invisible than in that moment.

I was on the porch watching them lead Nijel to a car when another man—taller and thinner than my mate—came running through the woods. "Whoa, what's happening here?" His eyes met mine, and I saw no question there. No surprise. He had to know who I was, which meant that this was Bennett the reindeer shifter. Nijel's friend.

Reindeer to the rescue.

"He's being arrested," I said, hurrying Bennett's way so I could drop my voice. I didn't want the police to hear. "He punched a guy at the bar last night because he'd gotten handsy with me, and now Nijel's being arrested."

"Protecting your mate isn't against the law in this town."

I glanced at my very angry-looking, very silent mate. "He didn't tell them why he hit the guy, and the one made a crack about Nijel fighting his way through town again. I don't understand."

Bennett sighed, his frown deepening. His concern obvious. "Yeah, well…he wouldn't tell them anything having to do with you. Not ever."

Could Nijel really be *that* private? To be willing not to spill the truth about the night to the police to save himself?

Apparently he was, because he let the police load him into the back of the car without saying a word. His dark eyes held mine for as long as they could, and then he was gone. Carted off to the station like some sort of criminal. Still silent.

"Did he tell them he wanted a lawyer?" Bennett asked.

Okay, so he hadn't been totally silent. Thank the fates for that. "Yeah, but nothing else. Not another word."

"Good. That's good."

"Why is that good?"

"Because it'll keep him from saying something stupid and getting into more trouble." Bennett sighed and cracked his neck, looking ready for action. "Come on. I'll drive us to the station."

Perfect. "Let me just shut Nijel's door."

"No need," Bennett grabbed my hand and took off at a fast clip through the woods. "No one would dare come to Nijel's house."

"Why not?"

The man shot a glance my way, one filled with confusion. "Because he's Nijel Carr—as in *Will beat your ass if you look at him sideways* Nijel Carr. At least, he was until about ten years ago or so. He's calmed down a lot."

I shrugged. "I'm not from here, so I don't know his past."

"Good. But people here? Those cops? They do, and they sometimes still treat him like he's that reckless, wild wolverine starting fights and brawling in the street."

No wonder Nijel didn't like to be around people. "He doesn't deserve that."

"Preaching to the choir, sister." Bennett tugged me through a copse of trees and onto the paved driveway of a little cabin much like Nijel's. Directly toward what I could only describe as a 50s boat of a vehicle painted bright red with gold trim and a white interior. It was the car equivalent of Santa's sleigh, and I was madly in love with it. "Load it up, lady. We've got a wolverine to save."

Yes, we did.

9

NIJEL

I was an asshole. A huge, idiotic asshole. The first day I have my girl at my home, the first time I bring her back to my den, and I get arrested. At least that particular event wasn't a first.

"You talking yet, Carr?"

I grunted toward the cop, knowing my rights well enough not to open my mouth. I'd already asked for my lawyer—I could tell them I had done any number of things and my so-called confession would be thrown out. Rights—I knew them.

Like I'd said, this wasn't my first time being arrested. Hell, it wasn't even my tenth.

"That's what I thought." The officer stood up and stretched, heading for the door leading into the actual station. "It's lunchtime for me. Try not to tear the place apart, would you? I've heard all about your rampages."

I'd have called him an asshole, but I was still feeling like the title was mine. Not that the guy was all that wrong. Wolverine shifters tended to be strong and never afraid of a fight. Add into that a bit of a temper and the unfortunate trait of attracting the attention of smaller guys with big egos who thought taking down the largest man in the room made them more important somehow, and I was what the local police would call a repeat offender. At least, I had been. I'd changed my ways after a particularly rough fight that had left my opponent seriously injured. The guilt of that, the feeling of needing to repent and apologize every single day, had forced me to change my ways faster than anything else could have. Except maybe finding out Lucy was my mate.

No—I was glad I'd been forced to wait. Been challenged to learn patience and control before she'd come into the picture. That man—that beast of a shifter with a lack of sense—hadn't deserved a woman like my mate. I still didn't, but I was at least humble enough to be willing to admit it and to try to be better.

Still, those years—that past—was a part of me. A part most of the town knew about. No wonder the cops had shown up at my house and arrested me instead of bringing me in for questioning. I was Nijel Carr. Fighter. Brawler. Troublemaker. This wouldn't be the first time some idiot had gotten mouthy and I'd swung. This was simply the first time that idiot had laid hands on my mate—an unforgivable offense in my eyes. My reaction had been justified, and once the cops knew why I'd punched the guy, I'd be released. I just had to wait for my lawyer to get there first, which was going to take a while. They hadn't even let me make my phone call yet.

It was going to be a long, boring day.

Lucy

Hours. Nijel had been gone for hours. Hours that added up to almost an entire day. Bennett had taken me to the station right after Nijel had been arrested, but to no avail—they had refused to let us in to see him. They'd also refused to even talk about the case. All we knew was Nijel was inside the police station somewhere, probably in a cell, and there was nothing we could do about it.

Once Bennett and I had given up getting to him, I'd stayed at Nijel's house all day, waiting for him to show up. He never had. I'd eaten his food, checked out his book collection, and stayed wrapped in his blankets with his scent dancing around me while I'd slept. The entire time I waited, I worried. Was he being questioned? Was he scared? Did he have anything to eat in there? I had never been to jail—I didn't know how the whole thing worked. My only experience was what I'd seen in movies and on TV, and that likely wasn't accurate.

I just wanted him home.

At some point—after growing weary of so much quiet—I turned on Nijel's television and found something to watch. Or at least something to make noise in the background as I paced the floor and thought about all I had to lose while chewing my fingernails down to the quick. I needed to come up with a plan, some way to help, some way to get him out. Nijel would not be facing this alone. I'd be there. I was his ride or die. His mate. I'd totally take care of him and wait for him if he ended up doing time, but I'd do anything in my power to stop that from happening first. I would—

A knock sounded at the door, yanking me from my own personal *stand by your man* refrain. I hurried across the floor, wanting it to be Nijel yet knowing that wasn't likely. Who knocked on their own door?

And yet…maybe.

My smile fell when the door swung open to reveal Bennett standing on the porch. "Oh. Hi."

"Gee, that's the greatest greeting I've ever received," he deadpanned, completely straight-faced. "You're obviously happy to see me."

I tried not to sigh. I failed, but I tried. "Sorry. I was foolishly hoping that was Nijel on the porch."

"Ah, the disappointment is justified, then." He glanced at the television, frowning. "What are you watching?"

"Some show about couples dealing with one being incarcerated."

"Is this research for you? Prepping for Nijel's time behind bars?"

My gut clenched, and I couldn't breathe. Behind bars. He was literally behind bars and may be for…who knew how long? Those people on the show—the phone calls and short visits once a month— that really was my future. Sort of. Maybe. Possibly.

I was going to be sick if I kept thinking that way. "Not really research," I said, hoping he didn't notice how I couldn't look him in the eye anymore. "Just something I'm finding relatable right now. Except for the drug addiction. There seems to be a lot of that going on."

"Indeed." Bennett grabbed the remote and turned off the television before taking a seat on the ottoman. "Sit. Relax."

I curled into the corner of the couch, biting my lip. "Have you heard anything yet?"

"Nothing from Nijel. A friend at the station said they're still waiting on his attorney and he's clammed up tight. No talking whatsoever." He leaned forward, his elbows on his knees and the prettiest green eyes I'd ever seen pinning me in place. "Tell me what happened."

The night before. Why Nijel had punched the tiger shifter with the roaming hands. Bennett was Nijel's friend—I felt sure he wouldn't mind if I told the man the truth. "We were at the Metro Lounge, hanging out in the VIP section with my cousins."

"Why VIP?"

"My cousin, Tilly, is mated to that action movie star."

Bennett nodded. "I remember hearing something about that. Okay—club, VIP, movie stars...go."

I really liked him. "Everything was fine, but I left to go to the restroom."

"Alone?"

"No, with my cousin Tilly."

"The one mated to the actor. Right. So, then what?"

"On the way back, a guy grabbed me and pulled me against him." Bennett's obvious shock made my gut twist harder. "I wasn't interested in him or accepting of his advances in any way. I was just trying to get back to Nijel."

He shook his head and leaned back. "Oh, sweetie—of that, I have no doubt."

Good. "So, he grabbed me, Nijel saw, the two had words, but the guy wouldn't back down and..."

Oh, I couldn't say it. My face burned, and every inch of my skin itched as if I needed to shower the memory off. As if the man had left his filth on my body.

"Are you okay?" Bennett asked, leaning closer. "I can call someone if you'd like."

"No, I'm fine. It's just—the guy grabbed me again. Right there in front of Nijel and Tilly's mate. He knew I was mated to Nijel, and he still yanked me against him and put his hand on my...rear."

Bennett blinked. "Rear."

It sounded like a question to me, so I said, "Yes, rear."

"Okay, so we're at the great-grandma level of vocabulary today."

I liked him, but I was not in the mood for his sarcasm. "It's been a rough one. If I want to say rear instead of ass or trunk or booty, I'll say rear."

"Fair enough." His brow came down, and he cocked his head. "So, wait—the guy knew you had a mate, knew Nijel—who was standing right there—was that mate, and he still grabbed you again and put his hand on your...rear?"

Okay, fine, the word sounded funny. Not that I'd admit that to him. "Yeah, he did. Nijel warned him off, and he still touched me."

"Did he have a death wish?"

"I don't know. It's all so strange."

"It is, but Nijel's reaction is not illegal."

That caught my attention. "But Nijel did punch him in the face. He fell flat on the floor."

"Oh, I'm sure he did. The guy's lucky Nijel didn't go all wolverine-smackdown on his...rear." Bennett smiled at me, obviously enjoying our little word debacle. "It's not illegal for a shifter to protect their mate. Period. Nijel didn't hit the guy until he crossed one hell of a line and grabbed you against your will, correct?"

"Yes."

"And do you think Renit will back him up?"

"I'm sure he will. He was right there, watching everything go down."

Bennett jumped to his feet, quite nimble for someone so lanky. "Then, let's go."

"Go where?"

"It's time to spring your man."

My heart skipped, and I jumped into action, grabbing my purse and shoes before...

"We need to stop at my place."

Bennett didn't appear to like that idea. "Why?"

I rose to my full height and slowly drew my hand down the length of my body. The body covered in Nijel's sweatshirt and a pair of his boxers. Making sure Bennett saw the angry, red tear tracks on my face from crying. Making sure he got the full picture.

"I'm a mess. If I'm going to have to fight for my mate's freedom, I'd like to do it looking more like someone who hasn't spent an entire day crying and watching bad reality TV."

Bennett was a man who knew when to talk…and when to keep his mouth shut. "We'll make it a quick stop."

"Fine."

And then we were off to save my mate from any sort of incarceration. Or at least try to. Once I stopped looking like a hobo.

We're coming for you, Nijel. Stay strong.

1 0

NIJEL

One day. Twenty-four hours. I'd spent one entire day and night in jail. I paced the cage those officers had put me in, for once unsure of what I should do. I hadn't talked—my lawyer had been real clear with me in the past that I should never talk. I'd called him to come get me out as soon as I'd been allowed to use the phone, but either there was a problem with that, or he hadn't made it to town yet. If it was the latter, he and I were going to have a long talk about my expectations once he got there. I had a mate to get home to—what was the holdup?

Just thinking about Lucy made my gut twist and my nearly constant growl deepen. My girl, my mate…alone. No one to protect her, and definitely no one to explain to her what was going on. She was an innocent—no way could she understand the ins and outs of dealing with false charges. And they *were* false charges. No one in this town would blame me for protecting my mate once they knew the truth. But Lucy—she only knew I'd been arrested. Had witnessed the cops putting handcuffs on me and placing me in the back of a squad car. Not exactly an image I wanted her to focus on.

As soon as I got out, I'd have some serious work to do to repair any damage the arrest had caused us. Until then, I just hoped Bennett or her family had stepped in to keep her safe for me. I hoped someone was

241

helping her stay calm and at home because no way did I want her at the station with me. That wasn't happening. This wasn't the place for her.

You ever have someone tell you to not even think something because just the thought would make it come true? I'd never bought into that bullshit, but pacing that cage with Lucy on my mind manifested her. Or she just showed up. Whatever. One second, I was really damn sure I didn't want her anywhere near this hellhole, and the next, she was there. Throwing open the door as if it were nothing more than a curtain and striding into the cellblock looking like some sort of angel sent straight from heaven. I'd never been happier to see her...

At least, until I noticed the officer—Carl, the same one who'd come to arrest me—at her side. Leading her. Taking her to the cell next to mine. And locking the door behind her.

What the fuck?

"No," I snarled, my voice filling the entire block. "Carl, what the hell is this? She doesn't belong here."

Carl didn't even look my way. "She's under arrest for assault and battery." Once he had Lucy secured, he moved to my cell door. And the bastard opened it. "She's admitted to the assault of Jacob Edwards, so you're free to go."

"The hell I am." I had no idea how I'd fallen into some sort of alternate universe, but I didn't like it. Not one bit.

Instead of leaving my cell, I rushed to the wall of bars separating mine from Lucy's and slid to the floor. Reaching through those cursed bars as best I could. The damn things didn't have much space between them and my arms were thick, but at least my hands and wrists were able to share space with her. To bring us close enough so I could lower my voice and whisper to her.

"What are you doing? You know I'm the one who punched that guy."

Lucy dropped to her knees before me, the two of us reaching through the impediment for each other. Both nearly whimpering when we finally touched. Might have just been me. And it might have been far louder than I cared to admit.

"Because of me." She tugged me closer, somehow magically finding a way to drop one of those sweet kisses on my lips. "Because you were protecting me."

I shot a glare at Carl, who at least had the decency to stand across the room and stare at the wall instead of watching us. Still, I kept my voice down. Not wanting to give them anything to hold me on. Wanting to get my mate the hell out of this place. "Lucy, I—"

"Are you ashamed of me?"

I nearly fell over. "Of course not. Never. You're a queen."

"Then why didn't you tell them you were protecting me? That you were defending your mate?"

"Because they'd have brought you down here and questioned you."

"So?"

Oh, my girl was stubborn. And smart—she wasn't going to let me go until I talked to her about this, even if I didn't want to. "Lucy, if they had brought you here, they would have separated us. I wouldn't have been able to protect you from them."

She smiled, slowly shaking her head. "Oh, my sweet, silly wolverine. I don't need you to protect me all the time."

That was a lie, but my mate was busy running her fingers over my face, so I let it go. I also whimpered again. Loudly. For fuck's sake, I missed her touch. I needed her so badly. I had no control around her— as evidenced by my near purr when those magic fingers scratched over my sideburns.

My mouth could not stay closed. "I want you safe and happy, my love. I need it more than I need air."

She never stopped touching me, thank the fates. "I *am* safe and happy…with you. But you have to let me help you when I can."

When she could—like now. Like backing me up when I told the truth about what happened. My lawyer was going to kill me, but whatever. I'd waited on him long enough. I wanted out.

"Fine." I turned, raising my voice so Carl could hear me. "Lucy didn't do anything wrong, and really, neither did I. I punched that fucker because he grabbed my mate and wouldn't let her go. He put his hands on her after she told him no and while knowing she was mated to me. The first part is a crime, the second proves my response wasn't."

Carl chuckled as he finally ambled our way. "We know—she told us everything. Next time, just tell us up front that the so-called victim was harassing your mate. There are laws in Kinship Cove about harming mated folk that protect the puncher instead of the punchee."

Which I knew, and yet I hadn't always had the best experiences with the law. "Yeah, well—not all places honor those."

Carl pinned me with a steely gaze, one that nearly set me back on my heels. "We respect the laws of mating in Kinship Cove. We also respect the autonomy of every female in our district. If she didn't want him to touch her, he shouldn't have touched her. Period."

Okay. I liked this guy. "Good."

"And just for the record, I know you're not the wild man you once were. I knew from the get-go that something was up with Jacob's report of what went down. We'll be bringing charges against him for assault against Miss Lucy and for filing a false police report. You can also file an impeding mating bond charge against him, Nijel."

That sounded like it meant more time at the station. "I don't want—"

"I do," Lucy said, looking fierce. "He shouldn't get away with bothering a mated woman, getting you in trouble for no good reason, and being so handsy with me. No one deserves what that guy did to us."

Well...okay, then. "Do we need to give statements or anything?"

Carl shook his head as he unlocked Lucy's door. "We already took one from your mate. We'll eventually need one from you as well, but it's been a solid day since you two have been together. I remember when I first met my wife—that mating bond needed some serious caring for. Our conversation can wait until tomorrow."

Thank fuck. As soon as Carl stepped out of the doorway to Lucy's cell, I rushed to my mate's side, picking her up and kissing her with everything I had. Running my hands over as much of her body as I could reach to make sure she was okay. Ignoring the quiet chuckle of the officer.

For a while, at least. "Okay, okay. Are we free to go, Carl?"

He shrugged. "Of course. Just try not to punch anyone else today. I don't want to deal with the paperwork."

I carried my giggling mate toward the exit, not setting her down for a second. "I make no promises."

When we made it outside—fresh air and sunlight...wow—we ran straight into Bennett. The reindeer I was a little pissed with.

"You should have kept her at home."

Bennett shrugged, casual as all fuck. "She didn't want to do that, and I wasn't about to force her. Sometimes, a change of plans is a good thing."

I set Lucy down, keeping her tight to my side, growling loudly. And I shook his hand. "Yeah, well...thank you. Sometimes, I guess you're right."

"That's what I've been trying to tell you for the past twenty years."

He had, and I'd never live down agreeing with him. But that was okay—he was the best friend a man could have. I owed him...a lot.

I also needed a ride from him. "Are you our chauffeur?"

Bennett shook his head, handing over the keys to his sledmobile. "I'm going to hang out in town for a bit—maybe get a coffee and cupcake from the bakery. Why don't you take my car?"

Translation—I don't want to be alone with an anxious and newly mated couple.

My sweet Lucy was obviously concerned about leaving him to his own devices, though. "How will you get home?"

Bennett shot her a wink and a sly smile. "I'll borrow Santa's sled."

Fucking reindeer quips—the man was full of them. "Fine, but call me if you need a ride or something."

Without waiting for an answer, I herded Lucy to Bennett's warm car, almost wincing at the audacity of the damn thing. Still, I'd put up with the red paint and gold trim if it meant making sure my mate was safe and home with me.

Once I had Lucy loaded inside, I raced to hop in on the other side, not liking being away from her even for those few seconds. This was going to be a long night of me clinging to her body. I could already tell.

"We'll be at your place in just a few minutes," I said, starting the engine and throwing the car into gear, trying my damnedest to ignore the Christmas music coming through the speakers. "Are you hungry? Do we need to stop for food?"

But my mate took me by surprise. "I don't want to go to my place."

"No?"

"No." She paused, looking at me with an intensity that stole my breath. "I want to go back to your house. I want to go home."

Ah fuck. Home. She was already calling my cabin in the woods home. That was what I'd wanted, but I would have sold it and moved into town if she'd asked me to. Hell, I would have moved to Times Square, New York, if she'd wanted. Fuck all the people and the lack of privacy—I just wanted to be with her.

And it sounded like she wanted to be with me, too.

I was one hell of a lucky wolverine. "I'll take you home, my mate. I have food there."

"I'm not hungry—unless you are."

Only for her. I grabbed her hand and kissed the back of it, turning toward the mountain road that would take us *home*. "Just for you."

"Good. Because I saw that huge bed of yours—I want to give it a try."

The vixen. My dick hardened in an instant, and I pressed on the gas a little harder. Driving a little faster. Rattling the jingle bells even more than usual. Fucking car. But no matter how fast I drove, I couldn't get to our destination quickly enough. Home had never seemed so far away. "You want to try out my bed, huh? You're tired?"

I knew she wasn't, and she proved that by leaning closer. By placing her hand on my thigh and running her fingers upward. Teasing me as I tried really fucking hard to keep Bennett's car on the road and not in a ditch. Motherfucking vixen.

As I nearly exploded when she whispered, "Sleep isn't on the agenda for tonight."

Speeding tickets be damned, I drove faster.

EPILOGUE

LUCY

My paws pounded the earth, my tail streaming out behind me. The woods behind the cabin had become my playground, a place for me to shift and be foxy every single day. The running, hunting, and playing brought me immeasurable joy, especially since the weather had turned nice and cold, and the snow had begun to fall. Christmas was coming. My very first with my grumpy mate. Not that he was grumpy with me. Ever.

As if my thoughts of Nijel brought him to life, a bush rattled, and a second later, a huge wolverine came barreling toward me. Had I not known it was my mate, I would have been terrified. Wolverines may look slightly cute with their big middle and wobble walk, but they were mean. Deadly. Vicious.

Nijel would never be that way with me.

Still, this was the game we played—I ran and he chased. My fox was far more agile than his wolverine, so I spun and zigzagged through the forest. The sound of the beast following me, of him gaining ground, only made me that much more excited. I loved to be his prey.

I was almost to the back porch when Nijel caught up with me. He actually tackled me, the two of us rolling across the snow-covered grass until we ended up at the foot of the stairs. Shifted. Human. Naked.

Oh, it was really getting cold out.

"You couldn't wait for me to get home before going on your run?"

Always so overprotective, my mate. "Nope. The snow was calling me."

He grunted, pulling me closer when I shivered. Warming me up with his big hands and thick arms. "Your body is calling me."

I grinned, leaning in to kiss him. Loving the way he responded to me. The way he clutched at my body and groaned through the kiss. The man truly loved me—every inch of me. He'd proven that again and again over the past few months. He listened when I spoke, laughed when I made a joke, and never raised his voice to me. He also loved my body each and every day, making sure I was sated no matter what else was happening around us. Poor Bennett had gotten an earful a time or two and complained that he had to keep his windows shut at night, but I didn't care. My man made me scream—I refused to hold back.

"My vixen," Nijel whispered when he broke the kiss, palming my cheek and staring up at me as if I were a gift. A joy. Something so very important to him. "It's cold out here. Let me take you inside and warm you up in our bed."

As if I'd say no. "Sounds perfect."

He grinned and jackknifed up, taking me with him. Rising to his feet with me in his arms as if I weighed nothing. As if he were the strongest man in the world. I often thought he was. He had a habit of picking me up—one I didn't complain about. Especially not when he was picking me up to facilitate some sort of sexual act. I may have been a virgin when I'd met him, but I definitely wasn't anymore. Not in the least bit. And I loved it.

"So, my sweet fox," Nijel said as he kicked the door closed behind him and strode toward the bedroom. "How was your day off?"

Joyous. Calm. Lonely without him. "Fine. Though, I missed you. How was work?"

He laid me down on his huge bed, chasing me up the mattress until I lay with a pillow under my head and him on top of me. Taking advantage of the calm before the storm, so to speak.

"I was away from you, so it was awful."

I smiled—how could I not? We were hopeless romantics and total homebodies, both of us just wanting to be with the other. It had been that way from the start—once we'd returned to his cabin from the jail all those months ago. Once we'd been reunited, I'd come with him to his cabin. And I'd simply never left. We'd spent every night together, woken up in each other's arms every morning. If we ran errands, we did them together. Our only separations came with work—a fact that had me wondering what sort of business we could open so we wouldn't need to be separated at all.

But as his hand slid up my thigh and he rolled to the side so he could access the most private parts of me, I tucked those thoughts away. This was our time—work could wait.

"You know," Nijel said as he rolled even farther, stretching to reach something on his nightstand. "I brought you a present."

"You did?"

"I did." He held up a… Well, it was something green and leafy with red berries on it. It was…I had no idea.

"What is it?"

"Mistletoe."

I grinned, pushing up so I could reach his lips. "Then, kiss me."

"Oh, I intend to." But he only gave me a quick, smacking kiss before dragging those lips down my body. Still holding the mistletoe over his head.

"I'm pretty sure mistletoe is meant for a kiss on the cheek, maybe the lips."

"That's because people aren't creative." He pushed my knees apart, settling between them. Holding the mistletoe over his head as he leaned in to drop a soft kiss over my clit. "I intend to kiss you all over tonight, mate. Every single inch. Starting right here."

I arched my back and moaned as he began doing exactly what he'd promised—kissing me. His hand soon joined the party as he slid two fingers inside me before flicking my clit with his tongue. My man wasn't playing around tonight. He wanted me to come—sometimes he would tease me with his attentions, would spend an hour with his face in my pussy as he pushed me toward my orgasm then backed away. Not tonight—tonight he dove in and drove me like a race car. Fingers, tongue, lips, and suction all coming together to wind me up. To make me grab his head and cry his name. To make me come all over his face.

"That was one," he said as he kissed his way back up my body, stopping at my breasts to lavish them with the same attention. "Let's see if we can get two before I slide inside you."

He continued his attentions on my breast even as he dropped a hand to once again control my pussy. Fingers inside, palm pressing against my clit, he worked me over. He sucked and licked and moaned against my breast as I writhed underneath him. As I rode his hand and spread my legs wider, needing him to fill me up. Wanting him so badly. And when I came that time, when he curled those thick fingers inside me and made me explode around him, I screamed. Loudly.

"Nijel," I gasped, tugging his shoulders. Wanting him so badly. "Now. I need you now."

"I know, my vixen. I know." He rose over me, watching as he moved his hips so his cock could nudge its way inside of me. As he groaned and gripped me, filling me up with every roll forward. Bringing us together again and again.

"I love you, my beast," I said once he was seated within me. So deep. The man could go so deep, and I loved it. Loved being filled by him.

"I love you too, my vixen." He pulled back and slid inside again, lifting my leg to rest on his shoulder. Opening me up wider and changing the angle until I gasped. Until he managed to slip even deeper inside of me. Until we were truly joined together, both heading straight for a blissful release. "Only you. Forever."

Which sounded pretty damn good to me.

Paranormal romance with a dangerously ever after.

FERAL BREED MOTORCYCLE CLUB

Wolf shifters, motorcycles, witches, and a threat lurking in the shadows.

Novels
Claiming His Fate

Claiming His Need

Claiming His Witch

Claiming His Beauty

Claiming His Fire

Claiming His Desire

Claiming Her Heart

Collections
Claiming Their Forever: A Collection of Shorts

The Feral Breed: Volume One

The Feral Breed: Volume Two

The Feral Breed: The Complete Series

FERAL BREED FOLLOWINGS

Stand-alone stories of characters first met in the Feral Breed Motorcycle Club series. Featuring cage fighters, dragon shifters, second chances, and young love.

Claiming His Chance

Claiming His Prize

The Gathering Tales

Come and enjoy tales from the biggest shifter event of the year as wolves from around the country fall in lust, in love, and in fate at The Gathering.

The Gathering Tales

The Devil's Dires

There's no escaping a Dire Wolf on the hunt…

Savage Surrender

Savage Sanctuary

Savage Seduction

Savage Silence

Savage Sacrifice

Savage Security

Savage Salvation

Motor City Alien Mail Order Brides

Where the men aren't human and the women are uninformed.

Cutlass

Hudson

Maverick

KINSHIP COVE: MATES & MACARONS

When shifters and humans mingle, the fates like to have a little fun.

Candied Wolf

Sugar Dragon

Honey Bear

Frappé Fox

Espresso con Eagle

Caffé Wolverino

Reindeer Ripple

Stand-Alone Romance

Masterson: A Vampire Sons Story

Fox Hunt: A Reverse Harem Romance

Sign up for Ellis Leigh's newsletter for release information, promotions, swag opportunities, and early access to free reads!

Free Reads…News…Good Stuff!

For new release announcements only, follow Ellis on Bookbub.

collar community know exactly what it is to have to rise from the ashes. Never giving up is part of life, like second base, second gear, and second chances.

POP THE CLUTCH

REV THE ENGINE (Coming Soon)

Sign up for Kristin Harte's newsletter so you never miss out on news and updates.

www.kristinharte.com/newsletter

Are you a Bookbub subscriber? You can follow Kristin there as well so you never miss a new release!

www.kristinharte.com/bookbub

ABOUT THE AUTHOR

A storyteller from the time she could talk, Ellis grew up among family legends of hauntings, psychics, and love spanning decades. Those stories didn't always have the happiest of endings, so they inspired her to write about real life, real love, and the difficulties therein. From farmers to werewolves, store clerks to witches—if there's love to be found, she'll write about it. Ellis lives in the Chicago area with her two daughters and a German Shepherd that never leaves her side.

When she's not writing paranormal romance, Ellis Leigh can be found writing romantic suspense as Kristin Harte and erotic shorts as London Hale.

Sign up for Ellis Leigh's newsletter for release information, promotions, swag opportunities, and early access to free reads!

www.ellisleigh.com/newsletter.

For new release announcements only, follow Ellis on Bookbub.

Come join my reader group for fun, snippets, secret handshakes, and discussions of what I'm working on and when that next book will be out.

Ellis' Elite Reader Group

www.ingramcontent.com/pod-product-compliance
Lightning Source LLC
Chambersburg PA
CBHW060924190726
48286CB00002B/626